I0722018

BUTTERFLY

MICHAELA GREY

For storiesthatfly. Thank you for being such a loyal reader all these years.

1

———

FELIX WAS SITTING in the back of the bar, out of sight of almost everyone and nursing a lukewarm beer when he saw them. The blond one was slim, similar to Felix's build but much shorter, and wrapped around his companion like a clinging vine.

His partner—Felix swallowed hard. His partner was *huge*. Easily six foot four, with dark hair that fell in soft curls into even darker eyes, a short, neat beard, and muscles to match his height.

And they were both looking at Felix.

Felix saluted them with his beer and an ironic tilt of his head. *Have fun*, it said. *Someone deserves to.*

He wasn't expecting the blond to disentangle himself and slide into the booth beside him. Up close, he had angelic features, hair so pale it was almost white, and piercing green eyes.

"Leo," he said. "I saw you looking at me."

"Who wouldn't?" Felix said, and took another swallow of beer. "You are easy on the eyes, my friend."

Leo clutched his chest dramatically as the big man slipped into the booth on Felix's other side. "French!" he said, pretending to swoon. "I've always wanted to sleep with a French guy!"

"French *Canadian*," Felix corrected. He eyed the other man. "And you are?"

"Fisher," the man said. "And he's always wanted to sleep with a French Canadian as well."

"It's the accent," Leo sighed. He leaned on Felix's shoulder and batted white-blond lashes at him. "What's your name, gorgeous?"

Felix debated. Neither seemed like hockey fans, but the last one hadn't either, and he still bore the scars.

"Just call me French," he finally said.

"Less of a mouthful than French-Canadian, and I can think of other things I'd rather have in my mouth," Leo said.

Felix snorted. Fisher was so close his thigh was pressed up against Felix's, but instead of feeling crowded or stifled, Felix felt… safe. He looked up through his lashes into Fisher's dark eyes.

"Come here often?"

Leo squeezed closer, running a hand up Felix's bicep. "Not as often as we should, if you're what they have on offer," he said.

"So are you two a couple?" Felix asked.

Leo waggled a hand. "Ish."

"More like no," Fisher said. His voice was so deep it reverberated through Felix's bones. "But we play together sometimes."

Leo propped his chin on his hands. "Do you wanna play with us?"

"It is a tempting prospect," Felix admitted. "What would it entail?"

"You, me, him, and our dicks," Leo chirped. "Anything you want."

"Anything?" Felix swirled the beer in its mug. "That is a dangerous offer, *ami*."

"You don't look like the kind to hurt me," Leo said, shrugging. "And if you *did*, I've got Fisher. Trust me, he will fuck you *up* if you do something I don't want."

Felix arched an eyebrow at Fisher, who also shrugged.

"Someone's gotta look out for him," he drawled. "Since he was born without a self-preservation instinct."

"So?" Leo asked, a hand drifting across Felix's thigh. "You wanna or not?" Slim fingers traced the outline of Felix's dick, and he twitched.

"Condoms," he managed.

Leo rolled his eyes. "Duh. But first—" He cupped Felix's chin in one hand and leaned in, giving him time to pull away. His lips were soft and tasted like grape chapstick, and he moaned as Felix got a hand free and wrapped it around the back of his neck, pulling him closer.

Distantly, Felix heard Fisher swear softly, but most of his attention was on Leo, currently doing his best to climb into his lap despite the table in his way.

"My turn," Fisher rumbled, and caught Felix's chin, pulling his head around. Their mouths fit perfectly together, Fisher's breath hot and his tongue soft. Felix melted against him, making a helpless noise high in his throat, and Leo cupped his hardening dick, rubbing it over the stretchy fabric of Felix's pants.

Felix couldn't figure out where to focus—the hand on his crotch or Fisher's mouth, so hot and demanding. He tore free with an effort, gratified to see Fisher was breathing as hard as he was.

"Not here," he rasped.

"Aw, no exhibition kink?" Leo pouted.

"I have no wish to be recognized," Felix said, smoothing his hair back.

Leo's eyes widened. "Are you a celebrity? Wait, I know all the local actors and musicians and I don't know you, so who *are* you?"

"Doesn't matter," Fisher interrupted, and Felix glanced at him, grateful. "You know I'm not famous but I don't wanna be recognized either. So let's get out of here."

Felix followed them from the bar, shrugging into his coat against the chilly Portland night. He shouldn't have gone out, should have stayed home and focused on his game, watched tape of the Ravens for tomorrow night, done anything else, but instead here he was, halfway to drunk and about to have sex with two men he didn't know.

"We're calling a car," Fisher said when Felix caught up to him. "And we thought we'd go to my house—it's not far. Do you have anyone you can tell?"

"Yes," Felix said, pulling out his phone. "Sa—" He caught himself. "My friend will want to know."

"Good," Fisher said. He rattled off the address

and waited as Felix texted Saint, who was probably at home wearing sweatpants, curled up on the couch with Carmine and their dog.

He got an answer back almost immediately. *Play safe and hydrate. Don't stay out too late. Text when you get home.*

Felix glanced up. "How much longer until the car is here?"

"Two minutes, according to the app," Leo said. "We could have some fun while we wait?" He took a step toward him, eyes intent.

"No," Felix said instantly, stepping back, and was startled to see Fisher getting between them at the same time.

"Back of a dimly lit, smoky bar is a little different from making out on the public street," Fisher snapped. "You know that, Leo."

Leo sighed, holding up his hands in a gesture of surrender. "Can't really blame me for trying. I mean *look* at you two."

The car arrived then, saving them from further discussion, and Leo slid into the front seat as Fisher and Felix got in the back. Felix folded his long legs in, watching with amusement as Fisher tried unsuccessfully to do the same beside him.

"Fuck—Leo, scoot your seat forward."

Leo complied, and Fisher sighed in relief. His knees still pressed into the back of the seat and he had to hunch a little, his hair brushing the roof.

Felix stifled a snicker. "We should have gotten the luxury ride, I think."

"God, your accent," Leo sighed as the driver accelerated away from the curb. "Fish, you hear how he drops his H's?"

"Leo," Fisher said warningly, as Felix shifted his weight.

Fisher glanced at him, an apology in his eyes. Felix nodded, twisting his mouth ruefully. He could already tell Leo was going to be a handful.

FISHER'S HOUSE wasn't very big—maybe two bedrooms, Felix thought, unfolding himself gratefully from the cramped backseat and stretching. It was a bungalow with a wraparound porch and a porch swing sized for two in the corner. Felix followed Fisher and Leo up the flagged stone path, past beds of neat flowers in perfect plots ringed by small white stones that gleamed in the moonlight.

Miraculously, Leo waited until they were inside and Fisher was locking the door behind them before swinging to Felix and demanding, "Say something to me in French."

Fisher sighed but didn't object. The lock clicked and Felix tried to think of something to say as Fisher herded them down the immaculately kept hall into a similarly neat living room.

"Ah… *t'as des beaux yeux*," he said.

"It's like music," Leo sighed. He was only a foot away, eyes bright in the dim room. "Will you talk dirty to me in French while you fuck me?"

"Jesus, Leo," Fisher sputtered. "I had no idea you had such a language kink!"

Leo shrugged, clearly unrepentant. "Someone's mouth needs to be on someone's dick, I'm not picky about whose. Except yours," he said, pointing at

Felix before he could speak. "You need yours to keep talking."

Fisher rummaged in an end table drawer and came up with a string of condoms. He wrapped one huge hand around the back of Leo's neck and pulled him into a soft kiss. Felix watched, spellbound, as Leo went up on tiptoe, wrapping his arms around Fisher's neck and pressing close.

Fisher unbuckled his pants. Heat slid through Felix's belly as Fisher pushed them down over his thighs. Leo stepped away and Felix made an unthinking noise at the sight of Fisher's cock. It was long and thick, hanging heavy between his thighs, and Felix took a step forward, glancing at Leo.

"I have to use my mouth," he said. "I have to taste him."

Leo giggled, pulling his own clothes off. "Not really a surprise. You can make it up to me later."

Felix folded to his knees and looked up through his lashes to Fisher, staring down at him as if mesmerized.

"Condom," Felix said regretfully. As much as he wanted to *truly* taste Fisher, he wasn't risking that.

Fisher didn't move for a minute. Then he shook himself and held out the strip. Felix took one and scooted forward until he was face to face with Fisher's cock, flushed deep red and leaking thick, slow drops.

Felix licked his lips and rolled the condom on, watching the way Fisher's thighs tightened and his muscular abdomen jumped as he struggled to hold still. Felix took a moment to prolong the tension, stroking Fisher's shaft and breathing warm air along his thigh.

There were noises, beside them, and Felix glanced over to see Leo naked and on his knees too, a bottle of lube in one hand and the other between his legs.

"*Calisse*," Felix whispered, and Leo moaned, head falling back and exposing the long line of his throat.

Fisher didn't move, didn't make a noise, but Felix could *feel* the want rolling off him in waves. It was delicious. He leaned in, holding Fisher's eyes as he sucked the head of his cock into his mouth. Fisher groaned deep in his chest, one hand coming up as if unconsciously to cup the back of Felix's head.

Felix gave himself over to it, running his tongue along the head and the sensitive area just underneath, adding teeth for the barest hint of a scrape just to hear Fisher jerk and swear thickly. He didn't move away though—instead he planted his feet and rolled his hips forward, pressing deeper into Felix's mouth as if daring him to do more.

Felix almost laughed and ran his hands up Fisher's thighs, squeezing and kneading the heavy muscle, mouth busy. It was sloppy and messy and from the way Fisher was trembling, filthy words falling from his lips as if unaware of them, he was just as into it as Felix was.

Hands at Felix's waist startled him and he jerked back, Fisher groaning in protest, to see Leo working on his belt. He had it free quickly and the zipper down, clever fingers pulling Felix's aching shaft out through the slit in his boxers. The condom went on just as quickly and then Leo was crouching to take him in his mouth and everything was soft wet heat and pleasure flashing through him.

Fisher twitched, his patience clearly tested, and

Felix murmured an apology, kissing the head of his cock swiftly and then swallowing him down again.

He used his hand this time, concentration too shot for him to focus on bringing Fisher off with just his mouth. Over the roaring in his ears, he could hear noises, filthy and wet, and he pried an eye open just in time to see Leo pull off and sit up.

Felix tried to say something, he wasn't sure what, but Leo put his hands on Felix's chest and shoved him backward. Felix went over in a startled sprawl and Leo was on top of him before he could get his bearings, dragging his pants down over his thighs and straddling him.

He sank down without hesitation and Felix cried out, bucking up into the tight, viselike heat as Leo rolled his hips, working him deeper in steady motions.

"Beautiful," Fisher breathed, and knelt by Felix's head. His hand was on his shaft, a question in his eyes, and Felix opened his mouth by way of answer. Fisher fed his cock inside, taking such obvious care not to choke him that Felix wanted to kiss him. He would later, he decided, and tilted his head so Fisher could slide deeper.

Leo adjusted his angle and made a choked noise, flailing for purchase. Fisher caught him with one hand, holding him upright, and Felix gathered the last remaining brain cells in his possession and grasped Leo's cock with one trembling hand. He wasn't going to be able to do much, he knew, but it didn't seem to matter. Leo sobbed, eyes losing focus, and came in heavy wet spurts across Felix's belly. The tight clench of his ass was enough to push Felix over, and he planted his feet flat on the floor and shoved up hard once, twice, spilling into the condom as pleasure lit his nerves.

Leo lifted himself off and fell backward just as Fisher swore and jerked the condom off. Felix turned his head just in time to watch him come, catching the jets in one huge palm, hunching forward as he shuddered through it. Then he fell sideways, collapsing to the carpet beside Felix.

FELIX STARED up at the ceiling, trying vainly to catch his breath. Leo was a heavy weight across his legs, and Fisher was facedown, eyes closed and breathing unsteady. Felix finally stirred, suppressing a groan, and Fisher opened his eyes.

"Okay?"

Felix nodded. He felt good—brain blessedly quiet, exhaustion curling through his limbs. "I should go."

"I'll call you a car," Fisher said, and rolled to his feet, unselfconscious in his nudity as he stepped over Leo's limp body.

"What about him?" Felix asked.

"He'll be out for a while," Fisher said. "Just push him off, he won't even notice."

Felix huffed a laugh and maneuvered Leo gently off his legs, slipping a pillow from the sofa under his head before rising to wipe at his stomach with a grimace and follow Fisher, who'd disappeared into another room.

The kitchen, Felix discovered when he stepped inside, zipping his pants. Fisher was still naked, bent over rummaging in the refrigerator, and Felix sighed appreciatively.

"Your ass is amazing," he said.

Fisher laughed, backing out of the refrigerator with a jug of water. "I work hard on it, so thanks." He poured Felix a glass of water and handed it to him as Felix tugged his shirt on over his head. "Car's on the way. It'll be here in three or four minutes."

Felix drained the glass, the water sliding down his throat cold and sweet, and set it back on the counter. Fisher was watching him, eyes bright in the dark kitchen.

"I had fun," he said quietly.

"Me too," Felix said, holding his eyes. He wanted to kiss him again but he wasn't sure if it would be welcome.

Fisher took a step closer. "Kiss goodbye?" he suggested, lips quirking.

"Yes *please*," Felix said, and closed the distance between them. The kiss was scorching, threatening to melt Felix's bones as he clung to Fisher's shoulders. He could feel Fisher's cock, somehow impossibly thickening against his thigh as he swept his tongue through Felix's mouth.

The phone chimed on the counter, startling them apart, and Fisher laughed ruefully, looking down at himself.

"Can I have your number?" he asked. "Just… in case you'd like to play again."

"With you and Leo or just you?" Felix said.

"Either," Fisher said steadily. "If we play alone, he'll know, I promise."

Felix deliberated. He normally didn't play with the same person—or people—more than once, but…. He swept his eyes up and down Fisher's body, the broad shoulders, defined abs, muscled thighs and that gorgeous cock, still half-hard.

"Sure," he said before he could change his mind. "Yeah, I'd like that."

The phone chimed again and Fisher grabbed it, tapping a quick acknowledgment. "Give me your number now, the car's leaving in two minutes if you don't get out there."

Felix gave it to him and grabbed his coat. Fisher followed him down the hall and to the door.

"I'll text you," he murmured. He was just inches away and Felix couldn't stop himself from going up on tiptoes and brushing a quick kiss across his mouth.

"I look forward to it," he said, and left.

2

————

FISHER TOOK A SHOWER, then pulled out sweatpants and a ratty T-shirt. He dressed, then padded
back out to the living room. Sure enough, Leo was
still sound asleep in a sprawl of arms and legs, a
pillow under his head. French must have put it
there, Fisher realized, warmth building in his chest.

"Hey," he said, stooping and patting Leo's cheek.
"Come on, wake up."

Leo moaned and turned his head away. "Go
'way."

"My house," Fisher said. "Not going anywhere.
Wake up or I'll shove you in the shower and turn it
on cold."

"I hate you," Leo said, opening his eyes to glare
balefully up at him.

"I know," Fisher said cheerfully. He held out a
hand and Leo took it, letting Fisher haul him easily
to his feet. Leo clutched at him, blinking, and affection caught in Fisher's throat. "Come on," he said,
and led him down the hall to the bathroom.

He was sitting on the bed when Leo emerged, rumpled and pink, wet hair standing up in spikes. Fisher patted the mattress and Leo made an agreeable noise and slid in beside him.

"Was that what you needed?" Fisher asked.

Leo snuggled into the pillows, looking highly pleased with himself. "Perfect," he declared. "Exactly what I was looking for."

"So what do we think of our new friend?"

Leo yawned. "Liked him," he said. "You gonna play with him again?"

"Might," Fisher admitted. He studied Leo's face, the eyes already drooping over his straight nose and soft mouth. "Okay if it happens without you?"

"Y'know I don't care," Leo slurred, snuggling into the pillows. "Think he liked you better anyway. But if he wants to… with me, let me know."

Fisher kissed the tip of his nose. "I will. Sleep."

Leo hummed and relaxed into unconsciousness.

Fisher lay awake awhile longer, arms behind his head. Even without the scorching hot sex, he'd been drawn to French, with his bright, dark eyes, that perfect mahogany skin and incredible cheekbones, not to mention his gorgeous tattoos. There *was* something familiar about his face, a faint feeling of having seen him somewhere before, but the attraction was far more than that. Fisher was fascinated by his duality, the way he focused so sharply, drew responses from his partners with an almost cruel precision, but also did little things like put a pillow under Leo's head so he'd be more comfortable.

He wanted to see him again. There had been humor in French's dark eyes, even though they hadn't talked much. Fisher wanted to see his smile. He thought it would light up that beautiful face, and he wanted to find out.

He fell asleep smiling at the thought of making French laugh.

3

———

FELIX WOKE up to a text on his phone. *It's Fisher*, it read, with a smiley face. Felix rubbed his eyes, trying to wake up enough to focus on the screen. After a few minutes of trying and failing to come up with a response, he saved Fisher's details and tapped out a quick *hi* before rolling out of bed.

Gameday meant practice. His routines weren't as rigid as Saint's, although few were, but they still helped him focus, drill down to that bright, shining purpose when he was in net where he existed only to stop the puck.

So he ate breakfast, leaning a hip against the counter and tapping the floor with his toe as he worked through drills in his head and Henry rubbed against his legs, purring. Then he went to the living room and stretched until his muscles felt warm and loose. He'd keep doing random stretches throughout the day to keep himself limber, and it was his favorite part of the day, at least right up until the game started. He loved the feeling of his muscles warming up, the ease of still, at twenty-six years old, being able to drop into the splits and fold flat to the floor. The repetition of the stretches helped him get his head on straight, helped him ignore the chatter and bustle of his teammates around him.

When he felt sufficiently warmed up, he popped back to his feet and headed for his car.

The practice rink wasn't too far. He caught sight of Saint and Carmine walking through the gates and couldn't resist honking at them. Saint flipped him off but Carmine just laughed.

Felix parked and hopped out to join them, wrapping an arm around Saint's neck in greeting. Saint squirmed free, laughing. His dark hair was longer these days, falling forward into his brown eyes, and a smile lit his face much more often lately. It made Felix's heart light to see, and he turned to the cause, pretending to pummel Carmine's ribs.

Carmine yelped, hands up as if he couldn't flatten Felix with one hand, and Felix ducked around his defense to poke his belly.

"Getting slow, old man," he said, dancing backward.

"Well, *you* had fun last night." Saint grinned at him as Carmine grumbled and prodded surreptitiously at his stomach as if to reassure himself his washboard abs were still there.

"I can't just be in a good mood?" Felix countered, holding the door to the rink open.

"When you're in *this* good a mood, it's because you had some mindblowing sex," Carmine said. "I just hope it was safe, sane, and consensual. And no blowup giraffes were involved."

Felix clutched his chest, pretending to be

wounded. "Miette will be crushed. You know she's the best part of having sex with me."

They were laughing as they entered the locker room, blending seamlessly with the clamor that rolled out to envelop them.

Kasha caught sight of them first, face lighting up as he bounded to meet them. Felix caught him in a hug, staggering backward under his weight.

"Jesus, Kash, it's been two days," Carmine said, sounding amused.

"I missed you," Kasha said, disentangling himself from Felix. "It was so boring, all alone. No one to talk to." His English was improving rapidly, although his Russian accent still thickened his words and rounded his vowels. He made puppy eyes at Saint, who seemed unaffected.

"And yet you survived," he said, and patted Kasha's cheek.

Kasha pouted and turned to Carmine for support.

"Whoa, hey, don't look at me," Carmine said, holding up his hands. "I'm on his side, remember? Besides, we took you to the zoo and bought you a giant stuffed giraffe that time. Personally, I think we're *great* parents."

"Zoo was last year!" Kasha complained.

Felix took pity on him. "We'll go out tomorrow, Kash, eh? You and me, who else do you want there?"

"Saint," Kasha said immediately. "Even though he's mean. And Carmine and Jason. Yes?"

"I'll see what I can do," Felix promised.

"Playdate scheduled!" Carmine said, and Kasha punched him.

PRACTICE WAS the usual raucous affair, Felix in his crease with the goalie coach, Ned, for the first hour as the rest of the team worked on passing drills and shooting on him. Felix focused on what Ned was saying, stopping the pucks snapped his way by whoever was in position.

Then they broke into skating drills and Felix and Vanya, the backup goalie, went to work with Ned in earnest.

Felix was dripping sweat when Ned finally called a halt and sent them to the showers. Clean and damp, he sat down on his locker and checked his phone. Fisher had texted him again.

Busy tomorrow?

Felix looked up. He'd promised Kasha— "Jason," he called. The big defenseman looked up, raising a crooked eyebrow in inquiry. "Go out with Kasha, me, Saint, and Carmine tomorrow?"

"Sure," Jason said easily. "Where we going?"

"Haven't decided yet," Felix said. "I'll let you know." He turned back to his phone.

Promised elsewhere tomorrow, sorry.

No worries, Fisher responded immediately. *Day after?*

Felix grimaced. Another game. *Not trying to avoid you, I promise, but... busy then too.*

Popular :), Fisher said.

Not deliberately. Felix stroked the case of his phone, thinking. He had nothing but practice on Sunday, before they left for their next road-trip on Monday. *Sunday?*

At the risk of sounding like I have no life, sure, Fisher said. *My place still work?*

Yeah. Felix ducked a flying towel without looking up. *I'm free after noon.*

See you then :)

"Who you talk to?" Kasha asked, flopping beside him.

"I'm scheduling a sex marathon," Felix said, straight-faced, and Kasha choked. Felix patted him on the back. "Don't ask questions you don't want the answers to." Slipping his phone in his pocket, he stood. He had a nap waiting for him. "See you at the rink, kid."

"Dammit, Saint!" Kasha complained.

"You're a kid until someone younger comes along," Saint called from across the room, focused on the skate in his lap. "Accept your fate."

Kasha grumbled. "Vanya is twenty-two. Why *he's* not kid?"

"Maybe because Vanya knows how to tie his own skates," Carmine said, tousling his hair.

Felix left them bickering and headed for his car.

Home and in bed, sheets cool and soft against his skin, he texted Fisher. *How's Leo?*

He's good :) thanks for asking.

Just us on Sunday? Felix sent.

That okay?

Yeah, Felix replied. His blood heated at the thought of having Fisher's attention focused solely on him. *See you then,* he sent, and put his phone away before he ended up too turned on to sleep.

4

THEY PLAYED the Ravens that night. The Ravens were a dirty team, prone to illegal hits and diving, and Felix had been run into and knocked over more times than he could count. That had improved since Carmine joined the team, but Felix still got dressed in his gameday suit with a set jaw, working through his mental exercises with grim determination. They weren't helping. His stomach was uneasy, butterflies in his chest as he drove to the rink and went inside, an automatic smile on his face for the cameras.

The locker room was as loud as usual, but Felix could read the underlying tension in the voices as they chirped each other. He scanned the room and made a quick executive decision. The room needed to lighten up, and that meant he needed to act. Pranking Saint was out of the question—he had enough to deal with, and upsetting his routines in any way was the best way to spark a meltdown. But Carmine—Carmine was definitely fair game.

He kept several things in his locker for quick and

dirty pranks. Tape to put on blades, baby powder to dump in helmets, shaving cream for filling skate boots—Felix debated for a minute. He wanted to keep this to the room, not out in public, so the tape was out. Baby powder would take a while to clean up, as would shaving cream.

Cup of water, then. He waited until Carmine left the room for the game of two-touch, then grabbed a small styrofoam cup and ducked into the hallway to fill it at the drinking fountain. Elias and Jesper, their fourth-line center and his left wing, watched him as he came back in, but neither said anything—they were all used to his hijinks by now, and they were probably relieved they weren't the target.

Felix set the cup on top of Carmine's pads, just out of sight. Carmine was prone to reaching up and grabbing the pads without looking, which made him a prime target. Then he went back to his locker and began his stretches again, focusing on quieting his mind.

He wasn't afraid of being hurt. Pain was part of the game, and something every player accepted. He was still young and he bounced back quickly. But the Ravens weren't just a rough team with a penchant for body checks—they seemed to actively target whoever was the biggest threat. That was usually Saint, but when Felix was having an especially hot streak, he'd found more than one Raven "accidentally" slamming into him while driving to the net.

Well, their intimidation game wasn't going to work. All it did was make him more determined to shut them out and send them home with their tails between their legs.

There was a clatter and a startled roar from across the room, and Felix jerked his head up. He hadn't even realized Carmine was back. He was glaring at Felix, dripping wet and sputtering, shirt plastered to his chest as the other players clapped and hooted.

Felix grinned at him and Carmine's glower redoubled. Saint, deep in his pre-game ritual, hadn't even looked up. Jason held out a fist and Felix bumped it with his own. The rookies were trying—unsuccessfully—to hide their laughter. The atmosphere was already lighter, some of the tension lifting. *Perfect.*

IT LASTED until they hit the ice for warmups. Felix was in his crease, shaving it down with his skates and then running through his drills with mathematical precision, but he kept a watchful eye on the Ravens at the far end of the rink, milling in a white, blue, and black crowd.

A particular set of broad shoulders caught his attention and he clenched his jaw. Everyone on the Seabirds hated Simon Fall. He'd made Saint a target every time they faced off, and the last time they'd played, he'd run Carmine into the goalpost, fracturing several ribs and taking him out for a solid six weeks.

Simon met Felix's eyes and winked. Felix stared back, unblinking, and Simon's smile widened as he turned to take shots on goal with the rest of his team.

"Don't let him get to you," Carmine said, appearing as if out of nowhere. "You know he's just trying to yank your chain."

"I'll yank *his* chain," Felix muttered.

Carmine slapped him on the back. "We won't let him anywhere near you, don't worry."

Felix shoved him away with his stick. "I'm not afraid of him, dick. I just don't *like* him."

"Pretty sure his mama doesn't like him," Carmine said cheerfully. "We'll still keep him off you."

IT DIDN'T WORK out quite that way, though. The Ravens were playing as dirty as ever, drawing penalties and diving every time a stick even got close to them. After the fourth penalty, Felix was clenching his teeth so hard he was distantly worried about cracking a crown. The referees were either blind or they'd been paid off, as they ignored a Raven blatantly tripping Jason and then blew the whistle when Kasha jumped the offending player.

When the dust settled, the faceoff was to his right. Saint lost the puck drop to the opposing center. Felix stayed ready as teal jerseys went into the scrum to try and get it back. A white jersey broke off and drove for the net, too fast for the forwards. Jason, in front of Felix, lunged, but the Raven spun, hopping neatly over Jason's reaching stick. In almost the same movement, he lifted the puck up over Felix's elbow.

Felix, occupied with trying to track where the puck was, didn't realize until too late that the Raven wasn't stopping, that he was following the puck into the net.

He collided with Felix as he was twisting for the puck, sending him over backward. His head bounced off the post, making his ears ring, as two hundred pounds of fast-moving hockey player landed on top of him.

They went down in a sprawling pile of arms and limbs, the breath driven forcefully from Felix's lungs.

There was a split-second pause as he tried to make his limbs work, and then hands were there, dragging the other player backward. Simon was laughing as he got hauled out of the net, but he wasn't laughing when Carmine's fist connected with his jaw. Felix made it to his knees and scrambled sideways as more players collided and gloves flew.

It took awhile for the referees to sort everything out and separate the combatants. It took even longer for the penalties to be assessed, as Saint and the Ravens' captain talked to the referees. Felix waited, skating in small circles to keep his muscles warmed up, seething silently until the players were back in position for the puck drop.

"LOOK ON THE BRIGHT SIDE," Carmine said in the locker room, slinging an arm around Felix's shoulders. "We won *and* I got to punch him. I don't see a downside."

"The downside is he's a dirty player who ran me over because he doesn't give a shit," Felix snapped.

Saint caught his eye. "Are you hurt?"

"Not the point."

"No, but are you hurt?" Saint insisted.

Felix sighed. "No. My hip is sore and I have a bruise on the back of my head, but mostly I'm just angry."

Carmine slapped him on the back. "I know what will help with that."

THREE BEERS LATER, shoved into the back of the deep booth of their favorite bar, Felix had to admit Carmine sometimes had good ideas. Saint looked alarmed when Felix tried to communicate that.

"Don't tell *him*," he said. "He'll start trying to make all our decisions for us. It'll end in tears and probably something burning down."

"Kasha's more likely to set stuff on fire," Felix pointed out. A thought occurred to him and he snorted a laugh.

Saint raised an inquiring eyebrow and Felix waved his mug, only spilling a little.

"Nothing, cherry," he said. "Only… I met someone who reminds me of Kasha a bit. I was imagining what mischief they would get up to if they met."

Saint looked both horrified and vaguely fascinated. "Is this the guy you went home with last night?"

"One of them," Felix said, and smiled into his beer.

Saint sighed. "You really are going all out, aren't you?"

"Meaning what?"

"You know what," Saint said, fixing him with a gimlet stare. Felix averted his eyes and drained his glass, but Saint was not to be stopped. "It hasn't been that long since that asshole broke your heart. I'm all for you having fun, but I don't want you to get hurt more."

"I play safe," Felix protested.

"Not what I meant and you know it." Saint was every inch the captain as he regarded Felix, a worried frown creasing his perfect brow. "I just… don't want you putting a bandaid over your broken heart and pretending everything's fine."

Felix scowled. "Just because you're in love and things are rosy doesn't mean you get to tell me how to live my life."

"That's not what I'm doing," Saint protested. "Felix, I *know* what P—"

"Do *not* say his name," Felix hissed.

Saint visibly regrouped. "I saw you, after," he said, under the noise of the bar. "I know what you went through."

"You don't know anything," Felix snapped. Guilt lurched in his stomach when Saint flinched, but he bit back the apology and pushed at Kasha on his other side to let him out. Kasha, built like a still-growing brick wall, barely budged, and Felix bit back a snarl and jabbed him in the ribs. "*Move,*" he snarled.

Kasha jumped and scrambled out of the way. Felix slid from the booth and left without looking back.

If life were kind to him, he would have made it

out of the parking lot without at least *one* of his teammates chasing him down.

Life was rarely kind to him.

Vanya got there first, skidding around the side of the building with his big eyes wide with worry. "You okay, Butterfly?" he panted.

Felix sighed and forced a smile. "I'm fine, Vanya. Just tired of socializing. Go back inside."

But Kasha was right behind Vanya, just as distressed, and on their heels was Carmine, brow furrowed. Felix threw his hands in the air.

"If my team could just once stop being a pack of meddling grandmothers, that would be *fucking fantastic!*"

Kasha stopped dead and Carmine ran into him.

Felix spun on his heel and took off before they could sort themselves out.

He caught the first taxi he saw and dragged out his phone. He needed to stop thinking, stop seeing Saint's worried face, stop—

My evening opened up, he texted. *You free?*

Fisher's reply took less than a minute. *Come on over :)*

Felix gave the cab driver the address and sat back, knee jiggling as he stared out the window, chewing on his lip.

5

———

HE TOOK the steps to Fisher's house in a single jump and Fisher was swinging the door open before Felix had his fist raised to knock. Felix took a quick step and a hop. Fisher caught him effortlessly and Felix kissed him hard, wrapping his legs around Fisher's waist. Fisher's mouth was hot and wet and he kissed back without hesitation, swinging the door shut and carrying Felix down the hall. He took him through the living room, Felix barely sparing a glance at their surroundings, and into the bedroom, where he toppled him onto the bed.

Felix landed with a bounce and Fisher was there immediately, crawling on top of him, knees and elbows bracketing Felix's frame.

"What do you want?" he asked, kissing down the side of Felix's jaw.

Felix shivered at the drag of his lips against stubble. "Oh—*calisse*, I want—"

Fisher made an encouraging noise, dragging

Felix's shirt aside and latching on over his collarbone, sucking hard.

"*Fuck*—" Felix gasped, writhing. He was already hard, uncomfortable in his dress pants, and when Fisher brushed the back of one hand over his erection, Felix jolted. "I want to come," he managed finally. "I want—I want to stop thinking. Please."

Fisher hummed and rolled off to strip. Felix did the same, kicking his tangled pants off to the side and falling back to the bed as Fisher crawled on again, eyes dark with purpose.

He reached past Felix and dropped a strip of condoms on the bedspread. Felix wrapped his arms around Fisher's neck, pulling him down into another kiss, this one even more heated and searing. Fisher's cock was hard against Felix's thigh, and he groaned into Felix's mouth.

"God, you're—" He tore away, panting for air.

Felix couldn't help preening. "I'm what?"

"So fucking *hot*," Fisher said, kissing him again hard before sitting up to grab the condoms. "And somehow the fact that you know it doesn't make you any less hot."

Felix's laugh turned into a yelp as Fisher rolled the condom into place with his mouth. He brought his hands up, tangling them in Fisher's hair, and he groaned as Fisher sank down, taking his length all the way in, until the head was bumping against the back of his throat.

Felix swore in French, hardly aware what he was saying as Fisher kept going, dropping down and lifting up, lips and tongue working Felix's shaft until his legs were shaking and he'd forgotten everything.

The game, the fight with Saint, everything was erased in the molten white heat rolling over him.

"Close," he said, clawing at Fisher's shoulder, but Fisher just took him deep again, swallowing around him, and Felix sobbed a breath and came, toes curling with the force of it.

Fisher eased off but didn't stop until Felix was twitching from overstimulation. Then he lifted his head, wiping his reddened mouth.

Felix held out a hand but Fisher shook his head. He sat up and straddled Felix's thigh, tracing appreciative fingers along the heavy muscle.

"You don't look this jacked with your clothes on," he said, taking hold of himself. His other hand was still roaming as he began to stroke—over Felix's abs, dancing along his softening cock, trailing through the hair at his groin. "You're beautiful, French."

Felix swallowed hard. "Next time, will you fuck me?"

Fisher jerked like he'd been hit, coming with a helpless noise on Felix's stomach. He fell forward, catching himself with a hand by Felix's head, eyes closed as he shuddered through the aftershocks.

Felix watched him, exhaustion finally seeping in and replacing the formless frustration and anger in his head.

"*Merci*," he murmured after a minute, and Fisher bent to kiss him.

"Feel better?"

Felix hummed, stretching. "Can I use your shower?"

"You're welcome to stay a little longer," Fisher

said, but Felix smiled and wriggled out from underneath him.

"Another time," he said lightly. "Speaking of, do you still want to meet Sunday?"

"God yeah," Fisher said. He propped himself on one elbow, gloriously unselfconscious, and Felix allowed himself a good long ogle before bending to scoop up his clothes and dispose of the condom.

Fisher was half-asleep when Felix reemerged, one long arm tucked under his head, limbs relaxed and face soft, unguarded.

"Don't get up," Felix said, touching his thigh. "I'll let myself out. You sleep." He bent and dropped a fleeting kiss on Fisher's mouth. "See you Sunday."

IN THE CAR on the way home, he checked his phone, which had three missed calls and multiple texts. Mostly from Saint, but a few from Kasha and Vanya, and one from Carmine. Felix tapped on that one.

He's worried, Carmine said. *Please just tell him you're okay so he'll stop eating himself alive.*

Felix sighed, resting his forehead against the cool glass. He didn't *want* to talk to Saint, who only wanted the best for Felix, who only worried because he cared, who was the best friend Felix had ever had and didn't deserve what Felix put him through.

He opened Saint's messages and tried to compose a reply. It took him most of the drive to figure out what to say and he was still only halfway through when the car pulled up in front of his house.

Felix tipped the driver, climbed out, and gave up. He dialed Saint's number as he trudged up the path to his door, and Saint answered immediately, despite it being three a.m.

"Are you okay?"

Carmine said something in the background, sounding sleepy.

"I know," Saint snapped. "I *know*, okay? I worry too much, whatever. But I need to—"

"I'm fine," Felix said wearily. He pushed his door open and stepped through into darkness. There was no sound from Henry—probably off sound asleep somewhere. Felix kicked off his shoes and padded into the kitchen. "Listen," he said, fishing for water in the fridge. "I'm sorry."

"No," Saint protested. "I pushed too hard. *I'm* sorry. I didn't mean to make it worse, Fee, I hate it when you're upset."

"Well, I'm not anymore," Felix said. He took a long drink of water and sighed. "I know I'm too touchy, cherry. I'm trying not to be."

"After what he did, you have every right," Saint said. He sounded less strung taut. "I could kill him, I swear to God."

"Karma will get him," Felix said, leaning back against the counter.

"That's an idea," Saint said, sounding suddenly intrigued.

"*No*," Felix snapped. He couldn't help the half-laugh. "You're not sending Carmine after him either."

"Fine." Saint heaved a sigh. "*Je t'aime*, Fee."

"*Je t'aime aussi, cherry*. Now go to sleep. I'll see you tomorrow—pick you up at ten."

Henry wandered into the kitchen as Felix hung up, and Felix bent to scratch him under the chin briefly.

"Evening, *bâtard*," Felix said.

Henry yawned, displaying sharp white teeth, then sat down and curled his tail around his paws, blinking sleepy golden eyes.

Felix pulled his shirt off and headed for the bedroom. He stubbed his toe on the couch as he went through the living room and hopped on one foot, swearing under his breath. He was still getting used to his new place, which was smaller and had a very different layout to his old house. He didn't need that much space when it was just him and Henry—he'd bought the other place with the money from his first signing, back when he was young and impulsive and thought a big house was a sign of wealth.

He liked the new place better, even if the circumstances that had driven him to buying it were less than ideal. Felix snorted, pulling a T-shirt from the dresser and tugging it on over his head. 'Less than ideal' was a nice way of putting it.

There were only two bedrooms in the new house, but they were both huge, with twelve foot ceilings, and Felix's king bed looked very inviting. He flopped face-first onto the mattress and Henry leaped lightly up behind him, stepping onto Felix's hips and flexing his claws as a rumbling purr started deep in his chest.

Felix closed his eyes and fell asleep.

6

KASHA WAS WAITING outside his apartment building when Felix pulled up the next morning, bouncing on his toes. The tip of his nose was pink with cold, and he was already talking when he slid into the car.

"Hi Butterfly, are you okay? Where are we going? Is it zoo again? I'm gonna pet donkeys. And goats! You sure you're okay?"

Felix put the car in drive, careful to hide his amusement. "I'm fine, Kash. Sorry about last night. Just having an off day, I guess. And where we're going is a surprise. Have you eaten breakfast?"

Kasha shook his head, glossy brown curls falling over his forehead. "Too excited."

"You're a professional hockey player and a growing boy, you must eat," Felix chided, and pulled into the nearest drive-through.

Four breakfast sandwiches later, Kasha leaned back in his seat with a satisfied sigh and looked at Felix, concentrating on traffic.

"What happen last night?" he asked.

Felix gripped the wheel a little tighter and forced calm into his voice. "Nothing, kid. Just… personal stuff."

"You're team. *Family*. Can I help?" Kasha's voice was soft, utterly serious, and Felix snuck a glance at him to see him gazing back, eyes dark and sincere.

Felix sighed. "It is not… a happy story."

"I can handle," Kasha said firmly. "I'm not little kid."

"I know you're not." Felix took the turn into Saint's driveway, gazing unseeingly at the gate as it rolled slowly open. "I don't like to talk about it because it wasn't…. Some shitty stuff happened. I was stupid."

"What did you do?" Kasha asked, sitting up straighter.

"I fell in love," Felix said baldly. He parked outside the house and turned to Kasha, who looked curious and uncomprehending. "He lied to me from day one, told me he wasn't a hockey fan, didn't even like sports in general, had no idea who I was, when in fact I found out later he'd… well. I suppose you could say he stalked me. Found out where I would be and when, and manufactured our meeting."

Dismay crept over Kasha's face.

"He faked it really well," Felix continued, ignoring the stab of pain at the memory. "Pretended not to care about anything to do with hockey except that it was important to me. So I bought it, yeah? Especially in a hockey town, finding someone who doesn't care that you're famous and make a lot of money is pretty fucking special, yes?"

Kasha nodded, mouth drooping. Felix

unbuckled and Kasha followed him out of the car as Steel, Carmine's dog, came bounding around the corner to meet them.

"So what happen?" Kasha asked, dropping to his knees to greet Steel properly.

Saint opened the door before Felix could answer. "We're almost ready, come on in."

Felix took the out gratefully and stepped inside, touching Saint's shoulder as he passed. Saint looked like he hadn't slept well, dark shadows under his eyes, but his smile was genuine and his touch unhesitating when he pulled Felix into a hug.

"Carmine's getting his shoes on," he said, ushering them through into the kitchen. "Coffee? Breakfast? We have plenty."

"We ate on the way," Felix said.

"Where are we going, anyway?" Saint asked.

"Japanese gardens," Felix told him.

Kasha perked up. "I'm never go there before! And you can tell me more about this ex, yes?"

Felix glanced at Saint, who raised an eyebrow. Felix shook his head, and Saint nodded infinitesimally.

"Sure thing," Felix said to Kasha as warmth spread in his chest. Saint had his back. He'd help distract Kasha anytime he remembered to ask for the story. Felix wouldn't have to lay his pain out for anyone else to pick through.

HE WAS STILL THINKING about that when he got home. He liked Fisher—a lot. Henry wound between his legs and Felix bent to pet him absently.

Fisher seemed solid. Safe. But Felix bore the scars of "solid and safe". He wasn't risking that again. He needed to lay down some ground rules.

PRACTICE WAS THE NORMAL CIRCUS. Felix's hip was still sore from Fall's hit, so after Coach dismissed them, he stopped by the trainers' room. He spent an hour getting worked over, the trainer helping him open his hip adductors and regain flexibility, and when she was done, he was a pleasant puddle on the table.

He levered himself upright, gave her a fistbump, and headed out.

A quick stop at home to grab a sandwich and feed Henry, and he was out the door and heading for Fisher's house.

Fisher answered the door in a pair of soft, weathered jeans and a long-sleeved T-shirt that did a lot to showcase his very excellent arms and chest. Felix gave him an appreciative once-over and Fisher's lips quirked as he stepped back to give him room to come inside.

The house was as spotless as ever but there was one difference this time—Felix rounded the corner and stopped dead at the sight of a sleek greyhound asleep in front of the fireplace.

"You have a dog!" he said, delighted.

"I do," Fisher rumbled, putting a hand on Felix's lower back and urging him forward a step so he could slip past him. "Her name is Maya, and as you can see, she's an excellent guard dog. Are you hungry?"

"Can I pet her?" Felix asked. Maya had raised her head at the sound of voices and was examining Felix intently. She was a solid nut-brown, with a white chest and white toes like she'd stepped in paint. "Hi, *mon pitou*," Felix told her, and she rose languidly to her feet, yawning and displaying rows of very white teeth before padding over to sniff the hand he held out.

"That's more her decision than mine, as you can see," Fisher said, sounding amused. "Would you like some lunch?"

"I actually already ate," Felix said. Maya was as silky soft as she looked, leaning rapturously against Felix's leg as he rubbed her ears. "How come I've never met you before, eh?" he asked her, and Maya licked his hand, her tail wagging in graceful sweeps.

"Well, to be fair, you've only been here late at night when she was already kenneled, and you've already discovered that she doesn't really give a shit about who's in my house."

"You're perfect, don't listen to him," Felix told Maya, and Fisher laughed.

"Can I at least get you something to drink?"

"Sure," Felix said, straightening reluctantly to follow him into the kitchen. Maya tagged along and Felix sat down at the table in the corner as Fisher rummaged in the refrigerator. Maya put her head on Felix's knee and Felix went back to petting her.

"Water? Juice? Soda?"

"Water's fine," Felix said. He accepted the glass Fisher handed him and took a quick sip, marshalling his thoughts. "So I think we need to talk."

Fisher raised an eyebrow, sinking into the chair opposite him. "Already?" He pitched his voice high.

"Baby please, I can change, I promise, I'll do better. Just tell me what to do."

Felix kicked at him, smothering a laugh. "Shut up, you ass. I just want to make sure we are on the same page, yes?"

Fisher grinned at him and made a go-ahead motion.

"This—" Felix gestured between them. "It's just sex."

Fisher arched that dark brow again and inclined his head.

"Nothing more, I mean," Felix continued.

"No relationship," Fisher offered.

"Yes, exactly. I don't want—" Felix swallowed. "I'm not ready for that. I may not ever be. So I think it's best if we keep personal details to a minimum. You don't ask me what I do. I won't ask what you do. No names other than what we've already given each other."

Fisher nodded slowly. "I can work with that, I guess."

"You guess?" Alarm caught in Felix's chest. "Is it not what you want?"

"It's fine," Fisher assured him. "Really, it is. You're ridiculously hot, I'm down to fuck you six ways from Sunday anytime you want. But—"

"But what?"

"I *do* want a relationship someday," Fisher said bluntly. "Not today, not for a while, not until the right person comes along, but when I meet him, this, us—" He repeated Felix's gesture. "It'll have to end."

Felix relaxed. "Okay. That's… okay. You tell me,

it's over. I'll understand. And in the meantime… do you wish to be exclusive?"

Fisher eyed him. "What do *you* want?"

"Exclusivity implies relationship, to me," Felix said carefully. "I might want to play with someone else. Would that bother you?"

Fisher shrugged, folding his hands on the table. "Contrary to the impression I may have given you, I don't really get out much. I spend a lot of time with work and I tend to take it home with me, so unless Leo drags me somewhere, I don't actually hit the bar scene that often. But I'm not going to be bothered if you do, as long as you communicate and play safe."

"And same for you," Felix said. He leaned forward and touched Fisher's knuckles with one finger. The hair curled crisp and tight, Fisher's skin warm under Felix's touch.

Fisher shivered. "Are we done talking?"

Felix smiled at him, letting the want shine through plainly on his face. "We are definitely done talking, *ami*."

"Oh thank God," Fisher said, and surged from his chair.

7

"ARE you sure this is something you can do?" Leo asked again.

Fisher chopped carrots a little more aggressively. "I already told you I can. Why are you pushing on this?"

"Because that's why you keep me around," Leo said, kicking his feet. He was perched on the counter, watching as Fisher prepared dinner. "That and occasionally excellent sex."

"*Always* excellent sex," Fisher said, nudging his knee. "Don't sell yourself short."

"Well of course it's always excellent," Leo said, grinning at him under the silvery fall of his hair. "I just meant it doesn't happen that often. Because you're a homebody and a stick in the mud and any other term for boring you can think of. But we're off-topic. *You* want a relationship. You want a perfect little nuclear family, with the white picket fence and the porch swing and cocoa at Christmas and stockings over the fireplace and dirty diapers and little league and—" Fisher got a hand over his mouth and Leo immediately licked his palm.

Fisher made a disgusted noise and yanked his hand away. "I don't want that *now*."

"But you wouldn't say no if it came calling." Leo's eyes were knowing.

"Yes I would."

"Liar." Leo kicked his feet again. "You're domestic as fuck, Fisher, and you want someone to share that life with you."

Fisher sighed, defeated. "Yeah. I do. Happy? I do want that. But I also want French. We're ridiculously compatible in bed. He's hot and funny and I very much enjoy the time we spend together, especially since most of it's naked. I'm not going to get hung up on him or start wanting my apple pie life *with* him, because I know it's not what he wants. Why can't I just enjoy hot sex on acceptable terms until the right guy *does* come along?"

Leo hopped off the counter and went up on his tiptoes to wrap his arms around Fisher's neck. "I just don't want you to get hurt, Fish," he said against his ear. "Because I love you, and you're my best friend, and as *your* best friend, part of my job is helping you protect yourself."

Fisher hugged him back. "I'm not gonna get hurt," he muttered.

"You're gonna get hurt," Leo countered, taking a step back. He looked old beyond his years suddenly, weighed down with bitter truths learned the hard way. "But maybe we can keep you from completely wrecking yourself. Now. Tell me more about this compatibility in bed."

———

8

"Good morning, Mr. Fisher!"

Fisher turned from the chalkboard as Samantha bounced through the door. "Good morning, Samantha, how was your weekend?"

"We went to the zoo! And I sat on Tommy." She giggled, twining a long strand of brown hair around her small finger. "Twice. It was an apsidents."

Fisher crouched, smiling at her. "Accident. Sound it out."

"Ax-i-dent," Samantha said dutifully.

"Good job! Now was it really an accident?"

Samantha tugged harder on her hair and Fisher gently untwined the strand from around her finger, slipping a small foam ball into her hand instead.

"The first time was," Samantha finally admitted. She looked guilty but not really repentant. "He's loud, Mr. Monty. And Mama's always busy. And Nanny Laura tells me to 'innertain myself' alla time. He kept getting in my way and spoilin' my games. It's his fault."

"En-ter-tain," Fisher said, and waited until Samantha repeated the word. "Good job, you're using such big words! Now, do you really think it was his fault?"

Samantha pushed out her lower lip, looking mutinous.

"How old is Tommy?" Fisher asked.

"Two," Samantha muttered.

"And how old are you?" Fisher prompted gently.

Samantha sighed. "Six."

"Mhmm. Do you think Tommy meant to mess up what you were doing?"

"Prob'ly."

Fisher held back a laugh with an effort, keeping his face calm. "Do you think maybe Tommy loves his big sister very much and wants to spend time with you, but maybe he doesn't know how to show it yet?"

Other students poured through the door as Samantha deliberated. Fisher waved but didn't address them, waiting for Samantha's reply.

"Maybe," she finally said.

"And do you think maybe it makes him sad if you're mean to him? Remember how sad you were last month when Martine said she didn't want to play with you?"

Samantha drooped.

Several parents were hovering near the door, clearly wanting to speak to Fisher. He patted Samantha's hand.

"Think about it, okay? Maybe we can come up with something fun you can do with Tommy, something you'll both like. I have to talk to the grownups really quick. Can you find your seat and we'll talk about it later?"

"Okay, Mr. Monty," Samantha said, and flung her small arms around his neck.

Fisher patted her back and stood.

"Good morning, ladies," he said to the women clustered in the doorway. "What can I do for you today?"

Margaret Charpentier batted her eyes at him and held out a Tupperware container. "Martine and I made cookies over the weekend. We thought you might like some."

"Martine!" Fisher called, and she came bouncing over, dark hair up in pigtails and every ribbon perfect on her frock. "Did you make cookies, Miss Martine?"

She dimpled at him. "Sugar cookies, Mr. Monty! Mama helped a little though."

"Well, thank you," Fisher told her, tucking the container under his arm. "I'm sure they're absolutely delicious."

Martine bounced off again and Fisher smiled goodbye to her mother before turning to the next parent waiting to talk to him.

"It's just such a shame you don't have a wife to take care of you," Laurel Hollingsworth lamented. "Such a *waste*!" She pushed a container of lasagna into his arms and smiled up at him and Fisher coughed and turned to put his gifts on the table behind him.

"I'm pretty busy," he said, turning back to her. "I don't really have time for dating in general right now."

"Such a waste," Laurel sighed.

Katherine, the hall monitor, cleared her throat quietly from the doorway. "Fisher, may I have a quick word?"

Fisher stepped into the hall to see a tall man with a little boy clinging to his leg. He didn't recognize either of them, but he gave the man a smile and dropped to a crouch to greet the little boy.

"Hi," he said. "I'm Fisher. What's your name?"

The boy hid his face in his father's leg, clutching him tighter, but Fisher didn't move, keeping the smile on his face. After a minute, the boy glanced at him, revealing bright blue eyes almost hidden behind thick glasses.

"Max," he said, almost inaudible.

The man touched his shoulder. "Speak up," he said.

Max took a deep breath and squared his little shoulders, meeting Fisher's eyes. "Max," he repeated more loudly.

"It's so great to meet you, Max," Fisher said, his smile widening. He glanced up at Katherine, a question in his eyes. *Is he mine?*

Katherine nodded, and Fisher switched his attention back to Max.

"How do you feel about hamsters, Max?"

Max's eyes widened. "You h-have a h-hamster?"

Fisher leaned in. "We have *two*," he stage-whispered. "And whoever is the best helper gets to feed them. Would you like to meet them?"

Max looked up at his father. "Can I, Daddy?"

"May I," his father corrected. "Yes, you may."

Fisher stood and put out a hand to Max, who took it immediately. "I'll be right back," he said to

Katherine and Max's father, and led Max into the room.

Once he was settled in front of the hamsters and Samantha had been beckoned over to make his acquaintance, Fisher went back to the hall, where the man was waiting by himself.

"Sorry about that," he said. "I like to make sure the kids know they're my priority at all times." He held out one hand. "Fisher Montgomery."

The man held Fisher's hand a beat too long before letting go. "Calum Stewart." His eyes, a colder shade of blue than Max's, were calmly appraising. "New to the area, my wife's job just transferred us over. Obviously we tried to get into Primrose House but they didn't have any openings, so now we're here. I've heard good things about you, Mr. Montgomery. I specifically requested Max be put in your class."

"Call me Fisher," Fisher said, skin prickling. Calum's eyes were almost hungry, not subtle about looking him up and down as if getting his measure. He was a few inches shorter than Fisher and Fisher probably outweighed him by forty pounds. So why did he feel on the defensive? "Anything in particular I need to know about Max? Allergies, fears, favorite things?"

"He likes Transformers, really anything with cars or robots," Calum said. "No allergies, but he has a silly thing about the texture of satin, he hates it. Just ignore it, he'll get over it." He shifted his feet but didn't move.

"We'll take good care of him," Fisher said, keeping a smile in place.

Calum appeared to finally get the hint. "The

office has my phone number. If you need anything, feel free to let me know."

Fisher turned back to the classroom, resisting the urge to wipe his hand on his pants.

"Who's ready to start the day?" he asked, and fifteen 6-year-olds' hands shot up in unison. "Oh, very good," he said. "You didn't make a single noise! Let's talk about our weekends. Samantha, who should go first?"

Samantha stood, chest puffed with importance at being chosen for this task, and surveyed the room. "Jeffrey," she finally declared.

"Jeffrey, you're up!" Fisher said.

HE SPENT the morning channeling the children's energy into healthy outlets, settling disputes, and admiring artwork, until it was time for lunch and they were gathered up by Katherine.

Alone, Fisher sat down at his desk and contemplated the glitter on his pants. Damn stuff was like herpes. He was occupied in trying to brush it all off when someone knocked on the open doorframe. Fisher glanced up to see a curvy woman about his age, dark brown hair with bangs cut too long, almost hiding her curious brown eyes.

"Hi," she said.

"Hi!" Fisher said, rising. "Are you a parent? Are you picking someone up? I don't think we've met—"

"No no," the woman said, flapping her hands. "No, I'm your new assistant. Wren Fairchild."

"Oh right!" Fisher crossed the room and held out a

hand for her to take. "They told me you were coming but I lost track of time. It's great to meet you, Wren, won't you come in? You can put your stuff there—that's your desk. I'm sorry I wasn't here to meet you during your hiring process, but I've heard good things."

Wren stowed her backpack and looked around the room. "It's a really nice setup," she said, tugging on her braid.

"Thank you. We get a lot of leeway to personalize our spaces. You come highly recommended—why did you want to work at the Saint Mary Conservatory?"

"Well, it's one of the best, isn't it?" Wren said. "I was looking at Primrose House but they don't have any openings right now. It's hard to get in there because no one wants to leave."

"Saint Mary's is pretty good too," Fisher said, smiling at her. "The kids are at lunch right now, but when they get back, we're going to work on their birdhouses. Everyone except Jeffrey, because he's afraid of birds, so he's building a squirrel feeder. You'll want to learn their likes and dislikes, what they're interested in and what they don't have time for. I like to encourage the girls to pursue interests in math and science, and the boys to allow themselves to enjoy more traditionally 'feminine' things like dancing and art. No one gets buttonholed in my classroom—everyone is free to pursue their own passions."

Wren nodded earnestly. "I have two little sisters at home. I helped raise them and it gave me a love for helping young minds develop. I'm really happy to be here, Mr. Montgomery."

"Call me Fisher, please," Fisher said, smiling at her.

THEY SPENT the lunch hour tidying the room and getting to know each other. Wren liked to knit and watch reality television and she loved hockey.

Fisher hid the initial twitch of distaste."Oh yeah, the Seabirds?" he asked, stacking chairs. "How are they doing this year?"

"Pretty good," Wren said. "My dad has season tickets so I go when I can. I'm not a diehard fan, though, I like the Kingfishers too, even though they're our rivals. Do you follow hockey at all?"

"Not a bit," Fisher said. "I had a—" He caught himself. "I knew someone who went pro, way back in high school. I... don't have good memories of the sport. It's very violent."

"It can definitely be physical and aggressive," Wren agreed. "But it's also fascinating and surprisingly cerebral. They have to be able to think and react in nanoseconds. They're skating at over twenty miles an hour and reacting to plays while moving that fast. And playmakers like Saint are even more impressive."

"What's a playmaker?" Fisher inquired. Even with the topic being hockey, he was enjoying the way her eyes lit as she talked and how she'd forgotten her shyness.

"Well, you know how the team all has to work together, and they have drills and routines, right? They practice over and over until things mesh. Most guys rely on that routine. If he sees a linemate making a particular move, he knows what he'll be expected to do on muscle memory, and he does it. But a playmaker—they think five steps ahead. They're not just out there reacting—they're *creating* the moves. They're setting up their teammates and driving the offense. A good playmaker is worth his weight in gold, and Saint's not just good—he's great."

"Wow," Fisher said blankly.

Wren blushed. "Sorry." She tugged on her braid again. "I got carried away."

"No, it's interesting!" Fisher said. He set the last chair on the stack and turned to find the broom. "I love hearing about people's passions. Do you play?"

Wren shook her head. "I wanted to when I was younger, but genetics worked against me. I played in college, thought about maybe even going pro, but I'm not very athletic." She gestured at herself. "It required a level of dedication that I just wasn't ready to put in, I guess. Hey, I have tickets to the next home game. Do you want to maybe come with me? There'll be a few of us."

"Oh, I don't—" Fisher hesitated. "I don't really know much about it." He winced, knowing how feeble it sounded.

"I can tell you!" Wren said. "The seats aren't great but the Birds always make home games fun. It'll do you good to get out of the house."

"Thank you for offering," Fisher said, smiling at her. "And don't take it personally, okay? I can see how much you love the game. But I—" How much to say? "That hockey player I knew in high school?"

"Ohh," Wren said, as if a light had dawned. "Bad breakup?" There was nothing but sincere sympathy on her face. "I had a girlfriend a few years ago who dumped me because I didn't like to workout. Which I guess is fair, you've seen me—" She gestured at her curves again.

"You're perfect," Fisher said instantly. "Her loss."

Wren dimpled, looking delighted, and Fisher glanced around to make sure no one else was within earshot.

"I guess you could call it that," Fisher said. "He wasn't out, and he was *obsessed* with hockey in general, but specifically in making it to the NHL. It's a long, boring story but basically it left me with a bad taste in my mouth. It's too long to go into here, really."

"Let's go out some weekend," Wren said. "Have some drinks, talk about our taste in partners. I'm bisexual, which means I'm capable of disappointing two genders instead of just one." She grinned at Fisher's startled laugh.

"I'm glad you're here," Fisher told her, and she blushed, tugging on her braid. "No, I mean it," he insisted. "You're already fitting right in."

They finished clearing up the mess, Fisher directing Wren on how to help. Finally, they were done and glanced around the room in satisfaction.

"Perfect. See you tomorrow?"

Wren smiled up at him. "I think I'm gonna like it here."

Someone rapped knuckles on the door and Fisher looked up.

"Do you have a minute?" Turner Scott was standing there, one eyebrow lifted.

"Of course," Fisher said. "Wren, you can head out. I'll lock up when I'm done."

Wren nodded. "Hi, Mr. Scott. Um, thanks again for the job."

"Well, you came highly recommended," Scott said, giving her a nod in return.

Turner Scott wasn't a big man, but he liked to think he was. It showed in the way he squared his shoulders, puffed his chest, walked on his tiptoes like he thought it added inches to his height. He settled himself in one of the small chairs kept near Fisher's desk with his lips pinched together, tugging his vest back into place as Fisher sat opposite.

"How can I help you?" Fisher asked.

Scott shifted his weight, trying to find a comfortable position. "You need adult-sized chairs in here."

If he added adult-sized chairs, the parents tended to stay too long, happy to keep chatting on about this or that as long as they had Fisher's attention, but he couldn't say that to the man who'd hired him.

"I'll look into it," he said instead.

Scott pinched his mouth again. "Some of the parents have come to me with… concerns."

"Oh?" Fisher kept his posture loose, his expression calm. "Is something wrong?"

"Not exactly," Scott said.

"Are the children not performing to standards?"

"You know they are," Scott snapped. "You also know you're our best *and* most popular teacher."

Fisher spread his hands. *So?*

"This is a good Christian school," Scott finally said. "As such, we expect you to conform to the code of ethics and decorum set forth in our handbook."

"Decorum—have I behaved in any unsuitable

way?" Fisher asked, throttling back the fury with an effort.

"Of course not."

"Then what's the problem?"

"A few parents have expressed concern that you're telling their boys it's okay if they want to wear girls' clothing, and encouraging their girls to pursue more… traditionally masculine activities."

Fisher took a deep breath, flattening his hands on the table and letting the air out slowly through his nose. *This is a good job*, he reminded himself. *It pays well and you have student loans. Do* not *talk back to the prissy little man with the God-complex.*

"I apologize if my teaching methods have been unseemly in any way," he said when he was sure he could keep his voice even. "I believe in teaching children to keep open minds."

"Well, not so open their brains fall out," Scott said, and laughed at his joke.

Fisher forced a smile. "Of course not."

"In any case," Scott continued. "Just try to remember that the parents of these children expect us to behave in a certain… manner. A seemly manner. We believe in raising boys to be gentlemen, and girls to be ladies. Alright?"

Fisher definitely didn't trust his voice, but he managed a nod.

"Oh, and one more thing," Scott said, standing. He tugged his vest down again. "I think you could be a little friendlier to some of our mothers."

"Are you seriously implying I'm not—"

"No no," Scott said, waving a hand. "You're perfectly polite. But you get a lot of interest, and you don't spend much time speaking to them."

"Because I thought my job was teaching their children," Fisher said through his teeth. "*Not* flirting with their parents."

"No one's telling you to flirt!" Scott said hastily. "Just… keep them happy."

Fisher took another deep breath. "Noted. Is there anything else?"

"That's all. See you tomorrow." Scott nodded once and made a quick exit.

9

———

FELIX STRETCHED his legs out with a sigh. He hated flying, but at least the plane was built with hockey players in mind—he had plenty of legroom.

He wondered idly what Fisher was doing. Even though they'd agreed on no personal details, Felix couldn't help the curiosity. Maybe he was a personal trainer. He had the muscles for it. Or maybe a bodybuilder.

On impulse, he pulled his phone from his pocket.

I hate flying :(

Fisher's response was gratifyingly swift. *How long is the flight?*

Felix calculated. *About eight hours longer. Kill me now.*

But then where would I get mind-blowing sex? Fisher countered.

Felix snickered, glancing surreptitiously around the plane to make sure no one had noticed before he composed his reply. *Leo would be offended. I think I'll tell him.*

Don't you dare, Fisher sent back. *He'd kill ME, or at least make my life unlivable for a while. Speaking of sex, when are you getting back to town?*

Felix laughed out loud, clapping a hand over his mouth to keep the noise in. *Didn't I wake you up with a blowjob this morning before I left?*

That was at three a.m., Fisher pointed out. *Pretty sure that counts as yesterday. I just need to know how long I'm going without, here.*

Felix rolled his eyes. *You don't have to go without just because I'm not in town.*

Fisher didn't reply for several minutes. *I know :)*, he finally sent.

Saint sat down next to Felix, who jumped and locked his phone.

"Can I help you?" Felix said, sharper than intended.

Saint arched a brow. "I can't sit by my best friend?"

"Usually you want something when you switch up your routine," Felix said. "And since you're not loving it up with Carmine—" Saint made gagging noises and Felix fought a laugh. "—I must assume you want something. So…?"

Saint glanced at Felix's phone, clutched in one hand. "What's his name?"

"Why do you assume it's a he, cherry?" Felix countered.

"Because you're more attracted to men, something *you* told me."

"I'm never getting drunk with you again," Felix muttered, slumping in his seat.

Saint waited, brow still arched.

There was no use trying to outwait him. "He's just a friend," Felix finally said.

"Uh huh. Let me guess. He's a very *hot* friend who you sleep with."

"There's not much sleeping," Felix admitted, lips twitching, and Saint laughed, making several heads turn.

"Knew it. Tell me about him."

"His name is Fisher," Felix said with a sigh. "But truly, he is just a friend. There is no relationship."

"More of the benefits than the 'friend with', eh?" Saint asked. His eyes were keen but amused, and Felix smiled back at him.

"You want to see him?"

Saint rolled his eyes in response, so Felix unlocked his phone and scrolled through his pictures. He'd been over in the afternoon that day, and after they were done, Fisher had brought them both water and then collapsed on the couch, still sweaty and naked, facedown with his head turned so he could see Felix, who was on his back on the floor.

Felix had emptied half the bottle of water and then groped for his phone. Only one of Fisher's eyes was visible but it had creased with his smile as Felix took a picture of him from the shoulders up.

"I need proof that you can get tired," Felix had teased, and Fisher had laughed, making a half-hearted attempt to flip him off.

"Oh shit," Saint said, taking the phone. "Good *taste*, Fee. Damn, he's gorgeous."

"He is, no?" Felix smiled and accepted the phone back.

"What does he do?"

Felix sobered. "Oh, ah… I don't know."

"You don't *know*? How long ago did you meet?"

"Three weeks? Three and a half."

"And you still don't know what he does?"

Felix squirmed. "It's… better this way. Safer. No one gets their heart broken."

"He's okay with this?" Saint straightened. "He knows what *you* do, right?"

"Ah—"

"*Felix.*"

"He didn't recognize me!" Felix said defensively. "There's *nothing* hockey related at his house. He's never brought it up—not that we talk much—"

Saint's brows were pinched together, his mouth tight with worry. "Fee—"

"You saw what happened last time," Felix managed. His throat was tightening. "I don't—I can't—"

"They won't all be like that," Saint said. "You can't just… throw out the entire concept of a relationship because of one rotten apple."

"You *know* what he did," Felix hissed. "He—"

"I know," Saint interrupted. "Fee, I *do* know. I was there, I saw it happen. I picked the pieces of you up off the floor, remember?"

"And for that I should thank you?" Felix snarled. "Saintly Saint, always repairing the broken? Have you been fitted for your halo?"

Saint flinched. "That's not fair," he said in a low tone.

The fight rushed from Felix all at once and he folded over, covering his face, as the guilt flooded in. "I'm sorry," he managed through his palms. "Saint, I'm so sorry." He sat up, turning to catch Saint's hands. "It is the worst aspect of me, the way I hurt you when you speak truth I don't like. Forgive me, cherry, please."

Saint squeezed his hands. There was still hurt in his brown eyes, but the small smile he summoned was real. "I've known that about you since we were fifteen. If it was a deal breaker, I'd have kicked your ass to the curb a long time ago."

"*Je t'aime*," Felix said helplessly. "You know the worst of me but still you stay."

"It's not like I've never hurt you either," Saint said. "But are you sure you know what you're doing?"

Felix sat back in his seat with a sigh. "I *never* know what I'm doing. Of all things, that is a given."

Saint patted his arm. "Well, I'm right there with you."

"Everything okay with Carmine?"

Saint sighed. "Sure. I mean yeah. No, it is."

It was Felix's turn to arch a brow. "Truly."

"It *is*," Saint said. "It's just…." He shifted his weight, touching his thumb to each of his knuckles in turn—a calming ritual he'd developed when they were teenagers. "He's gonna get sick of me."

"Has he said something? Done something? Made you think—" Felix put his hands on the armrests, ready to leap to his feet and thrash Carmine for making Saint doubt himself for even a *second*—

"No! Felix, stop!" Saint grabbed his arm, pulling him back down into the seat as everyone turned to stare at them.

"Keep it down," Roddy called from across the aisle. His sleep mask was still firmly in place, head back against the seat cushion. "Some of us have small kids and need sleep."

"Just because you don't know what birth control is doesn't mean that's our problem," Carmine yelled from several rows up, making everyone laugh. "What is it they say about your failure to plan not being my emergency?"

Felix sank back into the seat under the raucous noise of everyone teasing Roddy. "If he hasn't said anything, then why—"

Saint slumped, hair falling into his eyes. For a brief moment, they were fifteen again and Saint was admitting to him in a tiny whisper fueled by too much of their billet father's pilfered whiskey that he was gay and Felix was the first person he'd ever told.

Felix took his hand again. "Talk to me, cherry."

"You're the only one who's ever stuck around," Saint said in a whisper. "Until now. And you don't have to live with me, which is probably why you haven't killed me."

"Not true," Felix said flatly. "I *did* live with you, remember? And you never once did anything bad enough to warrant murder."

"Well, we never had a romantic relationship, either. Carmine—" Saint shook his hair out of his eyes.

"Carmine loves you," Felix said. "Do you doubt that?"

"No. No, never." Saint's eyes softened. "I know he does. I just—I keep waiting for the other shoe to drop."

"Well, stop it."

That startled Saint into a laugh and some of the tension in his shoulders eased.

"I mean it," Felix said, smiling back at him. "You're perfect, cherry, and he knows it. He's the lucky one, and I promise you he knows *that*, too."

Saint wrapped an arm around Felix's shoulders and hugged him briefly. "You'll tell me if anything goes wrong with your new friend?"

"Yes," Felix said resignedly. "So you can fuss and mother hen me and threaten to kill him. I know how it works."

"As long as you do." Saint let him go and stood, winking at him before heading back down the aisle to rejoin Carmine.

Felix waited until he was gone before he turned back to his phone and tapped out a quick message. *I'll be back in three days. Free on Thursday?*

Absolutely :), Fisher sent back, and Felix smiled and locked his phone again.

10

———

FISHER HAD glitter in his hair. Felix hadn't noticed it at first, too busy dragging him into the bedroom and pulling off his clothes, but now, with the afterglow warm in his bones and his mind quiet, the setting sun caught glints of purple and red in Fisher's black curls, and Felix blinked, looking closer.

"What—" He plucked a fragment from the mess and held it up on his fingertip, peering at it. "Is that *glitter*, then?"

Fisher laughed, one muscled arm tucked under his head. "That damn stuff gets everywhere."

Felix squinted at him. "Are you secretly a drag queen, *pêcheur*?"

"I could rock a pair of stilettos," Fisher said comfortably.

"Mm," Felix agreed, dropping his head back onto the pillow beside him. "Do wonders for those lovely legs of yours."

Fisher's laugh vibrated his chest and he patted

Felix's thigh. "Hungry? I was going to make salmon for dinner."

Felix's mouth watered. "Only if I get to pet Maya and not help you cook at all," he said.

"No good in the kitchen?" Fisher sat up, smiling down at him.

"Hopeless," Felix agreed, returning the smile. "And also lazy."

"Well, as long as you pet Maya where I can see you and appreciate the view, I'm okay with this arrangement." Fisher swung his legs out of bed.

"Oh, I am to be eye candy, then?" Felix said, feigning offense. "I'm good for nothing else?"

Fisher snorted a laugh and threw himself back on the bed, straddling Felix and pressing him into the pillows. He bent, bringing their faces together, and Felix swallowed hard. Fisher's eyes were flecked with gold, he could see from this close, his breath warm and sweet and a smile quirking the corner of his mouth.

"I think we've established you have other… qualities," Fisher said, and kissed him.

It was like Fisher's mouth switched off Felix's brain. All thought ceased when their lips were touching, when Fisher's tongue was softly probing Felix's mouth, quick and teasing, when he made a noise low in his throat and deepened the kiss.

Felix arched into it, wrapping his arms around Fisher's neck and hanging on until Fisher tore away, breathing hard.

"No, nope," he said, sitting up on his heels. "We already did that, and I'm hungry."

Felix pouted at him, rocking his hips up to grind

his growing erection against Fisher's ass. "Dinner can wait, no?"

Fisher shivered, eyes drooping shut. "Fuck, you're—"

"I'm what?" Felix prompted, trailing a finger over the thick line of Fisher's cock.

"Hard to say no to, for one thing," Fisher gasped, and dropped to kiss him again as Felix laughed quietly, triumphantly, and rolled them so he was on top.

AFTER, he sat in one of the dining room chairs, one knee drawn to his chest and his chin propped on it, as Fisher puttered around the kitchen. Maya was curled at Felix's feet, her head on his sock. Felix unlocked his phone and scrolled his social media, checking his mentions. He got enough of them that he didn't respond often, but he liked to find the fans that didn't get much attention, the kids, the single mothers, the fifty-something dads, and reply to them.

He was in the middle of composing a message to a twelve-year-old on Twitter who had asked him why he used the brand of stick he did when Fisher laughed softly.

"What?" Felix asked, raising his head.

"You're as flexible as my—" Fisher caught himself. "You're flexible. I've never seen anyone over the age of ten sit like that."

His what? Felix couldn't ask. *Wouldn't* ask. Instead he sent Fisher a slow smile.

"I find it helps with certain… activities."

Fisher pointed the whisk he was holding at him. "It sure does, and you're just staying over there out of the way while I do this so I don't burn the damn fish."

Felix laughed to himself and went back to typing. He'd just hit post when a new notification caught his eye.

Anyone know where @butterfly_39 is living these days?

Felix stiffened. Why anyone would *tag* him in posts like that, he'd never understood, but it happened far too often, often enough to make him consider deleting social media altogether.

A reply popped up. *Dude, not cool.*

Thank you, hockyluvr27, Felix thought wryly.

The first person responded almost immediately. *Just wanted to see the outside of his place! His old house was sick.*

Felix's skin crawled and he locked the phone, dropping it on the table. The noise made Fisher glance up.

"Everything okay?"

Felix forced a smile. "*Oui.* Will you tell me about the glitter?"

"If I tell you about the glitter, you'll know what I do for a living," Fisher countered. "As I recall, that's a rule *you* put in place. Why are you asking?"

"Because it makes me curious," Felix admitted. "And probably no harm would come from knowing a *little* more about you, if our relationship doesn't change."

Fisher gave him a look but didn't say anything.

"Plus I like games," Felix said, grinning at him,

and Fisher's lips twitched. "So will you tell me if I'm right?"

"*If* you're right," Fisher said. He stirred the sauce, adding something to the pan.

"Fine." Felix considered. "You are… a makeup artist."

Fisher laughed, head falling back and shoulders shaking. "I can't contour for shit," he finally said when he'd sobered. "Leo despairs."

Felix grinned and drummed his fingers on the table. "Wedding planner. You work with satin and lace and terrible mothers all day."

"The terrible—" Fisher stopped. "No. Not a wedding planner, but weirdly closer than you might think."

"That explains absolutely nothing," Felix said, nettled, and Fisher grinned at him.

"So do I get to guess what you do?" he countered.

Felix narrowed his eyes. "I won't tell you if you're right," he warned.

Fisher sighed. "And you say you like games."

"Go ahead and guess then," Felix snapped, bristling. "You won't get it right anyway." He told himself the way Fisher brightened didn't affect him at all.

"Actor," Fisher said immediately.

Felix burst out laughing and Fisher scowled at him.

"I am a *hopeless* actor, *pêcheur*," Felix said through his giggles. "I tried once, in high school. Missed every cue, forgot all my lines. The director fired me, said she had a desk chair that would do a better job." There was a reason he was never tapped to do anything in the commercials the media team shot other than smile widely and stop pucks.

"Ouch," Fisher said, snickering. "Okay, hm. Something fairly prominent publicly, I'm guessing."

Felix very carefully didn't react beyond raising a neutral eyebrow.

"You're a lawyer," Fisher said. He sounded pleased with himself.

Felix made a gagging noise. "Do I really look like a lawyer?" he demanded. "I think I'm insulted."

"Your clothes are expensive enough!" Fisher said, fighting a laugh. "Fine, fine. One more guess." He poked at the fish, lips pursed. "Oh, I've got it! Pack it up, I've figured it out, I know *exactly* what you do."

Felix held very still, careful not to let the sudden panic show. "And what is that, *pêcheur?*" he asked when he was sure his voice wouldn't give him away.

"You're in politics," Fisher announced triumphantly, grinning at him, and the rush of relief that swamped Felix was dizzying. "Think about it," Fisher continued. "You're obviously well-off, you don't want to be recognized, you travel all the time. Clearly, you're a closeted politician and you've got your sights set on somewhere high up, maybe the White House."

"*Pêcheur,*" Felix said, chewing his lip in a desperate attempt to keep from laughing. "I'm *Canadian.*"

"Oh right. Forgot about that."

"You... *forgot* I was Canadian."

"Well, it's not something I spend a lot of time thinking about!" Fisher said defensively. "You're just… you know. You." He made a vague gesture in Felix's direction. "But fine, I give up. You win."

"I like winning," Felix said, grinning at him.

Fisher smiled back and turned to flip the fish. "Anyway, it's not like I care," he said over his shoulder. "As long as you're not a professional athlete."

Ice slid down Felix's spine. He took a sip of water to steady himself. "Why not?" he asked, praying his tone sounded casual.

Fisher shrugged, back still turned. "I hate sports in general," he said, taking the pan off the heat and sliding it into the oven. "Football bothers me because of all the TBI that everyone just seems to ignore."

"TBI?" Felix asked, tilting his head when Fisher glanced at him.

"Traumatic brain injuries," Fisher said. "Concussions and stuff. Look 'em up, they're terrifying. And no one wants to talk about them because then they might have to change the way the game is played, make it safer, which of course means making it less interesting."

"Huh," Felix said. *It doesn't mean anything anyway*, he told himself. *We're not in a relationship, so it doesn't matter.* But the thought of Fisher hating sports, hating *his* beautiful sport, made him faintly ill. "Basketball? Baseball? All sports?"

"Never really understood the point of any sport," Fisher admitted, reaching into the fridge for a beer and tossing one to Felix. "All that effort, for what? To put the ball in a hoop or chase someone around a diamond, getting all sweaty and filthy? It doesn't make *sense*."

"And that goes double for hockey," Fisher was

continuing, oblivious to Felix's internal dilemma. "Maybe triple. Because not only do they go a *lot* faster, so they get hurt a ton more, but fighting's *legal*, which is the stupidest thing in the world."

"It's technically not," Felix pointed out before he could stop himself, and hunched his shoulders when Fisher glanced over again, raising an eyebrow.

"You know much about hockey?"

"I'm Canadian, as we just established," Felix said, a feeble attempt to seem distanced from the conversation. "It's in the handbook that we all have to like hockey."

Fisher laughed, setting another pan on the stove and turning to open the refrigerator. "Well, remind me never to move to Canada then. Anyway—" He emerged holding a carton of vegetable broth. "It's not something that takes up a lot of my thought, and anyway it wouldn't matter if you *did* play hockey, it's not like we're together. But on top of it being violent and dangerous and bloody, I have... negative associations with it in general. So I'm sure as hell never falling in love with a professional athlete, that's all."

Fuck you for thinking I can't act, Mrs. Bushnell, Felix thought viciously, and was ready with a smile when Fisher crossed the room and stepped between Felix's knees, returning the smile.

"Do you know many professional athletes?" Felix inquired, proud of himself when his tone stayed light and teasing. "Because maybe I could get some numbers, I have no such hangups—"

Fisher laughed and cut him off with a kiss. "Shut the fuck up," he growled against Felix's mouth, and

Felix wrapped his arms around his neck to kiss him back properly.

IT CHANGES NOTHING, he told himself on the way home. *We were never going to be a couple. And if he does find out, so what? He can't tell me what to do with my life, and if he'll stop seeing me over something this important to me, then I don't want him anyway.*

Still, he couldn't stop the clinging misery as he fed Henry and got ready for the flight in the morning, and it took awhile for him to realize exactly *why* he was so sad.

When it clicked into place, he glanced down at Henry, winding between his feet as Felix stood in the middle of his laundry room.

"Oh," he said, and his voice sounded small to his own ears.

Henry meowed, rusty and creaking, and Felix bent to pick him up. Henry began kneading his shoulder, eyes closed in bliss as his purr vibrated his lanky frame.

"It's because there's no *chance* for anything," Felix whispered against Henry' silky fur, and blinked against the stinging of his eyes. He hadn't thought about it too much, hadn't wanted to confront it head-on just yet, but the truth was, Fisher was exactly his type. And the tiny seed of hope had been planted that maybe, just maybe, he could learn to let go of what had happened with Paul and have a healthy, *happy* relationship with someone he already wanted to spend all his time with.

It was stupid, he told himself. He'd made it clear

from the beginning that there would be nothing more between him and Fisher other than sex. Fisher was fine with that, so why couldn't Felix be?

"I *have* to be," he told Henry, who kept purring. "It's fine. It is. Everything's fine. I can do this." He kissed the dome of Henry's skull and set him back on the floor to put his clothes in the dryer. He had a game to think about and footage to watch, strategy to plan.

11

"Why are you always on your phone these days?" Saint asked as they deplaned in Saskatchewan.

"My private life is none of your concern," Felix said, hastily shoving his phone in his pocket and putting his nose in the air. Fisher's pic-spam of him and Maya at the park playing with several kids and other dogs would just have to wait.

"Uh huh." Saint was hiding a smile but it showed in the dimple in his cheek, the way he tucked his lips in to keep them from curving up.

Felix peered at him. "You're smiling. What happened?"

"Fuck off," Saint said, shoving him. "Something has to happen for me to smile?"

Felix pushed him in return, ducking under his swing and shoving him back several steps. They fell into Carmine, who caught Saint with a grunt.

"Please don't injure our star forward before the game," he said, setting Saint back on his feet and winking at him.

"It's the Sentinels," Felix said, smoothing his hair. "I think we could probably manage without him. No offense, cherry," he added to a distinctly offended-looking Saint.

"Okay, I have to know," Carmine said. "Why do you call him that?"

"What, cherry?"

"You don't call anyone else that. Where'd it come from?"

Felix shot a glance at Saint, whose dimple had deepened. "You want to tell him?"

Saint looked at Carmine. "Felix and I were inseparable when we were billeted together."

"You're inseparable now," Carmine pointed out.

"Not like we were then," Saint said. "We were attached at the hip. So our teammates started saying we were married."

"Saint was the wife," Felix added.

"*Anyway*," Saint continued loudly, "*mon cherie* is a term of endearment for a lover. So Felix took to calling me *cherie* around our teammates just to fuck with them, and it ended up sticking. And morphing a bit, I guess."

"That's disgustingly adorable," Carmine said. He looped an arm around Saint's neck and pulled him close to whisper something in his ear, and Saint snorted a laugh.

Felix rolled his eyes. "Revolting."

"Jealous," Carmine said cheerfully, arm still around Saint's shoulders, and then they were at the bus and Felix couldn't find a counter argument in time.

"I hear they're trying to land Stromberg," he said

when they were in their seats, twisted sideways so he could talk to Saint and Carmine behind him.

"That Swedish kid?" Saint asked. "Shit, they get him, maybe figure out how to score occasionally, they might have a chance."

"Theo's no slouch," Felix said, always ready to jump to a fellow goalie's defense, even one he was going up against in a few hours.

"He's cold as ice," Carmine commented, and they both looked at him. Carmine shrugged. "Back with the Otters, we played them and someone rushed his net. I think it might have been Rory, come to think of it. Anyway, he took Wallin, the net, all of it out. Can't believe no one was hurt. But Wallin got up, brushed off his helmet, and just... *looked* at Rory." He shook his head. "He shut us right the fuck out that night, and it was all him, their defense was as shit as ever." He huffed a quiet laugh. "And then, right, Rory tries to apologize to him after, because he's an idiot but he's not an asshole. And Brick just looks at him and says in that cool voice of his, 'sorry for what, losing?' And just walks away. *Cold.*"

Felix snorted laughter. "That's Brick."

"I get the feeling if he's pissed off enough, he'll win the Cup on his own just to show the rest of 'em," Carmine said, resting a hand on Saint's thigh. Saint didn't move, but his dimple deepened.

"Are you going out with him after the game?" he asked Felix.

"Probably," Felix said.

"Good. Make sure he tells you where we need to get better."

"You know him?" Carmine asked.

"Played together in juniors," Felix said. "He's a little older, I was his backup. He's cold if you don't know him, you're right, but he's a good man, too."

Carmine rubbed Saint's thigh and Saint leaned against him.

Felix turned back around in his seat and pulled out his phone. He was playing Words With Friends with Fisher, and it was his turn.

THEO WALLIN ENDED up next to Felix on the blue line, stretching on his knees beside him.

"*Bonjour, ami,*" Felix greeted him. "How have you been?"

Theo glanced over. His blue eyes were already distant behind the mask, settling into the zone, but he smiled readily enough. "Been a while. Let's catch up, after."

"Loser buys," Felix said, rolling onto a knee to stretch his hamstring, and Theo sighed.

"I'll get my wallet ready."

A Sentinel player dropped to the ice on Theo's side to stretch. Theo said nothing, just turned to look at him, but the player flinched immediately and scrambled upright.

"Uh… sorry, Brick," he stuttered, and made his escape.

"Is he new?" Felix asked, hiding his amusement.

"Just called up."

"He'll learn," Felix said. He rolled to his feet and tapped Theo's pads with his stick. "See you after the game."

12

———

THEY ENDED up in a quiet restaurant not far from the rink. Out of his gear, Theo wasn't a big man, barely 5'10 and compact, his bearing as neat and contained as ever as he inspected a menu, lips pursed.

"Sure your team doesn't mind you ditching them?" he asked, glancing up.

Felix shrugged. "I go out with them plenty. They'll understand. How are you? How's your little woodcarving business?"

"Fine," Theo said, smoothing a strand of blond hair back. He was handsome in an unassuming way, his personality always tucked deep like the rest of his life. If they hadn't played together in juniors, Felix might never have gotten to know the man behind the icy persona he presented to the media, learned to appreciate Theo's dry humor and sharp insight. "I'm working on a patio set for Sunny right now."

They didn't make much small talk throughout

their meal, enjoying each other's company without feeling the need to fill the silences that fell naturally.

When they were done, Felix leaned back in his chair. "So what do you think of our team?"

Theo rolled his eyes. "Are we doing this?"

"Just like always," Felix said cheerfully. "Do we have a chance yet?"

"No," Theo said bluntly. He winced as if immediately regretting the word. "Sorry."

"Don't be sorry," Felix said. "Tell me why not. Saint will want to know."

"You're getting there," Theo said, picking up a napkin and toying with it. "Carmine was a good trade in so many ways. His ability to strip the puck is always good and he thinks three plays ahead. He reads Saint's mind, and his d-partner's too. Plus it's clear everyone respects and *likes* him. That's... important." He fell silent briefly, lips tightening.

"Your team loves you," Felix said quietly.

Theo flicked a glance at him. "But they don't *like* me very much, do they." It wasn't a question. "Except for Sunny, they're all afraid of me. I don't know how to—I don't have your gift of being a charming bastard."

"Not many do," Felix said, grinning.

"Anyway," Theo said, lips twitching. "Saint is... Saint. And you're good, I suppose."

"Try not to hurt yourself," Felix said dryly, and Theo laughed.

"But you need more defensive depth. More cohesion. I like your offensive lineup, but Carmine and Jason are the only strong d-pair you have. Your others fall apart at the first sign of trouble."

Felix grimaced. He wasn't wrong, that was the real bitch of it.

"You'll make the playoffs, but not the Final," Theo said. "Not with the team you have now." He hesitated. "Sorry."

"No, I need to hear it," Felix said. "Only so much I can do, but management listens to Saint. Maybe we can make some changes, get some stronger defense. So thanks. How have you been? Anything new and exciting in your life?"

"Is there ever?" Theo said dryly.

"You never know. *Something* might happen in Saskatchewan someday. A chicken lays an egg with a double yolk, or Farmer John cheats on his wife or something."

"Fuck you," Theo said, lips twitching. "It's *not* that rural here."

"How's your lovelife?"

Theo shrugged. "Same as ever, nonexistent."

"Think that'll ever change?"

"Unlikely." Theo didn't look too worried about it, but Felix could hear the underlying sadness in his voice. "Hard to find someone willing to accept how I've chosen to live my life and not come in trying to change it. Or me. Besides, I like things the way they are. I don't need the drama of dating. But tell me how *you're* doing," he said, setting the napkin down. "I haven't heard from you much since—"

Felix took a sip of wine to delay answering. It didn't work; Theo was still watching him expectantly when he lowered the glass, and Felix sighed.

"I'm fine."

Theo raised an eyebrow.

"I mean, I'm never falling in love again, but other than that I'm fine."

His attempt at humor fell flat.

"Felix," Theo said softly, and Felix bridled.

"You have no room to talk, do you? Still single after all these years all because you won't—"

"Stop." Theo's voice was sharp. "Stop right there. Don't lash out at me just because you're hurting."

Felix closed his eyes. "I'm sorry," he said quietly, and felt Theo take his hand, squeezing it gently. "I'm just—it was—" *I can't risk it.*

"He's a piece of shit, and he hurt you badly," Theo said. "It's understandable that you're… skittish now." He squeezed Felix's hand again, thumb stroking over his knuckles, and Felix opened his eyes to look at him.

There was a question in Theo's steady gaze, the way he was still holding Felix's hand, safely hidden from other patrons in their small booth tucked off to the side of the room.

It would be easy. Familiar. He and Theo had done this dance before, in and out of each other's orbit through the years, comfortable with what each of them could offer. And it wasn't like he and Fisher were actually together.

And yet—

Felix shook his head. "I'm sorry, *ami*, but I think not this time."

Theo's eyebrows went up briefly but there was no hurt in his eyes as he pulled his hand back, or in the smile he gave him. "I'll drive you back to your hotel," he said.

13

"Mr. Monty, Mr. Monty, guess what?" Martine was tricked out as neatly as ever, satin bow in her perfectly brushed golden curls. Fisher knew for a fact she hated it, that she got filthy and disheveled the minute she could, and he tried to help whenever possible, when he had a plausible excuse to give her mother that wouldn't get Martine in trouble.

"I give up," Fisher said, crouching to smile at her. "What?"

"Anthony asked his favorite hockey player a question on Twitter, and he *answered* him! Anthony won't stop talking about it. He says he wants to get his autograph." Martine glanced over her shoulder to make sure her mother was gone and then yanked the bow out of her hair.

"Wow, good for Anthony!" Fisher said. "Who's his favorite player? And what did he ask him?" He took the bow, tucking it into his pocket where it would be safe until it was time to help her get put back together before classes ended.

"Butterfly!" Martine exclaimed.

Wren gasped. "Martine, Felix Papillon talked to your brother?"

"Yes!"

Fisher glanced back and forth between them, uncomprehending. "Who's this?"

"Felix Papillon is the starting goalie for the Seabirds," Wren explained. "Which means he's super rich and famous and also *busy*, but he stopped to talk to Martine's brother. What did he say, Martine?"

Martine shrugged. "I dunno. Something about his stick? Anthony wants to go pro, he never stops talking about it."

"Well, that was really nice of him," Fisher said. "And what about you, do you play hockey?"

"Mama says girls shouldn't play hockey," Martine said.

Fisher kept his smile in place with an effort. "Would you like to know a secret?"

Martine nodded and Fisher beckoned her close.

"Girls can do whatever they want," he whispered in her ear, and Martine broke into a huge smile. Fisher smiled back. "Let's get our day started, hmm?"

Martine darted for her seat and Fisher stood, amused by the look on Wren's face.

"Is he dreamy?" he teased.

Wren started. "No! I mean, he *is*. But that's not —guys like that, professional hockey players, everyone's trying to get their attention. *Everyone*. And most of them, if they even *have* social media, don't talk to their fans."

"Why not?" Fisher was interested in the answer, but he could also tell that Jeffrey was edging closer to Max with clear mischief in his eyes.

"Well, they really are busy," Wren said. She caught Jeffrey's eye and shook her head. Jeffrey pouted but he retreated to his desk. Wren turned back to Fisher. "And they have to be really careful what they say, because of being in the public eye the way they are. They can't have opinions or, God forbid, say anything that seems remotely flirtatious to someone. Their media teams have them on pretty tight lockdowns."

Fisher grimaced. "That sounds kind of miserable."

"I guess they think playing pro hockey makes up for it. But more than that, Felix had something sh—uh, bad happen to him last year." Wren waved to Samantha, bouncing in the door. "His address was posted publicly," she told Fisher.

"Oh no! Did anything happen?"

"I don't know details," Wren admitted. "But he ended up having to move. So the fact that he's still willing to engage with fans after something like that happened? He's just… really nice." She caught Fisher's eye and her lips quirked. "*And* he's dreamy, fine."

Fisher laughed. Someone knocked on the door and he glanced up to see Calum.

"Be right back," Fisher said to Wren, and headed for the door.

"Hi," Calum said.

"Everything okay?" Fisher said.

Calum's eyebrows arched.

"Um, hi," Fisher said. "Sorry. I get worried about the kids, you know how it is."

Calum shrugged. "My wife handles most of it, so probably not. Do you have a minute?"

Fisher glanced over his shoulder at the classroom before turning back.

"I can spare a few," he said. "After school?"

"See you this afternoon then."

CALUM WAS WAITING when the last child left. "Tilda's in the car waiting for you," he told Max, and shooed him down the hall.

"Is Tilda your wife?" Fisher asked, stepping aside to let him in.

"God no," Calum said. "She's the nanny." He looked around the room, calculating and appraising. "Max is enjoying your class."

"I'm glad to hear it," Fisher said. "We definitely enjoy having him here." He rested a hip against his desk and waited.

"My wife is the CEO of a Fortune 500 company," Calum said. "I work in network security. I'm sought after by businesses all over the world for my skills."

Fisher made a neutral noise.

Calum came farther into the room, his bearing loose and calm, and trailed a finger over one of the children's desks. "It would be accurate to say our income is closer to eight figures than six," he said, as casual as if he was describing his favorite sandwich order.

"I—okay," Fisher said. "I'm not sure what this has to do with me—"

"I'm merely making sure you understand something," Calum said, turning to face him.

"And that is?"

"I get what I want."

Fisher kept the distaste off his face only by dint of years of practice. "Is this where I'm supposed to ask what you want?"

"You," Calum said bluntly.

Fisher froze.

Calum turned away, strolling down the aisle between the desks. "You're an attractive man, Fisher," he said over his shoulder. "Besides, I'm sure your classroom is in need of a few things? Maybe I can help with that."

Fisher finally found his voice. "I am *not* for sale," he managed.

Calum turned, eyebrow going up. "I don't want to buy *you*," he said. "Just a little one-on-one time *with* you."

"You're trying to bribe me," Fisher said through his teeth. "And I'm—" He swallowed nausea. "I'm flattered, of course, but—"

"Don't try and tell me you're not gay," Calum said, leaning a shoulder against the wall and putting both hands in his pockets. "I knew that within thirty seconds of meeting you. Do you have a boyfriend? Is that why you're so reluctant?"

"No, it's not—" Fisher shut his mouth. "I'm not —I'm not out. Not here. And I could never have a relationship with a parent. It's absolutely unthinkable and I could get fired."

"Lucky for you I'm not asking for a relationship, then." Calum straightened and took a step toward him. "I have no interest in leaving my wife and our very comfortable lifestyle."

"I don't—" There was panic in Fisher's chest, clogging his throat. "Thank you but—no."

Calum's lips twitched. "Fisher. It's cute that you think I was giving you a choice in the matter."

Fisher straightened, sudden fury swamping him. "If you're not giving me a choice, that's called rape, Mr. Stewart, whether you use force or not."

"Who said anything about sex?" Calum demanded, eyebrows winging upward. "That's a disgusting accusation to level and you should be ashamed of yourself. I want to spend some *time* with you. Maybe have dinner together occasionally. And if at some point you feel you'd like to have a physical relationship, well, I'd be quite… agreeable to that. But I would *never* force you into sex." He looked furious, spots of color burning high on his cheeks, and Fisher fumbled for words.

"You said I don't have a choice," he finally managed. "That implies—"

"Really, *what* is so onerous about having dinner with me every once in a while?" Calum asked. "All I want is for you to sit across the table from me so I can enjoy some intelligent conversation and a nice view once or twice a month. More if you find you actually like my company once you get to know me."

Just keep them happy. Turner Scott's parting words floated through Fisher's head and he clenched his fists.

"I think you'll find I'm quite bearable when you get to know me," Calum continued, taking another step closer. He was smiling now, head tilted, and Fisher looked away so Calum wouldn't see the loathing in his eyes. "And as I said, I'll make it worth your while. I've already placed an order to be delivered in a few days. New tables, new chairs for the children, even several adult-sized chairs so you can conduct your parent-teacher nights more comfortably."

Fisher opened his mouth and Calum held up a hand.

"Don't thank me."

Wasn't fucking gonna. Fisher snapped his mouth shut again and Calum nodded, smiling.

"Tell you what, why don't you think about it? I'll drop by on Monday to see how the new things look. I'm sure your very kind dean will want to thank me, in any case. You can give me your answer then." He took one step nearer and Fisher just barely stopped himself from recoiling.

"And if I say no?" he rasped.

Calum shrugged. "Well. I hope it doesn't come to that. I'd hate to have to speak to Mr. Scott about my concerns over what you're teaching my son, whether you're really an effective teacher or not. Especially not so soon on the heels of the very generous financial gift I made to the conservatory." His eyes glinted steel blue behind his glasses, and Fisher swallowed rage.

"You really are just... *so* attractive," Calum mused. He dropped his eyes to Fisher's mouth, licking his lips absently, and looked back up. "Have a good afternoon, Fisher. I'll see you in a few days."

FRENCH WAS LOUNGING on Fisher's front porch steps, but he took one look at Fisher's face as he stalked up the path and stood. "What happened?"

Fisher unlocked the door. "Were you waiting long?"

"Five minutes, if that. Fisher?"

Fisher pushed the door open and French followed him inside. "I have to take Maya out," Fisher said over his shoulder. "Sorry, can you wait?"

"*Fisher.*"

French was standing in the middle of the living room, feet braced and face tight. "Did someone hurt you?" he asked in a low voice.

Fisher scoffed. "Look at me. Who's going to hurt *me*?"

"There are different ways of being hurt," French said, tone still low. "And you—you seem hurt."

"I'm fine." Fisher bent to let Maya out of her crate. When he straightened, French hadn't moved. Maya stretched, her back bowing in a perfect curve, and Fisher's shoulders slumped. "I'm not—I'm not fine," he managed, barely more than a whisper.

French closed the distance between them and cupped Fisher's face in warm hands. "Do you want to talk about it?"

"Maybe at some point," Fisher said, and tugged one of French's hands up to kiss the inside of his wrist. French watched him with dark eyes and Fisher kissed that soft skin again. "Right now," he continued, "I need to take my dog out and then I need to fuck you. Is that alright with you?"

French smiled at him. "Yes," he said softly. "That's very alright with me."

"Then I'll be right back," Fisher told him, and headed for the door, Maya on his heels.

14

———

THEY LAY IN BED, legs tangled together. Most of the tension that had been running so high in Fisher's body earlier seemed to have dissipated, leaving him limp and exhausted, one arm over Felix's waist and face buried in his shoulder.

Felix stroked the sweaty curls out of Fisher's eyes, bending his head to see him better. "How are you feeling now, *pêcheur*?"

Fisher's eyes were heavy-lidded and he blinked slowly. "Better," he said after a minute. "Um. Thanks."

"For letting you give me an incredible orgasm?" Felix laughed quietly and was gratified to see Fisher's mouth curve slightly.

"Sorry about earlier," Fisher said after another pause.

Felix threaded his hand through Fisher's curls, winding one around his index finger and watching the strands cling to his skin. "Do you want to talk about it?"

Fisher turned his head, pressing his face against Felix's arm. "This, um… man at work. He—"

"Someone you work with?"

"No." Fisher resettled his grip on Felix's waist. "More like… a customer. He sort of… asked me out."

"I get the feeling that's not all that happened," Felix said. He was still running his hand absently through Fisher's hair, scratching his nails lightly over his scalp.

"Shitty enough that he did it while I was at work," Fisher said, closing his eyes. "I just met him recently and I got a bad vibe from him immediately but I thought maybe I was imagining it. I guess I wasn't."

"So he's a regular customer, you see him often?"

Fisher lifted a shoulder. "I see him… not as often as some, but maybe a few times a week?"

"And he pursues you like this? Your employers— do they not step in?"

"I—they can't. It's a small—business. Their priority is keeping the customers happy. They've told me before to do whatever I have to do to make that happen."

Felix propped himself on an elbow, suddenly furious. "They would have you whore yourself out, all so they can make more money? Is that—"

"I mean, they've told us to find ways to let them down politely." Fisher shrugged. "I tried. I told him it was inappropriate. He said no one had to know. I accidentally let it slip that I'm single, so I can't use having a partner as an excuse. I told him no. I said I was flattered—even though I'm really not—and that I declined the offer."

"And what did he say?" Felix asked, tracing a line of freckles down Fisher's shoulder.

Fisher heaved a sigh. "He said it was cute that I thought I had a choice."

Felix sat bolt upright. "What is this man's name? Where do you work? What is your boss's name?" He twisted, looking for his phone. "I'm putting an end to this *right now*."

Fisher rolled to his knees "French, *stop*."

When Felix ignored him, swinging himself out of bed to find his phone, Fisher followed him, grabbing his wrist.

"If you don't stop," he said, and there was something dangerous and low in his voice, "you're going to show me you're no better than him, that you can't listen to me either."

Felix froze. "That's not fair," he whispered.

"Isn't it?" Their faces were close together. Fisher's dark eyes were sad. "Neither of you are giving me a choice in anything right now. He thinks he can own me, and you think you can fix it. You're not letting me have a voice in my own goddamn life."

Felix cupped his face, suddenly ashamed. "I'm sorry," he managed. "Fisher, *mon pêcheur*, forgive me. I wanted only to help."

"I know, sweetheart," Fisher said softly. "Will you come back to bed with me?"

They curled up together again, on their sides facing each other. Felix wedged a knee between Fisher's thighs.

"Are you out at work?" he asked after a minute, when Fisher didn't seem inclined to say anything else.

Fisher shook his head. "It's… a very conservative

company. And the line of work I'm in, it's not—" He sighed and closed his eyes briefly. "I'm just not comfortable being out. But he… threatened my job. Said that he would complain about my, uh… job performance, or that he wasn't satisfied with my customer service, I guess you could say. And the s— business would take his side, because nothing matters more than that the customers be kept happy."

Felix swore in French, sharp and vicious.

"It's okay," Fisher said. "I can… handle it. I was just upset."

"*How* is it okay?" Felix demanded. "Why don't you just quit? Find somewhere you can be comfortable?"

"I—" Fisher sighed and rolled onto his back. "I like my job. I *love* my job. And people depend on me. I want to think I make a difference. If I leave—" He lifted a shoulder. "Plus I have student loans and a shitty car that'll need to be replaced soon and a mortgage. I can't just pick and choose, you know?"

Felix slid closer and kissed him. "I don't know what you do, *pêcheur*, but I know this—you do make a difference."

Fisher's eyes creased with his smile. "Oh yeah? How do you know that?"

Felix looped his arms loosely around Fisher's neck. "Because it's who you are."

"God." Fisher leaned in and kissed him again. "You're…. Thanks for listening. Are you hungry?"

"I'm a growing boy," Felix said as Fisher sat up. "I'm always hungry."

"Well, let's get showered and I'll cook for you."

15

"You're falling for him," Leo said. His eyes were keen, kicking his heels against the cupboard as he perched on the counter again.

"I'm not," Fisher said immediately. "Taste this."

Leo sipped obediently from the spoon and made a considering noise. "It's okay."

"So, not good enough." Fisher turned back to the stove. He really didn't want to have this discussion, but Leo was, predictably, undeterred.

"You told him about that piece of shit at the school. You turned to him for *comfort*. Fish—"

Fisher sighed, setting the spoon down and turning to rest his hips against the stove. "He was here, he listened. He still doesn't even know what I *do*, Leo."

Leo flung his hands in the air. "It doesn't matter!"

"Yes it does!" Fisher yelled back. "Because he doesn't *want* a relationship and I'm respecting that, okay? I am *not* falling for him! I know better, I'm not *stupid*, Leo!"

They stared at each other across the kitchen for a minute.

"Meat's gonna burn," Leo observed.

Fisher spun, swearing, and grabbed the spoon. Behind him, Leo hopped off the counter. His sock-feet were almost silent on the floor as he crossed the kitchen and wrapped his arms around Fisher's waist. He pressed his face to Fisher's spine and Fisher closed his eyes.

"Sorry," he muttered.

Leo squeezed briefly and let go. "Guests will be here soon. What do you need me to do?"

"Um, set up the coffee table with what we'll need —plates, napkins, that stuff. And get the movie queued up?"

"You got it." Leo padded out and Fisher poked the ground beef without really seeing it.

He liked French so much. And he would never admit it to Leo but it *did* hurt that French didn't feel the same way. He could see a future with French, and that was what stung the most. He barely knew him, not his life, but somewhere deep down, something in him called to French. *Recognized* him.

But it wouldn't happen. He wouldn't allow himself to want it, because that way lay heartbreak.

The doorbell rang and Fisher turned the heat down with something like relief, wiping his hands on a dishtowel as he headed to answer it.

Wren beamed up at him, bundled in an over-sized coat and a knitted scarf, matching hat pulled low over her dark hair. "Hi! This is Grace."

Grace was a Black girl a few inches taller than

Wren, with luminous dark eyes and purple lipstick that matched her overcoat perfectly.

"Welcome," Fisher said, shaking hands with both of them. "Come on in. Leo's in the living room, and Maya's there too, for the introverts."

He took their coats in the hall and there were delighted gasps from both girls when they rounded the corner and spied Maya, in her usual spot by the fireplace.

"Doesn't even shift her arse when strangers show up," Fisher said, shaking his head. "I want a refund. I'm getting a *real* dog next time. Grace, Wren, this is Leo. Leo, Grace and Wren. Wren's my assistant."

"Yes Fisher, you've mentioned," Leo said as he straightened from setting the plates on the low coffee table. "Hi, ladies, it's wonderful to meet you both. Would you like something to drink?"

Fisher left them to chat and headed back for the kitchen to check on the meat. The tortillas were warming in the oven, and the salsa and guacamole he'd made the day before were in the refrigerator waiting to be put in bowls.

"Who else are we waiting for?" Leo asked, coming in to grab glasses from the cupboard.

"Mille couldn't make it, but Rainbow should be here any minute."

"Oh good, I haven't seen her in ages!" Leo filled the glasses with ice and grabbed sodas. He stopped, hands full, and bumped Fisher gently with his hip. "Hey. Are we okay?"

The smile Fisher gave him was genuine. "Yeah, Leo, we're okay. We're always okay."

HE WAS in the middle of stirring the meat when the bell rang again. "Leo, can you get it?" he called, and heard Leo's rapid footsteps heading for the door.

A moment later, happy voices were raised and Fisher smiled down at the frying pan.

"He's in the kitchen," Leo said, and Fisher just had time to turn the heat down and brace himself as Rainbow rounded the corner and hurled herself at him.

"Sugar!"

Fisher caught her, grunting, and she beamed at him, almost as tall as he was, with a pastel pink wig that brushed her eyebrows in a Natalie Portman-style bob and set off her dark skin perfectly. She'd paired the wig with dark red lipstick and bright pink eyeshadow. Pink glitter highlighted the tops of her cheekbones, and huge gold bangles swung from her ears.

"You look amazing," Fisher told her.

Rainbow cupped his face and kissed him on the mouth. "It's so good to see you, sweetheart. Thank you for inviting me. How are you? Who are those two delicious tidbits in the living room?"

"Wren, my assistant, and her friend Grace." He pulled a bottle of wine from the rack and held it up for Rainbow's inspection. She pursed her mouth and nodded, and Fisher turned to find the corkscrew. "Leo, come help me pour!" he called as Rainbow settled herself at the kitchen table, wrapping her maroon and pink caftan around her sturdy body.

Leo skidded into the room a minute later, followed by Wren, who smiled hesitantly at Fisher.

"Can I help with anything?" she asked. "Grace is petting Maya."

"That's a full-time job," Fisher agreed. "Wren, this is Rainbow. If she flirts with you, you're allowed to tell her you're not interested. She won't take offense."

"I won't," Rainbow said, giving Wren a big smile. "Come sit down here by me, sugar, and tell me who you are."

"Oh, I—" Wren eased herself into a chair, looking unsure. "I work with Fisher."

Rainbow waved that off. "I didn't ask what you do. I asked who you *are*. What makes you happy? What do you think about?"

Fisher coughed. "Hockey players," he said, grinning.

Wren pointed at him. "Don't you *start*."

"What's this?" Rainbow demanded. "Hockey? Any hockey players in particular? Any I'd know?"

Wren turned back to stare at her. "*Do* you know any?"

Rainbow patted her wig. "Listen, I may be a good Southern girl, but the north got a few things right, and hockey players are one of them. And sugar, let me tell you—" She leaned forward and Wren matched it, her expression rapt. "Those boys like to get *freaky*." She winked and sat back as Fisher stifled a laugh in his wine.

Wren looked absolutely fascinated. "Do you follow the Seabirds?"

"I live in Portland, don't I?"

"Fisher doesn't," Wren said. "Says he doesn't like it." She brightened. "Hey, I have a couple of extra seats for the Ravens game next week. Do you and maybe Leo wanna come with me and Grace?"

"Does a bear shit in the woods?" Rainbow demanded. "Leo, you in?"

"Oh hell yeah," Leo said. "I don't understand it either, but I'm always down to ogle some hot guys." He hopped up into his favorite spot on the counter as Grace came in and took a seat by Wren. "Fisher dated a hockey player in high school. He's never been the same."

"Oh my god, you make me sound like a grieving Victorian widow!" Fisher sputtered. "I'm *fine*, thank you, I just—" He shrugged. "He didn't have time for anything else. *Everything* was about hockey with him, about making it to 'the show', he called it. So of course he was also *deeply* closeted, because the NHL wasn't ready for a gay player, and he didn't want to jeopardize his chances of being drafted. He wouldn't even acknowledge me in public because he was afraid someone would guess the truth." He kept his tone light, but it still stung, the way he'd always been relegated to the backseat, always pushed away in case someone saw, never good enough to be seen with in public. He'd hated hockey, deep and fierce the way only a teenager can, with a burning resentment borne from not being able to compete with it, not even being as tempting as broken bones, bruises, concussions, and worse.

"Did he make it to the NHL?" Wren asked.

Fisher shook himself from his reverie. "Yeah," he said, setting his wine down to stir the beef again. "He was drafted by the Riptide. Which meant it was all worth it, of course."

"Ouch," Rainbow said. "Is he hot?"

Fisher rolled his eyes and picked up his wine. "Of course he's hot, I have excellent taste."

"Followup question," Rainbow said. "Actually, two of them. How do you think he feels about drag queens who can rock his world, and how do *you* feel about me picking up your sloppy seconds?"

Fisher couldn't help the laugh that bubbled up, nearly dropping his glass. "Jesus *Christ*, Bow, why are you *like* this?"

Rainbow preened. "You wouldn't have me any other way, baby."

"No, I really wouldn't." Fisher blew her a kiss and turned off the heat as Wren leaned forward to ask Rainbow another question. He listened with half an ear to the conversation as he put the ground beef in a bowl and pulled the sour cream and shredded cheese out of the refrigerator. Leo butted in to add to whatever they were discussing, and Rainbow laughed, clutching her chest and leaning back in her chair as she shook with her mirth.

Fisher added cheese to a bowl and sour cream to another and wondered what French would think of his friends. Would he like them? *Well, he already likes Leo*, he thought, lips twitching, and pulled the guacamole out. *He'd probably think Rainbow's as great as I do. And it's impossible not to like Wren.*

"Five minute warning," he said aloud, and hooked his chin at Leo. "Grab this tray and take it to the living room for me."

"Using me for free labor," Leo complained, already standing.

"You sure you don't mind us eating in your living room?" Wren asked.

"That's what living rooms are for," Fisher told her. He topped up her wine, offering some to Grace, who shook her head. "They're for living in."

"So like, stains are proof of life or something?" Wren said, grinning up at him.

Fisher laughed again. "Something like that. Let's go eat and watch a dumb movie."

As they settled in, he pulled his phone from his pocket and checked it quickly. There was a text from French, so he opened it as Leo got the movie started.

It was a picture of French's back, taken over his shoulder as he was lying on his stomach in bed. He was shirtless, just the edge of the tattoo on his back visible, and there was a lanky Siamese folded into a perfect loaf on his hips, eyes closed and triangular ears glowing with the sun.

He insists on sleeping here, French's text read.

Something tugged low in Fisher's gut. He wanted to crawl into bed with French, kiss him all over that gorgeous back, make a map of his moles and freckles. He wanted to drowse away an afternoon with him, nothing to do and nowhere to be but with each other.

Get yourself under control, he told himself sharply, and locked the phone without replying. French wasn't an option and he never would be. Fisher had guests—currently bickering over the best toppings for tacos, he noted—and he didn't need to spend any more time wanting what he couldn't have.

He was ready when Leo appealed to him for an opinion on guacamole, and he didn't look at his phone for the rest of the evening.

"Ideal man, go," Leo said, pointing at Rainbow.

The movie was over and Fisher was pleasantly

full and a little buzzed. He stretched his legs out and laced his fingers over his stomach as Rainbow hummed into her wine glass.

"Muscles and money and stupid as fuck," she finally said. "I've got enough brains for both of us. You?"

Leo snickered. "Big," he said promptly. "Big like Fish but meaner. Fisher's too sweet."

"What the fuck is that supposed to mean?" Fisher demanded. "And how is me being nice a *bad* thing?"

"It's not," Leo said, and stuck his tongue out at him. "I just like a little… bite."

"I bite," Fisher protested, nettled. "I *can* bite."

"But it's not your first instinct," Leo countered. "I don't know, I just… I want someone who's big and tough but who falls apart for me. Like I'm the only one who gets to see that side of him. And hot. Like *stupidly* hot, just brain-meltingly nuclear." He shrugged and sipped his wine. "But it doesn't matter, I'm never settling down anyway. Your turn." He pointed at Wren.

"Oh… I don't…." Wren tugged on her braid. "I don't really know. Or care, I guess. As long as we care about the same things and they're sweet. *I* like them nice." She shot a mischievous grin at Fisher, who laughed and saluted her with his glass.

"Grace?" Leo inquired.

"My ideal man is a woman," Grace said, lips twitching.

"Absolutely fair," Fisher said comfortably. "Men are disgusting. Anything else?"

Grace shrugged. "Butch girls are my jam. I'm

weak for short hair and a leather jacket or good flannel."

"What about you?" Wren asked Fisher.

"Tall, dark, and French Canadian," Leo said into his glass, and Fisher shot him a filthy look.

"That's oddly specific," Rainbow said, perking up. "Details, my love."

Fisher sighed. "It's not a relationship. I'm not dating him."

"But you're seeing someone," Rainbow said. "Which means we want to know more." Wren and Grace nodded as Leo smirked.

"Leo—who I will be murdering later—and I met him at a bar," Fisher said. "We're... compatible in bed. That's all."

"What's his name? What does he look like? What does he do?" Wren asked.

"I don't know, tall, dark, and French Canadian, and I don't know."

"You don't know his *name*?" Rainbow demanded, sitting forward.

"*Or* what he does?" Wren added.

Grace looked fascinated, head swiveling to whoever was talking.

"I told you, it's *not* a relationship," Fisher said, somewhat desperately. "I call him French. He made it clear from the beginning that he doesn't want a relationship, so it's just... it's some fun for both of us."

Rainbow looked dubious. "You don't *do* fun, sugar. Do you have a picture of him?"

"I—" Fisher closed his mouth. "No," he finally admitted. "None that show his face, anyway." French sent him pictures a lot, but never any with identifiable details.

Rainbow arched her brows. "Interesting. Is he famous? A closeted musician or politician?"

"Pretty sure he's not in politics," Fisher said. "But he won't tell me what he does."

"A mystery!" Rainbow looked absolutely delighted. "Tell me everything right now."

"Nope." Fisher drained his glass. "We're very much off-topic, and we're not discussing my not-boyfriend. So, in regards to Leo's original question, I don't care about height or weight. Attraction comes from within for me."

"Way to make me sound like a shallow asshole," Leo muttered.

"Don't be a shallow asshole then," Fisher shot back. He grinned when Leo flipped him off. "I'm more like Wren, I think. As long as we care about the same things, that's what's important. But specifically, I want to spend my life with someone. I want kids. I want to *share* my life. I know it's boring but I'm ready to settle down. I want someone who makes me laugh, who challenges me. Someone I can trust. Steady, not flashy. Looks fade anyway. I want someone who I want to wake up next to for forty years."

He looked up when he was done to everyone staring at him.

"So soft," Rainbow said, clicking her tongue.

"Fuck off, men are allowed to be soft," Fisher retorted.

"Deal breakers!" Leo said, sitting up and crossing his legs. "Bow, you first."

"The usual." Rainbow lifted a shoulder. "Racism, homophobia. Grace?"

"Straight girls." Grace sighed.

"They will break your heart," Rainbow agreed. "Wren?"

"I don't think I have any," Wren said thoughtfully. "I mean other than the obvious."

"No, come on, everyone has deal breakers," Leo protested. "You're saying you wouldn't care if your dream guy had really bad breath, or he only listened to the Hamilton soundtrack on repeat for the rest of your life?"

Wren shivered and Leo crowed, triumphant.

"See, everyone has *something* that's a hard line. Fisher?"

Fisher narrowed his eyes. Leo returned his look with an innocent expression.

"Fine, I'll go. Transphobia and not liking cats. Oh, and saying irregardless."

"That's not a word?" Grace said, and Leo gasped in outrage before registering her twitching lips.

"I'm watching you," he warned, and switched his focus to Fisher. "Your turn."

Fisher sighed. The girls were watching them, clearly picking up on the tension and just as clearly not sure what to do about it.

"Someone who doesn't want to settle down," he finally said.

Leo sat back, his expression clearly saying *my job here is done.*

"More wine," Fisher said, pushing himself upright.

Alone in the kitchen, he leaned a hip against the counter and closed his eyes. Leo was right, but all he wanted to do was pull out his phone and text French. Or better yet, call him just to hear his voice. It took a few minutes before he was able to go back into the living room with the wine bottle and a smile on his face.

16

"Why do you keep checking your phone?" Carmine asked on the bus, leaning over the seat after Saint had gone up the aisle to talk to one of the rookies facing his first NHL game.

Felix twitched and shoved it back in his pocket. "I'm not. Mind your own business."

Carmine raised an eyebrow but didn't challenge the blatant lie. "So how are things with you?"

"You see me nearly every day," Felix pointed out. Had his phone vibrated?

"Does that mean I can't ask you how you're doing?"

Felix narrowed his eyes. "You want something."

"I don't want a damn thing!" Carmine protested, but there was something almost guilty about the way he wouldn't quite meet Felix's eyes.

Felix sighed and patted the empty seat beside him. "Come on, then."

Carmine hopped up and stepped around the seat to sit next to him.

Felix waited. One of the trademarks of a good goalie was patience, a willingness to hold perfectly still until it was time to act, and Felix was a *very* good goalie.

As expected, Carmine broke first. "Has Saint said anything to you?"

"He says things to me all the time," Felix pointed out. "He is my best friend *and* my captain, after all."

Carmine glared at him. "Don't be an ass," he hissed. "You know what I meant. Has he said anything about *me*?"

"What are you hoping to hear?" Felix countered. "How good you are in bed? Saint is not one to kiss and tell, you should know that by now."

A smile flickered across Carmine's mouth, there and gone again. "No, he definitely wouldn't do that." He slumped in his seat, running one big hand through his hair. "I guess I just—worry."

"About him, or about your relationship?"

"Both," Carmine admitted. He was scooted so low in his seat that his knees were pressed against the back of the bench in front of them.

"Are you *hiding*?" Felix inquired, and Carmine shot him a filthy look but sat up a bit.

"Do you think he's tired of me?" he said in a rush.

Felix laughed, making Carmine glare again. "Forgive me," Felix managed, waving a hand. "But you—and he—" He trailed off, giggling.

"*What*?" Carmine demanded.

"You think Saint could ever get tired of you?" Felix demanded, suddenly sober. "He does not give his heart easily, Caz, and when he does, he won't take it back unless you do something so terrible he can't forgive you." He leaned in, gratified when Carmine leaned slightly away. "Have you done something terrible, Carmine?"

"*No,*" Carmine said. "I mean, I only tipped fifteen percent the other day and I've felt bad about it ever since, but also he was literally hitting on Saint with me right there, and he 'forgot' my food when he brought Saint's, and when he did bring it out it was mostly cold, and anyway we're off-topic. I haven't done anything bad."

"Then are you planning to?"

"No!" Carmine squirmed in his seat. "It's just… look, we've been together for a year now. We live together, we're almost never separated."

"I know," Felix said. "I never see my best friend without you in tow, like a very large puppy. If you didn't make him so happy, I could be upset with you about that."

Carmine bit his lip. "Sorry," he said quietly. "No, really, I am. I didn't mean to… steal him or whatever."

Felix took pity on him, patting his knee. "You have proven time and again how much you care for him, Caz. I could never resent you. Now tell me what's bothering you."

"It's just… he's so good at everything, and he's only going to get better," Carmine said, his voice low. "I'm nearly six years older than him. I'll be looking at retirement when he's at the peak of his career. How can I ask him to stay with me? He could have… anyone, honestly. With his looks, and brain? There isn't a guy alive who swings the least little bit in his direction that wouldn't be all over that."

"As flattering as that may be to Saint, that's not

exactly the truth, is it?" Felix touched his knee again before Carmine could object. "No, my friend, you mean well. And it speaks to how much you love him, that you see him this way. But Saint is… not an easy person. No, don't bristle at me. He's quick-tempered, neurotic, demanding and difficult. Stop *glaring* at me, you know I'm right."

Carmine scowled but glanced away.

"What I'm trying to say is he's not some sort of fabled prize the whole world is panting over. There are very few who could truly understand him, and more, *love* him the way he deserves. But in any case he doesn't want this mythical 'anyone'. He wants *you.*"

"And when that changes, but he's too kind to tell me because he doesn't want to hurt me?" Carmine didn't look at Felix, head down as he pulled on a loose thread in his cuff.

"*If* that ever happened, I think you are far too smart not to realize it," Felix said. "But it won't."

"You know that how, exactly?" Carmine snapped. "Crystal ball? Fortuneteller in your pocket?"

Felix refused to be baited. "Because he came to me the other day worried about the same thing."

"Worried about… falling out of love with me?"

Felix rolled his eyes. "*No*, you idiot. Worried *you* would fall out of love with *him.*"

Carmine sputtered. "You—but—that's *ridiculous.*"

"Clearly." Felix touched Carmine's hand. "You're a good man, Caz. But promise me you'll *talk* to him. Really talk. Not get distracted by sex or staring into each other's eyes or whatever you do when you're alone—" He held up a hand when Carmine opened his mouth. "*Not* an invitation to tell me. But talk to him, Caz. Please? You both need to actually tell each other what's on your minds."

Carmine sighed and nodded. "Alright, I will. Thanks, bud. Hey, when you retire, maybe you should be a relationship counselor, you're pretty good at this stuff."

"The irony is *très tragique*," Felix admitted, fighting a smile.

"Speaking of which, Saint mentioned you'd met someone near the start of the season? How's that going?"

"Did he tell you it's *not* a relationship?" Felix asked. His phone buzzed, unmistakable this time, and he twitched.

"He said you're gooey over him," Carmine said, and grinned at the look on Felix's face. "Aw, the big mean French-Canadian doesn't want to admit he has feelings."

"Shut the fuck up," Felix said.

Carmine snickered. "Okay but seriously, when do we get to meet him?"

"Absolutely never," Felix said flatly. "Even if I *was* willing to mix my personal and public lives again, I would never introduce you to someone I was interested in romantically. They'd spend five minutes with you and I would never see them again."

"It's a gift," Carmine agreed, looking pleased.

Felix's phone buzzed again.

"We're just friends," Felix said. "We have clear boundaries. No relationship. It's just… physical." A memory rose unbidden, of Fisher half-dozing in bed the last time they'd been together. They'd had sex again after dinner and it had been more difficult than Felix had expected to tear himself away, despite knowing the plane left early the next morning.

"Just physical," Carmine echoed, sounding very skeptical.

Felix shook himself. "Was there something else?" he asked, knowing his tone was too sharp.

"We're here for you," Carmine said, instead of taking offense. "You know that, right?"

Felix sighed. "I know."

"You deserve love." Carmine sounded earnest, hair falling into his hazel eyes, staring at Felix as if willing him to believe it.

It made something inside Felix ache, a knuckle pressed against a bruise. "What if I don't want it?" It was almost a whisper.

"I think—" Carmine hesitated. "Well, it doesn't matter what I think."

"Yes it does," Felix said, surprising himself. "Saint says you're one of the most emotionally intelligent people he's ever met. So… tell me what you think, then."

Carmine glanced toward the front of the bus, where Saint was still talking to the rookie, then back at Felix.

"I think you *do* want it. And I think you're scared shitless of being that vulnerable again."

The bus was pulling into the airport. Felix still hadn't even looked at his phone.

Carmine stood, balancing himself in the aisle as the bus went around a corner. "It's okay to be scared," he said softly. "What matters is doing what scares us anyway."

Saint was coming toward them, looking quizzical. "You guys okay?"

"Just catching up on all the latest gossip," Carmine told him, and the smile they shared was downright disgusting. Felix made gagging noises until they were both glaring at him, then smiled up at them cherubically.

"Let's go play some hockey, eh?"

He managed to wait until he was in his seat before he pulled out his phone. Sure enough, the texts were from Fisher.

Sorry for the late reply, the first one read. *Had guests over last night, getting a slow start today.*

It wasn't even eight A.M. Felix snorted and read the next message.

That cat is almost as gorgeous as you. And he's clearly got good taste. :)

The plane taxied onto the tarmac and Felix tapped a response. *Plans this weekend?*

Not really, Fisher replied. *Work stuff, maybe going out with Leo.*

Something squirmed in Felix's belly. *Picking up?* Fisher couldn't see his face, hopefully he'd take the question as casual.

The reply took a minute. *Would you mind?*

Felix took a breath. Held it. Let it out. *Not if that's what you want to do*, he sent. *As long as you're safe.*

Fisher hadn't replied by the time the plane took off, and Felix finally put the phone away and went to bully Vanya into a game of cards.

17

———

THEY LOST to the Direwolves two minutes before the final buzzer. Felix didn't meet anyone's eyes in the locker room after, elbows on his knees and head down as Coach talked.

It was his fault. He was distracted, thinking about Fisher out with Leo, maybe finding someone, taking him back to Fisher's place, doing all the things with him that they'd done with Felix.

He'd done this to himself. He'd told Fisher he didn't want more. But was that strictly true? The thought of Fisher kissing someone else made Felix nauseous. But the thought of letting Fisher in, making himself truly vulnerable again, was even worse.

Saint sat next to him as Coach finished his speech and stalked off. He didn't say anything. After so long playing together, there wasn't really any need. Felix leaned against his shoulder briefly and Saint matched the pressure, a faint smile curving his mouth.

Back in the hotel, Felix kicked off his shoes, changed into sweatpants, and stretched out on the bed. There was nothing on his phone from Fisher, so he turned on the television and flipped idly through the channels, looking for something that would help him turn off his mind.

He settled on a stupid action flick, crossing his feet and lacing his fingers across his stomach. His ribs ached from the forward who'd knocked him over in his drive for the net, but it was bearable. He was almost asleep when his phone rang, startling him awake. Fisher's name was on the screen. Felix fumbled to answer without dropping it.

"Hello?"

No one said anything at first. There was a heavy, thumping bass in the background, shouted conversations overlapping and making it almost impossible to hear anything else.

"Fisher?" Felix said, sitting up.

"French?" Fisher sounded startled. "French, baby, hi! Why did you call me?"

"I didn't," Felix said. "You called *me*. Are you okay?"

"I'm fine, I'm *great*. Hang on." The noise got muffled, Fisher saying something Felix couldn't make out, and then a door slammed and everything went quiet. "Still there?"

"Still here," Felix confirmed.

Fisher sighed. "God, I love your voice. It's more than the accent, although that's sexy as fuck—it's, mm... how do I put it. It's like all soft and husky, and when you're really turned on it gets all raspy, and—" He cut himself off with a groan.

Felix swallowed hard. "Fisher, where are you?"

"Outside the bar," Fisher said. "But I'm going home. I want to talk to you."

The relief absolutely shouldn't have made Felix's head spin. "You—you're not—I thought you and Leo were gonna…."

Fisher made a dissatisfied noise. "He wanted to. I didn't. I just went to support him. Oh, hang on, the car's here."

Felix listened as a car door opened and closed and Fisher greeted the driver, his deep voice gravelly and warm. Then he was back.

"Five minutes and I'll be home," he said. His speech was just slightly slurred, words running together when normally they were clear and precise.

"How much did you have to drink?" Felix asked, amused.

"Just enough," Fisher announced.

"Enough for what?"

"For me to tell you just how fucking sexy you are," Fisher said, lowering his voice like he was confessing to a dark secret.

Felix couldn't help his laugh. "You tell me that all the time, *pêcheur*."

"I do? No I don't. I *think* it a lot though. It's your eyes. Or maybe your smile. Or—God, your hands. They're so beautiful, so graceful. God, and your—"

"Fisher," Felix interrupted, swallowing more laughter, "save it for when we're alone, yes? Don't subject your poor driver to this."

There was sudden silence.

"Sorry," Fisher said to someone else, muffled like he was holding the phone to his chest. "I hope I didn't make you uncomfortable. Although if you saw him, you'd understand."

Felix groaned and put his face in his hand. "Do you want to call me back, *pêcheur*?"

"Absolutely not," Fisher said firmly. "Unless—do you need to go? I don't know what you're doing, it's late, if you need to sleep or—"

"I'm fine," Felix said. "It's nice to hear your voice." It was, too. It settled something deep in his core to listen to Fisher talk, even when he was drunk and didn't really have a reason for it.

"Okay." Fisher sighed. "I miss you." Then, as if realizing what he'd said— "Sorry, shit, I didn't mean—"

"Don't apologize, *pêcheur*," Felix said. "I—" He took a careful breath. "I miss you too."

"You do?" Fisher sounded stunned.

"How could I not?" Felix countered. "You're so good to me. You're so *good*, so lovely, I just want to—"

"Wait," Fisher said, sounding desperate. "Wait, wait, just—hang on." The phone went muffled again, and then the car door slammed again.

A minute later, he was back. "Sorry, I'm back. Home, I mean. I'm home. Um. What were you saying?"

Felix laughed softly. "You want me to tell you nice things about yourself?"

"Mostly I just want to hear you talk," Fisher confessed.

"What would you like me to talk about?"

"Anything. I don't care. What you had for breakfast. Where you are right now. When you'll be back. Your cat. Just—"

"I had fruit for breakfast," Felix said. "Oatmeal too, it's S—my best friend's favorite meal. And an omelette with spinach and cheese."

"Oatmeal is your friend's favorite meal?" Fisher sounded nonplussed.

"Well, when we're working," Felix amended. "Not always. His boyfriend actually cooks for him. He's gained probably fifteen pounds since they got together."

"So you work with him?" Fisher stopped himself. "Sorry. I'm being nosy. Tell me… whatever you want."

"Where are you right now?" Felix asked instead.

"In the bedroom," Fisher said. "Just took my shoes off, I'm gonna lie down. You're not done, are you?"

"No, *pêcheur*, I'll keep talking." Felix waited until he heard rustling and a soft grunt. "Are you comfortable?"

"Be more comfortable if you were here," Fisher said. He sounded sleepy.

"I'm in Denver," Felix said. "But I'll be home tomorrow. Would you like me to come over then?"

"God, yes. French—"

"Yes, *pêcheur*."

Fisher yawned. "Y'know I don't—I don't care. Right?"

"Care about—what?"

"I've been thinking about it. You. The night we met, you said you didn't want to be recognized. So maybe you're not a politician—probably—but you're in… the public eye. At least well known enough that there's a good chance people would recognize you."

Felix couldn't move, couldn't breathe.

Fisher didn't seem to notice. "I just want you to know, I don't *care*. I don't care what you do, or if you make a lot of money, or—" He yawned again. "God, I'm drunk. Sorry. What was I saying?"

Felix made a huge effort and gathered his wits. "That you don't care. About… my secrets."

"Mm. I don't. You can keep 'em, I won't ask for anything you don't want to give me." There was rustling, like Fisher was turning over. "I know how scared you are."

"I—Fisher…."

"You are," Fisher said. He still sounded half-asleep, but somehow completely sure of himself. "You're terrified. My best guess is someone hurt you really badly, I don't know who or how, but it's left you scared shitless about ever taking a chance on someone else."

Felix draped an arm over his face, blinking away the prickling in his eyes. "I don't—"

"You don't have to say anything," Fisher said. "I'm not asking you for more than you can give. I just want you to know it's okay." He sighed. "Talk to me some more. Tell me a story."

It took Felix a minute to get his voice under control. Fisher's breathing was deep and steady in his ear, and finally Felix was able to clear his throat and start talking.

"When I was about fourteen, my papa took me fishing. We're Quebecois, ice-fishing is important to us. He built a wee shed, cut a hole in the ice, put in a heater, and we sat in there for hours. Maybe some kids would be bored, but I loved my papa so dearly. It felt like I never saw him."

"What does he do?" Fisher asked.

"He was a long-haul trucker," Felix said, his throat tight.

"Was? French—"

"It's okay." Felix swallowed and kept going. "We spent the whole day there. Started early in the morning, maybe four a.m.? We didn't get home until it was dark. And while we were there, Papa, he… he turned to me, and he said, '*Maman* and I love you so much. More than you'll ever know. And it doesn't matter to us who you love. You'll always be our son.'"

"Oh, French," Fisher breathed. "He knew?"

"He knew," Felix whispered, rolling onto his side. "*I* barely knew, but somehow he did. We barely spoke of it after that, except for him warning me to be safe, to not give away my heart to someone who didn't deserve it." *And then I went and did exactly that.* He kept his mouth closed on the words.

Fisher didn't say anything. Felix listened more closely to his breathing. It had evened out into the slow, steady rhythm of sleep.

"Goodnight, *mon pêcheur*," he murmured, keeping his voice low.

He lay awake a while longer, staring at the wall as his thoughts chased themselves around and around.

Fisher isn't Paul. He's nothing like Paul. He's never asked you for a thing. But would he, if he knew? Would he use you, too? Make you feel special, like you're giving him a great gift, like you're the only one good enough to help him? Take and take and turn vicious when you say enough?

Felix didn't *know*. And he couldn't bear the thought of finding out, of watching Fisher turn against him by degrees until what they had was sour and sick like curdled milk. It was safer this way, keeping himself separate, protected from the inevitable pain.

But oh, how he *wanted*.

18

———

FISHER WOKE up with a pounding headache and a creeping unease that he'd said too much. A quick look at his phone confirmed he'd called French the night before.

Fuck. What had he said? Had he let his guard down? Probably. Alcohol always loosened his filters, made him a little *too* honest. French had probably blocked his number already.

He flipped to his texts. One from Leo, confirming he'd gotten home safely, accompanied by a picture of a lurid hickey and then a selfie of him looking smug and thoroughly fucked out. Fisher rolled his eyes and went to the next message.

It was from Wren, asking if she could teach some of the more athletically inclined children how to play field hockey. Fisher smiled to himself.

Of course, he sent. *I'll put in a request for the equipment with the school and we can talk about starting a program.* They'd probably deny it, because there wasn't a lot of room in the budget, but he'd figure out how to tell Wren that later.

The next message was from French. Fisher swallowed hard and opened it.

Hangover? Nothing else.

Fisher stared at it for a minute. *What* had he said last night? Had he really bared his soul to his stupid-hot fuckbuddy or had he dreamed the whole thing? The one word text didn't exactly shed any light on the matter.

Nothing a few Advil won't fix, he finally sent back. *Did we talk last night?*

French didn't answer immediately, so Fisher took Maya out, then visited the bathroom and dug out some headache medicine. His stomach growled and he grimaced. A quick glance at his phone confirmed French hadn't messaged him again.

"That's fine," he said out loud. "Totally fine."

He cooked breakfast without looking at his phone, talking nonsense too loudly to Maya, curled up in her plush bed tucked in the corner of the breakfast nook. She listened to him with her ears pricked, head cocked like she could understand him, and Fisher tossed her a treat from the jar he kept on the counter.

"For being my best girl," he told her as she snapped it up. "And for not thinking I'm crazy. Or at least not telling me if you *do* think—"

His phone buzzed on the counter and Fisher froze. Goddammit, he was too invested.

He told himself he wasn't disappointed when the text was from Wren.

I'll bring what I have tomorrow :), it read.

Fisher sent her a thumbs-up and put the phone back on the counter to flip the bacon.

"It really is fine," he told Maya, who thumped her tail in response. "I mean, he's busy too, right? I don't know what he does but I know a lot of his time isn't really his own. What do *you* think he does, baby girl?"

Maya wagged her tail again, looking hopeful.

"No bacon," Fisher said. He pulled another treat from the jar and tossed it to her. She snatched it out of the air and crunched happily as Fisher flipped the bacon. "He travels all the time," he continued, resting a hip against the counter. "And you've seen how he dresses —money definitely isn't an issue for him." He caught Maya's stare and hunched his shoulders. "It's not *jealousy*." He turned to reach into the refrigerator and pull out the eggs. "It's just… it'd be nice not to have to… worry, you know? Of course you don't know, you're a dog. It's not like *you* have crippling student loans."

His phone buzzed again as he was cracking an egg into the skillet. Probably Wren again, or maybe Leo, although he highly doubted Leo could text with the hangover he *had* to be suffering from.

Once the eggs were frying, he picked up the phone. His traitorous heart flip-flopped when he saw French's name on the screen.

You don't remember?

Thought maybe I dreamt it, Fisher sent back. He chewed on his lip for a minute. *I didn't say anything too cringey, did I?* He hit send before he could change his mind and dropped the phone on the counter.

"I'm such a fucking idiot," he told Maya, and flipped the eggs.

French didn't reply for another hour, during which time Fisher ate, cleaned up the breakfast mess, took Maya for a run, and had a quick shower. When he got out, a towel around his waist as he dug for clothes in the dresser, his phone lit up on the bed where he'd tossed it.

Fisher managed to ignore it until he was dressed and his towel was hung up. Finally, though, he picked it up.

Sorry, French had sent. *Airports, you know?*

He was on his way back, then. Fisher took the phone into the living room and curled up on the couch, bare feet tucked under himself. French hadn't answered the question, but it wasn't like Fisher could ask again without making it weird.

The three little dots indicating French was typing popped up.

You've never been cringey in your life :)

Fisher put his head on his knee and tried to breathe through the relief. Maybe he hadn't ruined everything after all. When he was composed, he tapped a quick reply. *Clearly you didn't know me in high school.*

French didn't respond immediately, but this time it didn't make the anxious knot form under Fisher's breastbone. He hadn't scared French off. Whatever he'd actually said the night before, he could handle it. As long as French was still talking to him.

You're falling for him. Leo's voice was so clear in his head, he might as well have been in the room with him.

"Fallen," Fisher said out loud, and sighed. "Not that I'll ever admit it to anyone but Maya, obviously, but I'm pretty sure I'm in love with him."

Maya, now comfortably ensconced in her bed by the fireplace, lifted her head at the sound of her name.

"Go back to sleep," Fisher told her. "I'm just having a crisis, nothing to see here." He unwound himself and stood. He had lesson plans to refine; maybe that would help keep his mind off things he couldn't change.

He was immersed in creating an interactive chart for identifying living and nonliving things when someone knocked on his door. Fisher jerked and his pencil slipped, making a jagged streak through the bird he'd drawn so painstakingly.

"God*damn* it," he muttered, and set the pencil down, wiping the graphite on his hands off on his thighs as he went to answer.

French smiled when the door swung open, eyes warm as ever. "Ah… you said I should come over," he said, smile slipping when Fisher just gaped at him.

Fisher gathered his wits and reached for French's wrist, pulling him over the threshold. "Sorry, sorry, of course. *Hi.* I just—you didn't answer so I thought you were still at the airport."

French's smile returned. "*Portland* airport," he said. "I had to drop my bag at home and feed Henry, but I didn't want to wait any longer. Are—" He hesitated. "If you're busy, I can go—"

"Don't you *fucking* dare," Fisher growled, and hauled him into a kiss.

French laughed, arms going around Fisher's

neck. He tasted like peppermint and smelled like cloves, the sharply sweet aftershave he favored, and Fisher groaned and tugged him closer, one arm around his waist.

"Hi," he repeated against French's mouth. "How are you, how was your trip?"

French nipped sharply at Fisher's lower lip. "We can talk later," he suggested.

"Excellent point," Fisher said. He kicked the door shut and towed French through the house to the bedroom. The midday sun lit the room in a golden glow as he pushed French onto the bed and landed on top of him in the next breath.

I missed you. He didn't say it. French reached up and pulled his head down until they were kissing again, and Fisher closed his eyes, imagining French was feeling it too, that he'd missed him just as much, that the desperation thrumming in Fisher's blood was echoed in French's.

"Clothes," French demanded, yanking on Fisher's shirt, and Fisher almost laughed as he sat up on his heels to yank his shirt off. He helped French sit up enough to pull his own top off, and then froze at the sight of a purpling bruise covering the left side of his ribcage.

"What—"

"It's nothing," French said, reaching for him, but Fisher pulled back.

"French, what *happened?*"

French sighed, lower lip protruding. "Someone ran into me, knocked me over," he said. "I'm fine, *pêcheur*, really."

"Who do I need to kill?" Fisher asked, tracing the edge of the bruise with a featherlight finger.

French shivered and caught his wrist. "No one, *mon pêcheur*. It was an accident, I promise. Please will you get naked?"

Something hot and possessive rolled in Fisher's gut. The thought of anyone putting their hands on French, of touching him without French's permission, made him want to put his fist through a wall. Or the face of whoever had hurt the beautiful man currently doing his best to undo Fisher's belt.

He bent and French froze as Fisher kissed the soft skin an inch from the bruise.

"Say the word," he mumbled against French's ribs. "Just say it, and he's a dead man."

French's chest vibrated with his laugh. "I thought you didn't like violence?"

"Good point," Fisher said, lifting his head. "Turns out I'm willing to compromise a little."

French grinned at him, the sunlight painting his skin gold as his white teeth flashed. "Fisher, it's appreciated but can we *please* stop talking about a silly bruise and get back to what's important?"

"Well, if I must," Fisher sighed, and opened his belt.

19

———

FELIX ROLLED onto his stomach and set his teeth lightly in Fisher's bicep. Fisher twitched but didn't pull away, and Felix lifted his head.

"What are you thinking about, *pêcheur?*"

"You're assuming I *can* think right now," Fisher mumbled. He dropped a hand on Felix's head, lightly scratching his scalp. "Need a pacemaker, Jesus."

Felix snickered. "When you've got it, you've got it, eh?"

"You've definitely got it," Fisher said through a yawn. "How long can you stay?"

"I have the day," Felix said, nosing along Fisher's arm again. He wasn't trying to start anything, just enjoying the contact and simple intimacy. Not for the first time, he wished it could be real, that he could tell Fisher who he was and not have it matter. But as soon as he did, things would change. It didn't matter that Fisher said he didn't care. He *would* care. He'd care about the way the fans treated Felix, how they felt like they owned him at least in part. And he'd care about what they said about *him*, if it ever got out that they were dating. They'd be vicious. Tear Fisher to shreds. Judge him and measure him and deem him lacking, and Felix would watch the warmth in his eyes fade as the hurt crept in.

He couldn't bear it. He shook his head hard to dispel the thought and pressed his face to Fisher's warm chest.

"Hey, you okay?" Fisher asked gently, big hand settling on Felix's head again. "Where'd you go?"

"Nowhere," Felix said, lifting his head and forcing a cheer he didn't feel into his voice. "I'm here with you all day if you want me. Nowhere to be until Monday morning."

Fisher's smile slipped and his mouth twisted, but all he said was, "I was thinking of going to the farmer's market later. There's a good one down by Gresham. Wanna come with me?"

Felix considered. On one hand, hockey fans were everywhere, and the chances of being recognized were considerable. On the other, it was a beautiful day and the thought of getting outside, enjoying some time with Fisher, no other demands on his time, was… tempting. Plus Gresham was enough out of the way that maybe he'd be able to get away with it.

He was taking too long to answer. Fisher's smile shaded into something almost sad.

"Sorry," he said. "I forgot for a minute. It's okay, we can stay here."

"No!" Felix rolled to a sitting position. "Let's go out. It will be nice, getting some sun."

"Really?" Fisher touched Felix's thigh. "I didn't mean to push you—"

"Stop." Felix bent and dropped a kiss on his mouth. "Get dressed. Can we take Maya?"

WITHOUT BEING ASKED, Fisher pulled a pair of sunglasses and a snapback from the closet and presented them to Felix as they were getting ready.

Felix took them, turning the hat to examine it. It had a logo of a stylized lion on the front, frozen mid-roar. He looked at Fisher, oddly touched, but Fisher wasn't even looking at him. He was crouching to put Maya's collar and leash on, crooning to her as she wagged her tail. When he stood, Felix had the glasses and hat in place, spreading his hands in display.

"Perfect," Fisher said, grinning at him. "You look like you're going to a barbeque."

FISHER DROVE a small SUV with a space in the back for Maya and enough legroom for two tall men in the front. Felix gazed out the window at the trees as Fisher drove, appreciating the wind on his face. The leaves were orange and gold dappled between the evergreens, the bite of winter to come in the crisp air. Pedestrians lined the streets, tourists and locals alike out enjoying the weather before it turned bitter.

"I love this city," Fisher said.

"Have you always lived here?" Felix asked, turning to look at him.

"Moved here for college and ended up staying." Fisher flipped his turn signal on and slowed. "I did some traveling when I was younger, but nowadays I stick closer to home."

"Family in the area?"

Fisher slanted a glance at him but answered readily enough. "Just my found family. Leo and Rainbow, a few others."

"What were you thinking about, earlier?" Felix asked abruptly.

That earned him a startled look. "When?"

"When I mentioned Monday. You got tense."

Fisher's jaw tightened briefly. "That... guy. He said he'd be back for my answer on Monday. I guess you just reminded me that I have to figure out what to say to him that won't get me fired."

"Your job means that much to you, that you would consider—"

"I *wouldn't*," Fisher said sharply, turning into a small lot and putting the car in park. "But yes, my job *does* mean that much to me, okay? What I do is important. If I can figure out a way to keep this guy from pursuing me and *not* lose the job in the career I've worked for my entire life, that would be great! Besides, some of us have student loans and shitty cars and we can't just pick and choose what we *want* to do!"

"Okay," Felix said, his voice soft. "I'm sorry, *mon pêcheur*, of course it means a lot to you. Of course you feel trapped. Forgive me."

Fisher let go of the steering wheel and took a deep breath. "Sorry. I didn't—"

"No, you were right. I have privilege I take for granted and I speak without thinking. What are you going to do?"

He watched as Fisher rolled his shoulders, shaking the tension out, and pulled a smile into place.

"I'm going to browse the farmer's market with you," he said. "And make you a delicious meal this evening, and then after dinner, I'm going to fuck you." He lifted an eyebrow. "Unless you have a better idea?"

"I think that sounds excellent," Felix said. "Let's go browse some farmers then, eh?" He chalked Fisher's laugh up as a win and stepped out of the car.

THEY STROLLED the aisles of the market, hands brushing occasionally. Fisher bought a bushel of apples and insisted Felix share one with him as they walked. Felix licked the sweet juice off his lips and caught Fisher's eyes following the movement. He hid the amusement and covered Fisher's hand with his own when he offered him the next bite, holding it to his mouth and watching the way Fisher's throat bobbed when he swallowed.

"*After* dinner," Felix said, and Fisher glowered at him.

"You're doing that on purpose."

"You blame me?"

Fisher turned away with a snort instead of answering, but a minute later, he was buying a paper packet of roast corn and insisting Felix let him hand-feed him the first few kernels.

Felix savored the sweet-salt burst of flavor, letting his tongue linger on Fisher's fingers for a brief moment, knowing Fisher could read the mischief in his eyes.

Fisher coughed and handed him the packet. "Feed yourself before we get reported for public indecency."

There seemed to be no rhyme or reason for the way Fisher chose an aisle to explore, sometimes doubling back and at other times skipping entire rows. Felix just followed, his arms getting increasingly laden down with Fisher's purchases, and watched as Fisher inspected a stall brimming with gourds of various shapes and sizes.

"That time of year," he said, choosing several.

"You're one of those, aren't you?" Felix asked, accepting the bag when Fisher handed it to him.

"One of what? Who?"

"You decorate for every season, don't you? Jack o'lanterns on the porch for Halloween, a wreath on the door for Christmas?"

"Guilty," Fisher said, smile widening. "Plus winter potpourri on the stove and garlands above the fireplace."

Felix thought back to his own house, barely lived in with how busy he was. There were almost no signs that it was even *his*, anything more than a place to lay his head at night.

"It sounds nice," he said quietly.

Fisher's eyes softened. "Couple more rows and then we can go home so I can kiss you properly."

"That sounds nice too," Felix said, and followed him down the next aisle.

No one recognized him, and after the first few vendors, he'd stopped bracing himself for it, stopped trying to come up with plausible ways to deny his identity, and allowed himself to fully enjoy the view of Fisher from behind, his shirt stretched tight over his broad back, the swell of his perfect ass in his jeans. Even the way Maya's leash looped around his wrist looked good.

So it was something of a shock to feel a small hand tugging on his shirt as Fisher negotiated with a vendor.

Felix looked down to see a little girl wearing a miniature Seabirds jersey and staring up at him with big blue eyes, blonde curls wisping around her heart-shaped face.

"You're Butterfly," she said, and Felix flinched.

Fisher hadn't heard, still absorbed in whatever he was discussing, and Felix crouched to bring himself down to the little girl's level.

"How old are you?" he asked.

"Ten," she said proudly. "I'm a goalie too. My name's Emma."

"Good for you, *bébé*," Felix told her. "Can you keep a secret?"

Emma nodded, eyes big and earnest.

"I'm pretending I'm not me today. Do you ever do that? Pretend to be someone else?"

"I like being me," Emma said doubtfully.

"As you should," Felix said, glancing over his shoulder at Fisher, who hadn't turned. "But sometimes it's fun to pretend for a little time, to be another person, with another life."

Emma considered. "So if you're not Butterfly, who are you?"

"My name is French today," Felix said. "And I'm not a goalie, I'm just visiting a farmer's market with a friend."

Emma looked dubious, but shrugged, as if adults' inner workings were a mystery to her in any case.

"I'll give you my autograph if you promise not to tell anyone until I'm gone," Felix said, and Emma's eyes lit up.

He'd barely handed it to her and was straightening when Fisher accepted several parcels from the vendor and turned to find him.

"Did you make a friend?" Fisher asked, smiling at Emma.

Emma opened her mouth, looked at Felix, looked back at Fisher, and snapped it closed again. "I have to go," she announced, and scurried off.

Fisher blinked. "What a weird kid."

Felix hummed noncommittally. "Are we done, *cher*? I don't think I can carry much more, and I seem to remember you promising me something after dinner."

"We're done," Fisher agreed. "And I'll make it worth your while."

"I'm counting on it," Felix said, and they headed for the car.

20

THEY FELL into bed together after dinner and sex on the couch, pleasantly exhausted in every fiber. Fisher roused once to ask French if he needed to leave, and French shook his head, burrowing closer.

"In a bit," he mumbled.

Good enough for him. Fisher fell asleep listening to French's breathing, French heavy and warm in his arms.

HE WAS JOLTED awake by his alarm as French jerked upright and swore.

"What time is it?" he demanded, scrambling out of bed.

"5:30," Fisher said, rolling out of his side and rounding it to help French look for his clothes.

"I can't believe I fell asleep," French muttered, dragging his pants up over his hips. His hair was disheveled, falling into his eyes. Fisher located one of his socks under the bed and handed it to him.

French took it, murmuring thanks, and sat on the mattress to pull them on.

"Will you be in trouble?" Fisher asked, sitting next to him.

"*Non*," French said, bumping shoulders with him briefly. "But I will be given shit for it if it gets out."

"That friend you work with?"

"Yes, him. And his boyfriend. They bully me terribly." He slanted an amused glance at Fisher, who coughed a laugh into his fist.

"Something tells me you give it right back."

"Perhaps. Where's my shirt?"

"I think it's in the living room."

French hopped up and darted into the living room, pulling it over his head as he came back into the bedroom. He appeared through the neck hole, hair even more disheveled, and affection stole Fisher's breath.

"I have to go," French was saying, pulling out his phone. He frowned at it and tapped the screen a few times. "No, *no*." He looked up. "The soonest anyone can get here is twenty minutes. I have to go *now*." He went back to his phone, muttering under his breath.

"I'll take you," Fisher said.

French glanced up again, surprise in his eyes. "You have to go to work too, don't you? You'll be late if you take me all the way to the Pearl District."

Jesus, how much does he make? Fisher didn't let the reaction show on his face. "I wake up early to take Maya running and get some time to plan my day. It won't kill either of us to run this afternoon."

"I can call a cab," French said, but he was wavering.

"It'll take them a while to get here too," Fisher pointed out. "Your choice, but—" He stood and crossed the room to run his hands down French's arms. "I'm right here. Let me help you. We can be out the door as soon as I get my shoes on."

French leaned into him, chewing on his lip like he wasn't aware he was doing it. "You'll know where I live," he said, barely audible.

Would that truly be so bad? "I guess you're gonna have to decide whether you can trust me," Fisher said quietly. He waited as French fought an internal battle, holding perfectly still.

Finally, French nodded, sharp and jerky. "Alright."

"You'll let me help you? Take you home?"

"Yes," French said, and shoved at his chest. "Get your shoes on, *please.* We have to go *now.*"

"Can you take Maya out while I get dressed? It'll take her less than a minute, I promise."

"Yes, yes, of course." French darted for the living room as Fisher hunted for clothes.

He was dressed and pulling his shoes on when French came back inside, Maya on his heels. Fisher dumped her food in her bowl and grabbed his keys.

"Let's go."

HE DIDN'T QUITE SPEED, but he pushed the limits more than he normally would as French directed him, winding through Portland to the Pearl District.

"You know it's not personal, yes?" French asked once they were on the highway.

Fisher didn't look at him. "What, you not wanting me to know where you live?"

Out of the corner of his eye, he could see French hunching his shoulders.

"It's not you," French said.

"Okay."

There was silence for a minute and then French sighed.

"You don't believe me."

"It's not that," Fisher said. The roads were still fairly empty, thankfully. "I don't know *what* to believe, really. I only know what you've told me. And you must have a good reason for protecting your privacy so fiercely. So—" He glanced at French, who was watching him, dark eyes catching the street-lights' flicker. "I promise I won't tell anyone where you live. Does that help?"

French sank a little lower in his seat. "Can you go faster?"

"Not without risking a ticket."

French sighed again. "I'm sorry, *pêcheur*."

Fisher didn't touch that. "You work this early all the time?"

"No, we're going out of town again."

"Again? You just got home!"

"We'll be back tonight," French said. He was fidgeting, glancing at the clock on the dash and out the window as if willing the car to go faster. "The plane leaves in an hour, I should have been there already."

"Should I take you to the airport instead?"

"*Non.*" French's response was sharp, and Fisher hid the flinch.

"Right, that would probably be a bad idea."

French's phone rang and he twitched.

"Go ahead and answer it," Fisher said. "I imagine they want to know where you are."

French hit the call button and put the phone to his ear. "*Oui.*" The ensuing conversation was entirely in French, far too rapid for Fisher to follow, and within a minute, French had hung up, shoving the phone back in his pocket.

"Will Henry be okay?" Fisher asked.

He felt more than saw French's surprise.

"I—yes. I have a housekeeper, she'll feed him." He shifted his weight. "You care about my cat."

I care about you. Fisher lifted a shoulder and changed lanes to pass a slow car. "Just curious how he handles you being gone so much."

"He's an asshole who doesn't like anyone anyway," French said, sounding fond. "He's just as happy to be alone. I've thought of getting a kitten, though. To give him company. The exit's coming up."

Fisher nodded and took the ramp French indicated when it came up. The houses were set well back from the road, wide sidewalks and grassy lawns under heavy trees.

"This is nice," Fisher said.

"Fisher," French said.

"Yeah?"

"You're the only person I would have considered telling." There was something in French's voice, a desperation that begged Fisher to believe him. "There is *no one* else. No one else I would trust."

Fisher didn't reply immediately, but he reached across the gearshift and took French's hand. French gripped it, taking a ragged breath.

"If I ever meet the bastard who did this to you, I'm going to fuck them up," Fisher said conversationally.

French tightened his hold. "Up ahead," he said. His voice was slightly wobbly. "The white one."

Fisher parked on the street, French already unbuckling before the car was stopped.

"Thank you, *pêcheur*," he whispered. "I have to go, I'm sorry—"

Fisher pulled him in for a quick, hard kiss and let him go, gently pushing him away. "Go. Have a safe flight. Let me know when you get back, if you want."

"I want," French said, opening the door. "I always do. I'll see you later."

He loped for the house and Fisher watched until he was inside before accelerating away from the curb and doing a U-turn.

He drove home wondering what exactly had just happened. French had trusted him, let his guard down, and now Fisher knew where he lived.

"It doesn't mean anything," he said aloud to the empty car.

There is no one else.

"I'm so fucked," Fisher muttered, and took the exit.

He was only a few minutes late for work, which meant he was still thirty minutes ahead of the earliest students, but he was distracted and in a rush, juggling his charts and papers as he hurried down the hallway and nearly collided with Wren at the corner. She was carrying a huge bag over her shoulder and she stumbled backward, just barely avoiding running into him.

"Sorry, sorry," Fisher said, balancing his armload to dig for his keys.

"Everything okay?"

"Just running late," Fisher told her, and managed to get the door unlocked. "Whatcha got there?"

Wren hefted the bag. "Hockey sticks and some gear."

"*Right*, I forgot that you were gonna bring that. I should warn you that the school's likely going to decline the request to start an official program. Funds are tight."

Wren's face fell briefly but she squared her shoulders. "If they won't do it, I'll buy the equipment myself. I'll—I'll get donations from teams, used gear, things like that."

"That's the spirit!" Fisher said, setting his papers on the desk.

"I thought I'd see how many are interested and go from there." Wren's eyes were bright and she was almost bouncing on her toes. "I think it'll be a great way to help them get some exercise and also learn to use their bodies and brains."

"Well, Maxine's brother plays, she'll probably be interested if we can get her mother's permission."

They were discussing the logistics of how to spin it so Maxine could participate when someone knocked on the door.

A shiver went down Fisher's spine when he saw Calum standing there, Max clinging to his leg.

"Hi Max!" Wren said cheerfully. "Wanna help me sort the hockey equipment?"

Max gasped. "Are we playing hockey, Miss Wren?" He let go of his father and rushed to Wren's side.

Calum joined Fisher on the other side of the room. "Max loves hockey. Does the school have a program?"

"Wren's trying to gauge interest in getting one started. She's very passionate, she'll be great at it." Calum was standing a little too close, and Fisher took a discreet step away under the guise of reaching for a pen on his desk.

"I'll be happy to sponsor it," Calum said, and Fisher dropped the pen.

"You—oh, you don't have to do that—"

Calum shrugged, hands in his pockets. "Like I said, Max loves the sport. And it's a good tax write-off."

It felt like a trap, but Fisher couldn't figure out a way to turn it down. The school wasn't that well-off financially. They'd be more than willing to accept the gift, and it would mean Wren would get her program.

"Thank you," Fisher said reluctantly.

"I'll stop and speak to the dean on my way out," Calum said. "Have you thought any more about what we talked about?"

Fisher glanced at Wren and Max, absorbed in animated discussion. "I—look, I'm flattered."

Calum's brow lowered and he opened his mouth.

"I'm not saying no," Fisher said hurriedly, hating

himself and the man standing in front of him more with every word. "But I don't *know* you. And I need time to get to know you a little better before I give you an answer."

Calum watched him for a minute, mouth pursed thoughtfully. "As long as the answer is yes, then I suppose you can take a little time to decide."

So gracious of you. Fisher kept the bitter retort locked behind his teeth and nodded. "I have to get the day started."

"I'll be seeing you," Calum said, and left.

Fisher rolled his head, shaking the tension out of his shoulders, as Wren left Max going through the equipment and joined him.

"Max is a great kid but that guy gives me seriously bad vibes," she said under her breath.

"Yeah, you're not the only one," Fisher said. He summoned a smile. "Let's teach some kids."

21

FELIX GOT to the airport in record time. He hadn't even unpacked before going to Fisher's the day before, so he'd just grabbed the same bag and run for it. He'd use the laundry room in the hotel before the game.

Everyone was already on the plane when he got there, out of breath from running across the tarmac and up the steps at top speed.

A cheer went up at the sight of him, hoots and jeers following.

"What's her name, Butterfly?" Tye shouted.

"She *must* be special," Jason called. "You're never late!"

"Your mother is always an excellent host," Felix retorted, and Jason gasped.

"You've *met* my mother, don't take her name in vain like that!"

"Don't give me the chance to then," Felix suggested over the laughter of the others, and made his way to his seat, ignoring the jostling he was given by several players. He stowed his bag and flopped into the seat next to Vanya, ignoring Saint's gaze. Not that that would stop him.

Sure enough, the minute they were in the air and the fasten seatbelt sign was off, Saint was on his feet and crossing the aisle.

He jerked a thumb at Vanya, who scrambled out of his seat immediately so Saint could sit down.

"Pretty sure that's considered an abuse of power," Felix said.

"He'll live." Saint inspected Felix with sharp eyes. "What happened?"

"Overslept." Felix stretched his legs out and didn't look at him.

"First of all, you don't do that. Second, why were you speaking French when I called?"

"I'm bilingual, asshole."

"But you also know I'm not as fluent as you. You only use it with me if you don't want other people to understand what you're saying. So who were you with?"

Felix stared stubbornly at the bulkhead.

"Was it a hookup?"

"At six a.m.?" Felix said in spite of himself. "Do me a favor."

"I *knew* it. You were with Fisher."

"And what if I was?" Felix snapped. "Is that a crime?"

"You spent the *night* with him, Fee. That's not— you don't *do* that."

"I fell asleep," Felix said, somewhat desperately. "That's all it was. It doesn't *mean* anything." *Not like letting him drive me home does.*

"Would it be so bad if it did?" Saint said softly.

Felix looked at him. Saint held his gaze without flinching, waiting for an answer.

"Yes," Felix finally said. "It would. I won't *allow* it to mean anything, because if I let him in, *truly* let him in, he'll break me. When what he feels goes from love to hate, when he looks at me w-with pity, *disgust*, it will—" He rubbed his mouth with a shaking hand.

"You're so sure that's what will happen that you won't entertain any other possibility," Saint said.

"And *you* are convinced true love exists, that you've found it and therefore I will too," Felix shot back.

Saint stiffened. "Are you saying—"

"No. No, Saint, I believe what you and Caz have is real. But just because you *do* have it doesn't mean I ever will. Love like that, a bond like that, it's—" He shook his head. "Rare."

"People find it every day," Saint said, mouth set in a stubborn line.

"People *think* they find it every day," Felix countered. "Until the cheating, or the lying, or the abuse. Until it all falls apart."

"You know what that's called?" Saint snapped. "That's called a self-fulfilling prophecy. You've convinced yourself that love's a myth and no one will ever live up to your expectations, and you set your expectations so high that when they're human and they fail, you point to it and you say 'see? I told you!' Well, that's bullshit." He was glaring now, fire sparking in his brown eyes. "People fuck up, Felix. Everyone does. It's what you do *after* the fuckup that matters."

"Like you'd know," Felix snarled. "You and

Carmine are sickeningly perfect, aren't you? What do you know of fighting, or hurting each other?"

Saint gaped at him. "You think we don't fight? Felix, how stupid are you? Have you *met* us? I'm a neurotic asshole and he's the most stubborn bastard I've ever met. We fight *all the time.* Just last week, we couldn't decide on a movie to watch and we were both tired and in bad moods and instead of just turning it off and going to bed, we yelled at each other about it for twenty minutes and then slept in separate rooms."

"You did not."

"Hand to God," Saint said. "Neither of us wanted to admit we'd been wrong. We went to practice that day still not speaking to each other, and you had no idea, did you? Wednesday of last week."

Felix thought back. "I remember you seemed a little tense, but… you spoke to him. Played the scrimmage with him."

"Because we know how to make it work even when we're mad at each other. And by then, I was just mad at him being so stubborn and I wanted him to admit he was wrong."

"What happened?" Felix asked, fascinated in spite of himself.

Saint laughed quietly. "I think we both realized how stupid we were being at the same time. I looked at him and he was looking at me, and I remembered how much I loved him, how he pushes me and challenges me and never lets me back down from anything, how he makes me better in every way. The little stuff doesn't *matter*, Fee. Not when you have the right foundation."

"Not being able to agree on a movie is one thing," Felix said. "What Paul did—"

"Paul is a twisted sick fuck who gaslit you and emotionally manipulated you because he knew how to wrap you around his little finger. Which isn't your fault at all, by the way, he's also a charming asshole and I thought he was great for a long time, until I saw how you were changing."

"How did I change?" Felix whispered, crossing his arms over his stomach.

"You got suspicious, angrier." Saint looked sad again. "Like you were suspecting things weren't right, but you hated yourself for thinking it. You lashed out a lot more, too."

"I'm sorry," Felix managed. "For all of it, for believing him, for letting it happen, for not seeing sooner—" He swallowed back the tears, blinking hard, as Saint put a hand on his shoulder.

"I'll say it as many times as I have to," he said, his eyes steady. "It wasn't your fault. But you have to figure out what you're going to *do* about it. Are you going to be bitter and cynical the rest of your life? Never let anyone else in? Just assume everyone will be like Paul?"

"It's *safe*. I have you. I have Caz. The team. Why do I need more?"

"It may be safe but it's not what you truly *want*." Saint ran a hand through his hair, making it stand on end. "I'm sorry," he said abruptly, and Felix blinked, thrown.

"What?"

"I'm telling you what you want, what you have to do. I'm not letting you make up your own mind."

"You're worried about me," Felix said. "Because

you don't want to see me get hurt again. But I'm doing this so I *don't* get hurt again, Saint, can't you see?"

"Yeah," Saint said softly. "I'm just really afraid you're getting in too deep. You're halfway to in love with him—don't look at me like that, I've seen the way you go soft when you talk about him—and you're fighting it so hard you're tying yourself all in knots. You're convinced it won't work, while at the same time you're literally falling in love with him, and the whole thing's going to blow up in your face because those two things? They can't coexist, Fee."

"But it *won't* work," Felix whispered.

Saint's focus sharpened. "Why do you sound so sure?"

"Because I am. Because I haven't… told you everything."

Saint waited without moving as Felix tried to find the next words.

"Not long after we started… things, he was making me dinner, and—he'd had glitter in his hair earlier."

Saint blinked, momentarily diverted. "Wait, glitter?"

"Exactly," Felix said. "I was curious. Of course I was. So I asked."

"Did he tell you?"

"No," Felix admitted, scowling briefly. "But I made a few guesses at what he maybe did for a living that would cause glitter to be in his hair, and then he said I'd guessed so he got some guesses too. He didn't —he didn't get it right," he said hurriedly at the expression on Saint's face. "But after we joked about it, he said…." He swallowed around the remembered hurt. "He said, 'as long as you're not a professional athlete.'"

Saint's mouth fell open. "*Felix.*"

"He had an ex," Felix continued. "A long time ago. But he was hurt, and badly. And he hates all sports, but especially hockey. He… blames it. That's when I knew—" He drew a shaky breath. "I knew it wouldn't work. It would never truly work, even if I found the courage to tell him, to trust him."

"Felix," Saint said, and didn't continue, mouth working.

"It's okay." Felix patted his hand. "I wish… I do wish it *would* work. I think I could love him, Saint, so very easily. But I won't let myself, because I can't have that."

"It has to end," Saint said, looking miserable at having to say the words. "You're a grown man, I'm not trying to give you an ultimatum. If you want to keep doing this, you know I'll be there to help you heal after it blows up, just like I did with Paul. But Fee—I know *you.* I know you inside and out. I know what you need and what you want, and I know you're gonna get your heart broken if you don't figure this shit out. And for your sake, not mine, I don't want that. Because you didn't deserve it the first time, and if it happens *again*, I may have to kill someone."

Felix nodded. "You're right," he said after a minute. "I'll end it. Soon. I promise."

Saint squeezed his hand. "Caz," he called, and Carmine poked his head around the seats a few rows ahead. "Come tell Felix about that fight we had last week."

Kasha gasped. "You had fight? Caz, *no*. You're not fight with Saint!"

"Stay out of it," Carmine ordered, on his way down the aisle, and Kasha scowled.

"Saint is best," he muttered, crossing his arms. "Stupid Caz."

Saint winked at Felix and stood so Carmine could take the seat.

"So Saint doesn't like action movies," he began, and glanced up at Saint, still standing in the aisle. "Go away, I'm telling a story."

"Fine," Saint said, putting his nose in the air. "I'll go sit with Kasha. *He* appreciates me."

He sat down beside a visibly delighted Kasha and began talking to him in a low voice as Carmine watched him, a smile playing on his mouth.

"I've never met anyone with such a capacity for love before," he said to Felix.

"We are very, very lucky," Felix agreed. "So tell me about this fight."

SAINT WAS RIGHT. Felix knew that. But he didn't *want* to stop. Not yet. It wasn't just the sex, either. It was the feeling of being someone other than a professional hockey player with his name in the papers after every game, with speculation and gossip swirling around him like a cloud of stinging gnats. With Fisher, Felix didn't have to perform, stay professional, watch what he said with laser awareness so his words weren't twisted out of context.

With Fisher, he could relax. Stop being observed and simply… exist.

Felix wasn't ready to give that up just yet. He'd promised Saint, so he'd keep his word, but... not yet.

They lost to the Kingfishers in shootouts and returned to Portland exhausted. Felix checked his phone but Fisher hadn't texted.

What would he say, Felix wondered, if he told him? If he admitted he played the sport Fisher hated, that it meant more to him than anything else?

Would his eyes go cold, his mouth flatten? Would there be anger, betrayal, in his eyes? Or would he be disappointed, hurt that Felix had never told him? Would he tell Felix to go to hell? Or would he accept it, because Felix meant that much to him?

As the plane began its descent into Portland, Felix leaned his head back against the seat and entertained himself with a fantasy where he told Fisher the truth and Fisher had known for months, had memorized his game schedule, attended every home game in Felix's jersey to cheer for him.

The thought of Fisher wearing his name made Felix shiver, heat pulling low in his gut.

The plane's wheels hit the tarmac and he opened his eyes with a regretful sigh. It wouldn't happen. Fisher had said as much, made it *very* clear how he felt about hockey. There was no getting out of this with a happy ending. But that didn't mean it had to end immediately. He still had time, he could enjoy Fisher's company a little longer before he stopped things. He was delaying the inevitable, but was that a crime? He didn't think so, not if it meant Fisher kissed him again, *held* him again.

Still, maybe a little distance wasn't a bad thing.

When he was home, bag unpacked and laundry started, he sent Fisher a text.

Just got back. Early day tomorrow, and I have chores I've been putting off. Not sure yet when I'll be free.

Fisher's reply took awhile. Finally the message came through. *Are you regretting it already?*

Felix chewed on his lip, trying to figure out how to respond.

I'm sorry, Fisher sent before he could.

Felix hit the call button before he changed his mind and Fisher picked up on the first ring.

"I'm so sorry, that was uncalled for." He sounded miserable.

"No, it was a justifiable reaction," Felix said. "And understandable, that you assume I'm panicking."

"Are you? Panicking?" Fisher's voice was as deep and warm as always, but Felix could hear the nerves underneath.

"I was, a bit," he admitted. "At first."

"And now?"

"Not… as much. I've had some time to think about it, and I think… maybe you are not like my ex."

"Oh sweetheart," Fisher breathed. "I'm so proud of you. That couldn't have been easy to say."

Felix covered his face with an elbow and didn't reply. His heart was hammering in his chest like he'd been bagskated.

"If you ever want to tell me about him," Fisher continued, "I promise to listen without judgment. But right now I just really want to kiss you."

"That would be nice," Felix whispered. "I really

am busy tomorrow, but maybe I can see you Wednesday if you're free."

"I don't have plans," Fisher said. "Come over when you're ready; you know what time I get home. But right now… where are you?"

"In bed," Felix said. "Henry is off doing cat things, so I'm alone."

"What are you wearing?" Fisher asked, and Felix caught his breath.

"Oh—soft pants, a T-shirt. Not very sexy, sorry."

"They are if you're wearing them."

Felix shivered. "Are we doing this?"

"Do you *want* to?" Fisher countered.

"Very much," Felix admitted. "If you do."

"Do you have any idea how many times I've jerked off to the thought of your voice?" Fisher asked, and Felix smothered a laugh.

"As many as I have to yours, perhaps," he suggested.

"Glad it's mutual," Fisher said, sounding amused. "Take your shirt off."

Felix caught his breath and sat up enough to drag his shirt off over his head. His skin pebbled in the cool room and he shivered again, flattening his free hand on his stomach.

"You too," he managed.

He heard rustling, and then Fisher was back.

"Okay. Are you hard?"

Felix laughed. "You haven't even said anything dirty yet." He was *getting* hard, the sheer anticipation making his heart beat faster, but there was no reason to let Fisher win that easily.

"I am," Fisher admitted, and Felix's laughter cut

off. "Just thinking about you gets me so hard. I want you so much."

Felix groaned, sliding his hand down to cup himself.

"Getting there?" Fisher asked, sounding smug.

"Like you're—ah—not," Felix shot back. "Where are you?"

"Like on a scale of how aroused I am, or physically?"

Felix rolled his eyes. "You're not aroused enough if you can make stupid jokes."

"That's my superpower, baby," Fisher said, and Felix's brain stuttered briefly on the nickname, missing what he said next.

"Ah—what?"

One of the things that made Fisher so overwhelmingly attractive to Felix was just how perceptive he could be. When he was tuned in, Felix sometimes felt so *seen*, so understood to his core, that there was often no need for words.

It was no different now.

Fisher's voice deepened, sliding into a lower register that pulled at something deep in Felix's gut. "You liked that. I said I can always make stupid jokes, but I think you were too hung up on what I just called you to hear me. Weren't you?"

Felix blew out a breath that did nothing to slow his heart rate.

"Are you touching yourself?" Fisher asked.

"Through my pants," Felix managed. He was embarrassingly close to the edge already, skin so sensitive he thought a breeze might push him over.

"Take them off," Fisher said. "That's what I'm doing."

Felix struggled to obey, moaning softly as his erection slapped his belly and he curled his fist in the blanket beneath him. "Fuck, Fisher—"

"Your accent gets stronger when you're turned on," Fisher said, low and dark in his ear. "'Feesher.' I love it. Are you touching yourself yet?"

Felix worked moisture into his mouth. "N-no."

"Why not?"

"Waiting. For, um. You."

Fisher made a wounded sound. "Touch yourself, baby. Stroke your cock for me and think about me doing that to you next time, making you feel so good, there you go—"

Felix groaned, hips jerking as he stroked himself, eyes closed, imagining it was Fisher's hand on him, taking him apart slowly but surely, until nothing else existed except Fisher's touch, driving him out of his mind.

Fisher was still talking but Felix couldn't quite make out the words. He didn't need to to know he wasn't going to be able to hold on much longer.

"I'm close," Fisher gasped. "French, baby, I'm gonna—"

Felix sobbed as he came over his fist, hot spurts all over his belly as the bliss broke free. He dropped the phone somewhere in there, and it took a few minutes to come back to himself, the room slowly resolving into blurry shapes around him.

It was another minute of blinking at the ceiling before he realized Fisher was calling for him.

"French? Did I break you?"

Felix fumbled for the phone, dropped in the bedding, and got it to his ear.

"Hey," Fisher said, and his voice was so soft it made Felix's chest ache. "Doing okay?"

"Yeah," Felix managed.

"Feel better?"

"Mm." Felix draped an arm over his eyes with a sigh. "I hope I can see you on Wednesday."

"Me too," Fisher said gently. "Go to sleep."

"*Bonne nuit*," Felix said through a yawn, and stayed awake just long enough to pull a blanket up over himself before he fell asleep.

22

————

OCTOBER CREPT TOWARD NOVEMBER. The trees lost more leaves, the weather turning crisp and stinging and more rain blowing in.

The Seabirds kept inching their way up the standings, creeping toward clinching a playoff spot, but it was slow and halting. Kasha hit a hot streak in late October, racking up eight goals and five assists in six games, and the team rode the crest of that wave through Halloween and into November.

Felix still hadn't ended things with Fisher. *Soon,* he kept telling himself, but then Fisher would touch him, or just look at him, his dark eyes so warm, and Felix would find a reason to put it off a little longer.

Saint held his tongue, although Felix didn't miss the looks he threw at him when he thought Felix wasn't paying attention.

There was a fragile peace in the air as Thanksgiving approached. Fisher was hosting at his house for his friends who didn't have families to go home to, and he dragged Felix back to the farmer's market the weekend before to stock up on everything he needed, which included fresh cranberries that he apparently planned to jelly himself.

Felix played mule again, carrying the packages Fisher couldn't, following him up and down the aisles and watching the way Fisher's eyes sparkled as he described the menu and the guest list.

"Wren's going to her parents, but her friend Grace is coming to mine," he said as they carried everything to the car. "Along with Leo, Eileen, Rainbow, and Miller." They went around to the front, and Fisher hesitated before starting the car. "Would you—you know you'd be welcome if you don't have anywhere else to go."

He didn't look at Felix, probably bracing himself for a rejection, and Felix couldn't help leaning over the gearshift to kiss his cheek.

"Thank you," he said softly. "But my schedule is set. I'll be out of town that week for work."

"They make you *work* over Thanksgiving?" Fisher demanded as he started the car.

"How many times do I need to remind you I'm Canadian?" Felix asked, fighting amusement at his outrage. "It's not a holiday for me, *pêcheur*. Just another day." And anyway, they'd be in Calgary, playing the Riders. "But save some of that cranberry sauce for me, eh? I have to try this." A thought struck him. "You haven't mentioned that *connard* recently. Is he still bothering you?"

Fisher shot him a startled look. "That what? Oh —you mean the guy who hit on me."

"Yes, him. The asshole."

Fisher snorted. "He is that. He asked me for an answer last month and I told him I needed some time to get to know him." He put up a hand before Felix could speak. "I know, I know. And I'm not considering it, I swear. But he's backed off a bit, which is what I wanted. He's showing up more, though, finding reasons to hang around and talk to me before and after—" He cut himself off. "Anyway, we're kind of in a holding pattern. Eventually he's going to demand a yes or no, and I need to have something ready, some kind of escape strategy, since my bosses won't back me."

Felix swore under his breath. He could *help*, that was the worst part. It would mean Fisher finding out who he was, it would mean probably losing him, but he had money, he knew people. He could find this person, this cowardly fucker who thought he could force someone into doing his bidding, and make him stop, make him back off, keep him from ever getting near Fisher again.

And if he did, Fisher would never forgive him for not letting him deal with it.

He slumped in his seat, tugging on the belt and scowling.

Fisher patted his knee. "I'll handle it," he said. "I'm a big boy. How much longer do I have you today?"

"I should go home soon," Felix admitted. "Busy day tomorrow."

"Time for a blowjob first?" Fisher asked, eyes mischievous.

"There's *always* time for that, *pêcheur*."

FISHER GOT a text from Wren as he was getting ready for bed. It was a cold and rainy mid-December night, the weather dropping nearly to freezing for the first time all year, and he was looking forward to curling up with a book, a mug of cocoa at his elbow on his nightstand. French was busy, so all Fisher wanted to do was dive into his true crime stories and while away the quiet evening until bedtime.

Can't wait for tomorrow!!! Wren's text read.

Fisher set his cocoa on the nightstand and got into bed, propping up the pillows and getting comfortable before replying. *Aren't you at a game right now? Why are you texting me?*

Intermission, Wren answered immediately. *I'm just so excited!*

Fisher smiled, imagining the way her eyes must be sparkling. *Who's winning?*

We are. Butterfly's on fire.

That's the hot one, right?

There's more than one hot one, Wren retorted. *But yes.*

Fisher laughed. *Have fun. Tell me about it tomorrow!*

Rain pattered the window as he turned the phone off, soft pattering taps that were a comforting reminder that the world was big and cold, but he was warm and cozy. He had his family, his chosen siblings, and he had French. Sometimes he thought there was something French wanted to say, something big he was holding back, but it hadn't happened yet.

Fisher knew what he was hoping for, but he'd let French get there in his own time. There was no reason to rush.

He fell asleep smiling, imagining French telling him his true identity, confessing his love, asking Fisher if he'd be willing to have a serious relationship.

23

Wren was talking the minute she spied him in the hall the next morning. "Butterfly got a shutout and Saint got a hat trick! Plus Kasha got in a fight." She giggled. "I've never seen him fight before, he's kind of terrible at it."

"What's a hat trick?" Fisher asked, only half-listening as he got the door open and held it for her.

"It's when a player gets three goals in a single game," Wren told him. She headed for her desk and put her coffee and backpack down, bending to rummage in the drawer.

"Why do they call it that?"

Wren straightened, blinking. "You know... I don't know? I should probably know that."

"Call yourself a hockey fan," Fisher said, clucking his tongue, and dodged the pencil she threw at him.

"Oh hey, Leo was trying to get hold of you," Wren said as Fisher was laying out his updated lesson plans. "He seemed upset about something but he wouldn't say what."

Fisher dug in his pocket, frowning at his phone as he turned it on. "I overslept a little this morning, didn't have time to do anything other than take Maya out and get out the door myself. Haven't even checked—oh, he left me a message."

"Did he text you?"

Fisher flipped to the text app. "Just once, that he needs to talk to me. Doesn't seem *too*—"

Samantha charged through the door. "Mr. Monty, Mr. Monty, guess what?"

Fisher shoved the phone back in his pocket as Samantha rushed for him. Whatever Leo needed was just going to have to wait.

"Good morning, Samantha!" he said, crouching. "I give up, what?"

"My daddy's gonna be here today!" she announced, wriggling with excitement.

"Hey, that's great!" Fisher smiled at her. "Are you excited?"

Samantha shrugged. "I dunno, I guess?"

"Not a hockey fan, huh?" He leaned forward, lowering his voice. "Me either. Don't tell Miss Wren though, okay? We don't want to ruin her super-special day."

Samantha nodded gravely and Fisher winked at her before shooing her to her seat and standing.

"I just—" Wren took a deep breath. "I can't believe the Birds are coming *here*. That I saw them play last night and now I'm gonna *meet* them." Her eyes widened. "Oh God, I'm gonna make an absolute *fool* of myself."

"You'll be fine," Fisher told her. Kids were

coming through the door in a steady stream now. "They're used to people being awkward, I'm sure. And it's not the whole team, just a few of them."

"Do you know who yet?" Wren asked.

"Yeah, the coordinator got back to me, but I forgot all the names immediately." Fisher laughed at the look on Wren's face. "Relax, it'll be great. You'll be charming, they're all going to ask for your number and compete to sweep you off your feet."

Calum cleared his throat from the door as Max darted inside, making a beeline for Wren.

Fisher hid the twitch of revulsion and summoned a smile as he joined him. "Good morning."

Calum's eyes were as cool and calculating as ever, but he smiled. "Good morning. I understand the children are very excited about today."

"They sure are. I'm still not sure how you managed this, honestly."

Calum lifted a shoulder. "I seem to recall telling you that when I want something, I'm generally successful in getting it. You care deeply about the children you teach, as well as that flighty young assistant of yours, and if I can give you something that makes you happy, then perhaps—" He licked his lips. "Perhaps you'll give me something I've been wanting, too."

Fisher took a slow, steady breath. Just standing *near* the man made him feel filthy, like he desperately needed a shower. The thought of Calum actually touching him made him want to throw up.

"After school today," Calum said, eyes boring into Fisher's. "I've been patient, and you've had enough time to come to a decision. I'll expect your answer then."

He left without waiting for a response, which was probably just as well. The kids didn't need to see Fisher punching someone, no matter how richly that person deserved it.

24

THE MORNING PASSED QUICKLY, the kids almost all as excited as Wren was. Fisher couldn't even find it in him to resent the reason, not when it had them all so worked up, talking animatedly about the players and what they were going to do, speculating on if they were actually going to play hockey with them. More than one was worried about not being able to skate, and Fisher had to stop each time to assure them they hadn't frozen over the gymnasium, that if they *did* play hockey, it would be on the regular floor.

His phone rang as they were lining up to go to the gym, and Fisher swore internally, dropping back and signalling to Wren to take the children out the door.

"Leo?" he said.

"Fish, I have to talk to you." Leo sounded upset but not panicked.

The last child was out the door. Fisher followed, bringing up the rear of the train.

"Leo, I'm at work, you *know* that. We're heading for gym now. Is it an emergency? Are you okay?"

"I'm fine," Leo said. "It's not—look, I just need to talk to you. It's important. Can you call me the second you're home? I'll come over."

"Okay, sure. You're sure it can wait?"

Leo blew out a breath. "Maybe I'm imagining things. It's fine. We'll talk this afternoon."

Fisher put the phone away and nodded at Wren when she glanced back at him, a question in her eyes.

There were a number of parents in the stands, talking excitedly among themselves. To be expected, probably—this *was* a hockey town, and a chance to meet their favorite players was not to be sneezed at. Even Calum was there, sitting next to the dean and deep in conversation.

Wren and Fisher got the children organized, everyone sitting criss-cross-applesauce in two neat rows. Fisher was crouching to speak to Maxine, on the end of one row, when Wren grabbed his arm with a grip that made him wince.

"*They're here*," she hissed.

Fisher managed to pry her fingers loose before she bruised him, patting her hand. He was fighting a smile as he straightened and turned and the bottom fell out of his world.

A handful of men in teal and white Seabirds jerseys were coming in the door nearest Wren and Fisher, flanked by a camera crew, but those were all the details Fisher managed to retain, because that was *French* at the back of the group, laughing at something one of the others was saying. His white teeth were flashing, eyes crinkled in that delighted way he had when something really amused him.

There was no oxygen in the room. Fisher felt like he'd taken a baseball bat to the head, frozen in place as the group headed for them. He *felt* the moment French saw him, the shock that rippled through him as he missed a step and nearly fell. The man beside him caught him, saying something that sounded teasing, but French didn't seem to even hear him.

Wren cleared her throat, but Fisher didn't move. *Couldn't* move. Wren took a step forward instead, holding out her hand to the nearest player.

"Hi, um—hi. I'm Wren. Welcome to Saint Mary Conservatory, we're all so excited to have you."

French was still staring at Fisher, misery and what looked very much like guilt on his stupidly beautiful face, and all Fisher could do was stare back as the shock and betrayal writhed in his gut.

Wren was saying something. Fisher made an effort to listen, unable to look away from French.

"—Said this is Saint, the captain."

Fisher wrenched his eyes away and met Saint's eyes. He wasn't very big, almost short next to the men around him, but he had the easy bearing of someone used to being listened to. He also looked horrified, glancing between Fisher and French.

"You know," Fisher said before he thought better of it.

Wren shot him a puzzled look.

Saint's mouth worked. "Is there somewhere private we can go? Ah—Kasha, this is Wren. Will you help her by telling the kids our workout routine and getting them moving? Caz, you and Roddy stay too."

Bewilderment was in Wren's huge eyes, but Kasha was already moving forward, a hand out and a smile in place.

"Fisher?" Saint prompted quietly.

Fisher tore his eyes from French again and swallowed hard. *Focus*, he ordered himself. Why was it so hard to *think*?

"My classroom," he said aloud, and spun on his heel to stalk in that direction, not looking to see if they were following.

THE ROOM WAS DARK, and Fisher only turned on the light over his desk before turning to confront both men.

No one spoke at first. Fisher didn't think he could get actual words out past the hurt and fury, and French didn't seem any more inclined to break the silence.

Finally, Saint cleared his throat. "I've heard a lot about you, Fisher," he began.

"What's your real name?" Fisher demanded of French, who flinched.

"Felix," he said, an arm curled across his abdomen almost protectively. "Felix Papillon."

"Butterfly," Fisher said as the pieces clicked into place. "I *knew* I'd seen you somewhere before. God, I'm so fucking *stupid*."

Saint coughed. "Fisher—"

"Why are you here?" Fisher interrupted. "This is between me and *Felix*."

Saint turned to Felix and asked him something in French. Another shock of horrified recognition jolted through Fisher as Felix answered in a low, choked voice. *This* was French's best friend, the one he worked with, who'd called him the morning Fisher had driven him home.

"Alright," Saint said. "I'm going to go back to the gymnasium and help Kasha and Wren. Fee—"

"Go," Felix said, looking at Fisher. "I imagine this will not take long."

Saint winced. "Fisher—"

"What," Fisher said flatly.

Saint sighed. "Just… try not to judge too harshly. You don't have all the facts."

"I'm sure *Felix* can give them to me," Fisher said, and didn't miss the way Felix flinched again. There was a distant roaring in his ears, a howling wind scouring his mind clear of everything but the betrayal. Felix had known. He'd *known*, and he'd lied to him for *months*.

Fisher didn't look away. *Let him dangle*, he thought viciously. *Let him* hurt, *see what it's like.*

The door clicked shut behind Saint, and Felix gestured.

"Say it, then."

"Where should I start?" Fisher demanded. "You knew, almost from the beginning. You *knew* how I felt about hockey, about hockey *players*. And you let me think—you *lied* to me."

"I never lied to you," Felix cut in. "I didn't tell you, you're right. But I *never* lied to you."

"Oh, that makes it better," Fisher sneered. "Technicalities. Do you want a prize? You lied to me every time you touched me and let me think there could be something more, when the whole time you were hiding who you were. And don't you stand there and tell me you didn't think the same thing, don't you *dare*. I know what I fucking saw in your eyes, Fr—*Felix*. I saw the same thing I was feeling. And you let me think there was a *chance*."

Felix took a step back, arm still wrapped over his stomach. "I didn't—I never—" He cut himself off, rubbing his mouth with a shaking hand. "Fisher, you said—"

"What?" Fisher demanded. "What did I say? What did I *ever* say that would have made a betrayal like this justifiable?"

"You said you'd never fall in love with a professional athlete," Felix said. His voice was small, uncertain in a way Fisher had never heard from him before.

"Yes! I did! And you had a *perfect chance* right there to tell me who you were!"

"You would have kicked me out!" Felix shouted suddenly, lifting his head. There were tears in his eyes. "I didn't want to stop seeing you, Fisher—" *Feesher.* Fisher's heart throbbed painfully. "And when you said that, I knew—" He faltered. "I knew when you found out, it would be over. I didn't w-want it to *be* over. It was selfish, b-but—"

"You didn't give me a *chance!*" Fisher flung back. "You just made the decision for both of us, and you *lied to me.*"

Felix bowed his head, tears sliding down his cheeks.

"You let me fall in love with you," Fisher said, and Felix jerked like he'd been hit. Fisher kept going, tears stinging his own eyes. "You let me think—you told me where you *live*. Bet you're regretting that right about now, aren't you?"

A tear slid down Felix's cheek. "There are many things I regret," he managed. "But I still don't think you're like m-my ex. I don't think you would ever do anything to hurt me like he did."

Fisher took two quick steps forward and loomed over him. Felix stood his ground, looking up at him.

"You think I won't hurt you?" Fisher asked, low and dangerous.

Felix lifted his chin. "I think… I hurt you far more than you could or would ever hurt me. And I'm so sorry. For not telling you, for not—" He swallowed hard. "I wanted so much to say something, Fisher, but—"

"Get out," Fisher said. He took a step back and pointed at the door. "Get out of my school. Get out of my life. Don't you *ever* come near me again."

Felix's mouth worked, but he didn't say anything. He just turned jerkily toward the door, none of his usual grace on display as he stumbled to it. He hesitated, door half-open, but Fisher crossed his arms, raising his chin, and Felix crumpled in on himself and slipped through the doorway without speaking.

That's it, then.

Fisher sat down hard in one of the child sized chairs, covering his face. This wasn't happening. He was dreaming, and he was going to wake up in his bed, with French asleep beside him, and everything was going to go back to the way it was before.

Someone knocked on the door and opened it before Fisher could answer. He scrambled to his feet as Calum stepped inside.

"You never told me you knew someone on the Seabirds," he said, and there was something in his eyes like anger. Or maybe jealousy. "You told me you didn't have a boyfriend."

Something snapped inside Fisher, an almost audible sound, as blind rage swamped him. "I'm under no obligation to tell you *shit*," he spat, and Calum's eyebrows went up, then slammed together. Fisher didn't stop to let him speak. "You come in here and tell me I don't have a choice, that you want me and you're going to have me, you try to *buy* me, you threaten my job if I don't say yes, and you still somehow think I'd ever want to tell you the first thing about me?"

Calum's eyes were chips of blue ice. "You will regret that," he said, voice freezing in its calm.

"Newsflash, you fucking rapist prick, I regret *everything* about this day!" Fisher shouted, balling his fists. He took a step forward and Calum mirrored it, one rapid step back. "I regret the first time I laid *eyes* on you. Get the *fuck* out of my classroom. I will get a restraining order against you if you *ever* come near me again. *Get out of my sight.*"

Calum's jaw worked. "I hope you enjoyed this job," he hissed. "Because you just lost it. And I'll see to it you never work in this field again."

Fisher lunged but Calum jerked the door open and fled before he could get close.

So *that* was it then. Fisher stood very still for a minute, eyes closed. He would *not* let the tears fall, because he knew if he did, they'd never stop.

Moving on autopilot, he turned back to his desk and began gathering his things. The dean would be there any minute.

25

____

Numb. Felix wasn't feeling much of anything other than that. He felt like he'd been hollowed out, emotions scooped clean from him like a cored apple.

He didn't go home. Instead he drove, on autopilot, barely aware of his surroundings, to Saint's house. He let himself in with his key, the one given him for only the direst need. He thought this probably qualified.

There was no sound from Steel, who was probably crated in Carmine's absence. Felix took his shoes off and went to the living room, placing each step with care. His head felt loose on his shoulders and he wasn't entirely sure where his feet were. All he could see was the fury, the *pain* on Fisher's face, the disgust when he'd looked at Felix.

He found his favorite beanbag in the corner and curled up in the middle of it, drawing his knees to his chest.

You're as flexible as my—

Fisher's students. That's who Felix was as flexible as.

He closed his eyes. Fisher was a teacher. An elementary school teacher, from the looks of it. It suited him.

He hadn't wanted to go, when Saint had texted him to say that a conservatory had contacted the team's PR agent and asked if a few players could come to the school. He'd had a hard game the night before and he'd stopped a puck with his hip right after deflecting one off his collarbone. He was bruised and tired and all he wanted to do was take it easy until he could go see Fisher. Instead he'd been bullied into joining Saint and the others on a trip across town to a small school that was, admittedly, charming enough.

He was already over his annoyance at having to go when they walked into the gymnasium, laughing at something Carmine was saying to him. Seeing Fisher staring back at him across the gym floor had been like being run over by a D-man he hadn't even seen coming.

There had been a moment, one wild, fleeting moment where Felix had hoped for an outcome he'd known in his gut wouldn't happen. And then he'd registered the expression on Fisher's face, and the certainty had settled into his bones. It was all over but the shouting, as his mother would say.

Fisher hadn't shouted much. Raised his voice a few times, but even then, Felix had known instinctively that Fisher would never lay hands on him in anger.

Too good for you.

Felix held back the tears, clutching his knees

harder. He would *not* cry. He'd done this to himself. He didn't deserve to cry, to grieve. Not when he'd known it was coming, he'd been *warned,* and he hadn't put a stop to things in time.

His body ached dully, the aches and pains from the night before waking up again. Felix let himself sink into the hurt, starting a meditation chant his father had taught him when he'd first signed up for hockey. It was too simple to help him get in the zone most of the time, but right now he needed the comfort.

"You would have liked him, Papa," he said aloud to the empty room, and another tear slid down his cheek.

He had no idea how long he was there before the front door finally slammed open.

"Felix? Fee!"

There were running footsteps and then Saint skidded into view as Felix slowly, carefully, unwound himself and sat up.

"How did it go?" he asked.

Saint shook his head. "Don't. Don't do that. No, stay there." He kicked off his shoes, shoving them to the side as the front door closed again and Carmine's more measured steps came down the hall.

He stopped in the doorway, watching with sympathy in his eyes as Saint squeezed into the beanbag beside Felix, slipping a thigh between his legs and squirming until they were both comfortable again.

"I'm gonna take Steel for a run," Carmine said. "Felix—" He hesitated. "Hang in there."

Felix didn't have the energy to answer. Saint had

an arm around his waist, careful to avoid the bruise, his face pressed to the cap of Felix's shoulder.

"Did anyone say—anything?" Felix asked after a few minutes.

Saint shook his head. "They were confused, but Kasha and Caz put on a great show for the kids. I got to play goalie."

That almost made Felix smile. "I know how much you love doing that."

"Oh Fee." The sorrow in Saint's voice threatened to break the flimsy dam around Felix's emotions.

"Don't," he said, too harshly. He breathed through his nose for a minute until he had himself under control. "I did this to myself," he finally said.

"But I see *why*," Saint said, lifting his head. "I get it, Fee. He's—he's great. At least I'm guessing he is when he's not, you know… angry and heartbroken."

Felix screwed his eyes shut again, turning into Saint's frame. "I love him so much," he managed, the tears stinging fiercely again.

"It's pretty obvious he loves you just as much," Saint said into Felix's hair.

Felix shook his head without looking up. "Maybe he did. Past tense. He might have loved who he thought I was. But that's gone now."

Saint sighed. "Come on. We are way too sober for this." He hauled Felix, protesting, to his feet and chivvied him to the wet bar on the other side of the room, where he pushed him onto a stool.

"It's still *morning*," Felix said as Saint ducked behind the bar.

"First of all," Saint said, up on tiptoe to retrieve Felix's favorite brand of Scotch, "it's closer to midafternoon. And second, heartbreak does not acknowledge the passage of time, so why should we?"

Felix stared. Saint poured the Scotch, a serene expression on his face, and pushed the glass across the marble countertop.

"That was surprisingly deep. Have you been reading again?"

"Fuck off," Saint suggested, dimples flashing briefly. "Besides," he added as he poured a shot for himself, "we're off tomorrow too. So we can get as wasted as necessary. Knock that back already so I can pour you another."

Dumbly, Felix did as ordered. The Scotch burned a path down his throat and he blinked hard several times.

"Can you tell me what he said after I left?" Saint asked, topping up his glass.

Felix tossed back the next shot before answering. "It did not take long. He feels betrayed. He is… so angry."

"But the only reason you did it was because he literally said he wouldn't date a hockey player," Saint protested, brow furrowed as he refilled both glasses again.

"Exactly." Felix took the third shot and braced his hands on the counter. The room was already beginning to spin, just slightly. "I went and fell in love with him *knowing* how he felt about what I do. I let him think there was a chance. For us."

"No." Saint shook his head. "No, you told him from the beginning that there *wasn't* a chance. You set the boundaries early. You never changed them. Did you?"

Felix shook his head and swallowed the next shot. "*Non*, I never changed them. But apart from those few conversations, we also… didn't talk about them. I went to *farmer's markets* with him, Saint. Of course he thought we were dating. Or that we *could* date, I don't know." He put his face on his arms, the marble cool against his skin. "He invited me to Thanksgiving," he said, voice muffled.

There was a thump as Saint sat down on his own stool. "Wow. That's…."

"Yeah," Felix said against his forearm. "The worst part was I think if we had been in town then, I would have been tempted to say yes."

Saint rubbed his shoulder silently. "Farmer's markets, eh?" he asked after a minute. "Didn't you get recognized?"

"Only once, and I bribed her with my autograph to stay quiet until I was gone." He huffed an almost-amused breath, remembering. "Fisher thought she was very strange, because she looked at him when he came over, then me, and then she just… ran away."

Saint snickered. "You got off easy. There could have been a mob situation."

"I'm not you," Felix countered, lifting his head and reaching for his shot glass. He was feeling warm and floaty, the most jagged edges of the pain blunted by the alcohol as his head spun. "I hide behind a mask and my pretty face is not on twenty foot high billboards. I can go out in public without causing a riot. Mostly."

"Off topic," Saint said firmly. "What else did he say?"

Felix lifted a shoulder. "He shouted a bit. I tried to apologize but he didn't want to hear it. I can't blame him for that. He—oh, he asked if I regretted letting him take me home."

"Felix Édouard Papillon, you let him *take you home?*"

Felix scowled at him. "He's not Paul."

"*Still.* After everything that happened—"

"He's *not Paul,*" Felix repeated stubbornly. "He wouldn't. He *wouldn't.* I don't know how I know, especially when he was so angry, but he would *never.*"

Saint subsided, muttering under his breath as he poured again.

"Anyway, he told me to go away and never come near him again, and I left." More tears stung Felix's eyes and he blinked them away. "I should have listened. I should have—" He put his face down again as the tears welled and Saint put an arm around his shoulders.

"It's a stupid misunderstanding," he said. "We'll give him time to calm down, and then you can apologize again, properly. He'll take you back."

Felix heaved a sigh. "He won't, cherry. Not only did I lie to him, but I play the sport he hates most in the world and I won't give it up, not even for him."

"*Good,*" Saint said, startling Felix with his ferocity. "If you tried, I'd kill you myself." He nudged him with an elbow and pushed the full shot glass nearer when Felix lifted his head. "Still not drunk, come on. So *why* does he hate hockey so much, anyway?"

Felix swallowed the Scotch and wiped his wet eyes. "I don't know. He never really went into specifics. Just that he had an ex who played, and he had bad… associations with it. I know he doesn't like violence. The fighting and the hits bother him."

"But he runs a hockey program?"

"Wren runs it," Felix corrected. "It was her idea. He said yes because she loves it so much."

"Speaking of Wren," Saint said, "I think Kasha got her number."

"Did he now? Good for him. Fisher speaks— spoke—" He steadied himself. "—Of her often. He cares very much for her. I'm sorry I never met her."

"Probably for the best," Saint said. His words were slurring just slightly. "She'd have recognized you immediately, I'll bet."

"Then perhaps this whole *tas de merde* could have been avoided," Felix snapped. "Saved us both a lot of pain."

The sliding door opened and Carmine stepped through, Steel right behind him. His eyebrows went up at the sight of Felix and Saint at the wetbar but he just lifted his shirt and wiped his face.

"How we doing?" he asked when he emerged.

Felix held out one hand, palm-down, and waggled it vaguely.

"Fair enough." Carmine slapped him on the shoulder. "I'm gonna shower."

"Come drink with us when you're done," Felix said.

Saint lasted barely two minutes after Carmine was gone before he was squirming in place, casting quick glances at the far door like Felix hadn't been able to read him like a book since they were fifteen.

"Oh, go on," Felix finally said, exasperated. "Go be disgusting and in love."

Saint blushed, tips of his ears going dusky red, but he didn't move. "No. He'll be fine."

Felix rolled his eyes and shoved him off the stool. Saint went over with a startled squawk and scrambled back to his feet in the next breath.

"Seriously, *go*," Felix ordered. "Go talk about me and how worried you are and what you're going to do to mend my broken heart. I'll be fine for five minutes."

Saint wavered. "Five minutes," he finally said.

Felix flapped a hand at him. "Fuck off already. But no sex with me in the house!" he called as Saint headed for the door.

Alone, Felix considered his options. First things first—he poured himself another shot. Then he pulled his phone from his pocket. There were no messages out of the ordinary, and a little cursory Googling told him that no one seemed to have reported anything unusual happening at the Saint Mary Conservatory when the team visited.

That was good, anyway. Hopefully, Felix hadn't put Fisher's job in danger.

Fisher taught kindergarten. Felix moaned and put his head in his arms again. His traitorous brain was supplying him with rapid-fire image after image of Fisher surrounded by small children, helping them spell, or count, or learn algebra—Felix had only hazy memories of his own school days. Who knew what children were learning these days? But the thought of Fisher, maybe crouching to talk to a little girl or boy with a question, his eyes so soft and gentle—that was undoing Felix at the seams.

"I don't even *want* kids," he said despairingly. "See, Steel?" Steel, already curled in his bed in front of the fireplace, lifted his head at the sound of his name. "*That's* why it never would have worked anyway. Because he wants kids, and I don't. I'm not —paternal. I would be a terrible father. I've never even *thought* of having children."

Steel yawned and licked his chops.

"Exactly." Felix reached for the bottle and missed. Frowning, he recalculated and tried again, slower. He was successful that time, and only spilled a little when he refilled his glass. He lifted it and saluted his reflection in the mirror behind the bar. His eyes had deep shadows under them. "Fucking idiot," he told himself, and downed the shot.

He needed to apologize again. Properly. Fisher needed to hear exactly how sorry Felix was, how he'd never intended for any of this to happen.

He'd dialed, squinting at the screen, and was lifting the phone to his ear when it was whisked from his hand.

"Nope, nope, absolutely *not*," Carmine said, stabbing at buttons as Felix protested. He powered the phone off and put it in his own pocket, giving Felix a disappointed look. "You are *not* in a state to talk to anyone right now, but especially not him."

"I just want to apologize, do it *right*," Felix said.

Carmine's expression melted into sympathy as Saint appeared behind him. "I know, bud. But not when you're well on your way to drunk off your ass. Hey love," he said to Saint, who was going behind the bar again. "Got some bourbon for your favorite D-man?"

"Who *says* you're my favorite?" Saint countered even as he reached for the bottle.

Felix scowled at his shot glass as Carmine made

faux-offended noises. The noises cut off abruptly and Carmine cleared his throat. When Felix looked up, Saint was concentrating on the bourbon he was pouring with far more focus than it needed, and Carmine looked guilty.

"Sorry, Butterfly," Carmine said. "Didn't mean to… make it worse."

"Don't flatter yourself," Felix said, pushing his glass to Saint. "You've always disgusted me, the two of you. You don't have to stop just because I'm sad."

"Still, it's insensitive," Carmine insisted.

"Shut the fuck up and drink," Felix told him. "You have some catching up to do."

FISHER WAS WOKEN by Leo climbing in bed with him. Or more accurately, climbing on *top* of him and draping himself over Fisher's back.

"Time to wake up," he said in Fisher's ear, and Fisher buried his face in the pillow. Leo wriggled, shaking the bed. "Fisher, it's been a week and it's time to stop wallowing. Maya's forgotten what you look like."

Fisher turned his head just enough to glare at him over his shoulder. "I take her out multiple times a day, asshole."

"But when's the last time you went running with her?"

Fisher didn't bother to answer, burying his face again.

Leo sighed, warm against Fisher's bare shoulder blade. "C'mon, Fish. I know you got your heart broken, but hiding from life isn't going to help. You need some fresh air and sunlight."

"No."

"I am perfectly capable of annoying you out of this bed," Leo said placidly. "Don't test me."

Fisher took a slow breath. "Leo—"

"I know," Leo murmured, scooting forward so he could press their cheeks together. "I *know*, Fish. But you'll get through this. I'm gonna help. And the first step involves getting your fine ass out of bed and into the shower while I change your sheets."

"Or we could stay in bed," Fisher suggested, and pushed back against him.

Leo caught his breath sharply and rolled off fast, landing with both feet on the floor. He yanked the sheet off Fisher's legs in the next instant.

"Get the fuck up," he ordered, sounding furious, and Fisher sat up. Leo *looked* furious, spots of color high in his pale cheeks and fists clenched by his sides. Shame swamped Fisher, but Leo spoke before he could.

"You don't get to do that," he hissed.

Fisher opened his mouth but Leo cut him off.

"You don't get to *use* me to try to make yourself stop hurting," he continued. "You're better than that, Fisher." His voice gentled and he took a step closer. "I know you're grieving, but that's not okay."

"I'm so sorry," Fisher blurted. He covered his face, tears stinging. "Fuck, I'm—"

Leo stepped between his knees and wrapped his arms around Fisher's shoulders. Fisher pressed his face to Leo's thin T-shirt and let the tears fall as Leo rubbed his back.

When the worst had passed, he took a steadying breath. "I love you," he said against Leo's stomach.

"I love you too, asshole," Leo murmured. "You're not yourself right now. But don't ever do that again."

"I won't," Fisher mumbled. "'M gonna go shower."

"Excellent idea." Leo let him go and Fisher stood. There was nothing but affection in the smile Leo tilted up at him, and Fisher thumbed his chin briefly before turning to the dresser to look for clean clothes.

In the shower, he braced a forearm on the wall and let the scalding water rush over him, eyes closed against the steam.

It had been a week since his life had blown up in his face so spectacularly. He'd lost the man he loved *and* the job he loved in less than an hour. The first, he'd done himself. The second had been accomplished by Calum going directly to the dean and lodging a complaint against Fisher for 'inappropriate conduct'.

Should've punched him when I had the chance, he thought. *Accusing* me *of coming on to* him. *Ludicrous.*

There'd been nothing to be done. The dean had seemed regretful, but it was Fisher's word against Calum's, and the school had an at-will firing policy. They didn't have to give a reason for letting him go.

He could fight it, he'd been told by multiple people, including several parents who'd reached out when they heard the news. Laurel Hollingsworth was a lawyer, and Margaret Charpentier was married to one, and they'd both told him lawsuits could be filed, he could go to the union, there were things that could be done.

Fisher didn't want that. He didn't want the whole ugly mess dragged into the light, laid bare for everyone to gawk at and pick over. The dean had offered him a choice—refuse to leave, be fired, and take his chances in court, or quit and be given a good reference when any future place of employment called looking into his past.

Already bruised and brittle and so close to being broken, Fisher had taken the easier choice. Maybe he'd hate himself for it later, but he didn't have the energy or the heart to fight.

He turned off the water and stepped out, not looking at himself in the mirror as he toweled dry.

His bed was neatly made with fresh sheets when he came back out, but Leo was nowhere to be seen.

Fisher found him in the living room, on his stomach with his feet in the air as he talked to Maya, who had her head on her paws but was thumping her tail every time Leo finished a sentence. Fisher stopped to watch them and Leo glanced up, a smile spreading over his face at the sight of him.

"You look almost human again," he said, kissing the top of Maya's head before bouncing to his feet. "Hungry?"

"Not if you're cooking," Fisher said.

Leo grimaced. "Obviously not. I brought the ingredients, you're making the meal."

"I guess working in a grocery store has its perks," Fisher teased, mostly for the face Leo made. "How's that going, by the way?"

"Other than the fact that I hate people and dream of running away and never working another customer service job for the rest of my life?" Leo shrugged. "Fine. At least I get a discount." He followed Fisher into the kitchen and hopped up onto the counter as Fisher inspected the contents of the bags he'd left on the table. "So what are you making?"

"I don't even know what we have yet, give me a minute." When Fisher glanced over his shoulder, Leo was watching him, sadness in his bright green eyes. Fisher twitched irritably. "Don't look at me like that."

"Like what, someone who's had his heart broken? How would you *like* me to look at you?"

"Preferably as someone who doesn't want your pity," Fisher snapped. Leo had brought him an artichoke, some asparagus, tomatoes, and a bushel of carrots. With typical Leo-like lack of attention to detail, he'd most likely shoved the most colorful vegetables he could find in a bag and called it a day. Fisher sighed and turned to find a knife to start chopping them up.

"I don't pity you," Leo said softly as Fisher turned on the oven and set out the cutting board. "But I do think it's time to talk about this."

Fisher shut the drawer with more force than necessary. "No."

"We're talking," Leo said. He kicked his feet, crossed at the ankles, and met Fisher's flat glare with sunny equanimity. "You wanna go first or shall I?"

"There is *nothing* to talk about." Fisher grabbed the artichoke and began peeling it.

"*Au contraire*—" Leo caught himself just as Fisher went still. "Fuck. Sorry. But that right there proves we need to talk about this."

Fisher set the knife down carefully. "I'm a grown man, Leo, I can handle hearing words in... another language."

"You can't even say the *word* French!" Leo said accusingly.

"So what?" Fisher snapped. "You want me to

admit how fucked up I am? I'm fucked up, Leo, okay? He used me, he broke my heart, he did everything you said he'd do. I fell for him when I said I wouldn't, because I'm a fucking *idiot*. And now I'm jobless and worse off than when I started and in love with a fucking *hockey player*, and everything *sucks*. So what is there to talk about?"

"There's the fact that from everything you've told me, he's in love with you too."

Fisher spun. "So *what?*" he repeated. "Did you miss where he *lied* to me? Where he had every opportunity to tell me the truth and *didn't?*"

Leo bumped the cabinet with his heels, eyes steady on Fisher's. "That's exactly how I know he's in love with you."

That stopped Fisher. He sputtered but couldn't come up with words.

"You're a smart man, Fish," Leo said. "Think about it. If it *was* just sex for him, if you meant nothing more than somewhere to get his dick wet, why wouldn't he have told the truth? Why wouldn't he have risked it, even with the possibility of you kicking him out? He's rich, famous, incredibly good-looking—he could have anyone he wanted with the crook of his finger."

Fisher glared at him, but Leo just arched a brow.

"But he chose to stay, to see you, to be—I'm assuming—monogamous while he was with you, despite being clear upfront that he might want to sleep with other people." Leo paused. "Was he? Monogamous?"

Fisher nodded reluctantly. "At least as far as I know. But I *don't* know, Leo. He traveled *all the time*.

He could have been sleeping with new people in every city, and how would I have known?"

"God, I love you but you're *dim* sometimes," Leo sighed. "Fish, baby, try and think about it logically for a minute. I know you're angry and hurting, but just—use that big brain of yours. When he traveled, how often did you two talk while he was gone? Text or calling."

Fisher glowered at him but gave it serious, if unwilling, thought. "He'd go dark for at least five hours a night. I don't know about mornings as much, that was when I was in class anyway. But he'd usually text me when he woke up and then vanish for a few hours. We'd text off and on the rest of the time unless he was on the plane."

"So the first bit was likely when the games were on and he was playing," Leo said, nodding. "And mornings were probably for practices and traveling, maybe media shit."

Fisher stared. "Since when do you know hockey players' schedules?"

"Since my best friend fell in love with one," Leo retorted, kicking his feet again.

"Past tense," Fisher muttered. He turned back to the artichoke.

Undeterred, Leo continued. "Which means that other than games, practices, and actual travel time, he was in pretty much constant contact with you. But you still think he was running around sleeping with everyone else?"

Fisher hunched his shoulders and kept slicing. "Why not?"

"What do you mean?"

"I mean," Fisher said, turning around again,

"why would he have bothered? You said it yourself, he could have anyone he wanted. *I* was the one who wanted monogamy, not him. So what was in it for him?"

"You *can't* be this stupid," Leo said despairingly. "*Fisher.*"

"I just—" Fisher blinked a few times. "He said he didn't want it. Me. To settle down, be… whatever. More than fuckbuddies."

"Because everyone always says what they mean and never lies to themselves," Leo said, but he sounded sympathetic. "Maybe he *didn't* want that at first. You told me he'd been hurt. And by the way, if you haven't read some articles about him, you really need to do that. It's gonna explain a lot. But people change, Fish. What people *want* changes. Maybe he hadn't really faced it yet himself, but it sounds to me like he was coming around to the idea of being *with* you, really with you."

"Not enough to trust me," Fisher muttered. "He practically went into nuclear meltdown mode at the thought of me knowing where he lives. That fucking *hurt*, okay? We'd been together for like five months, I still didn't know his *name*, and he nearly had a panic attack at the idea of being that vulnerable with me."

"Of course it hurt. Hand me those baby carrots." Fisher obeyed and Leo ripped the bag open to pull one out. "But he did it, didn't he? He trusted you. I think that's pretty fucking significant, Fish." The carrot crunched as he bit into it. "Can I ask you something?"

Fisher almost laughed. "Can I *stop* you?"

"Why do you hate hockey so much?"

Fisher went very still. When he glanced over his shoulder, Leo was watching him, feet crossed at the ankles.

"It's…." Fisher sighed. "Complicated."

"Contrary to appearances, I'm capable of grasping complex issues and ideas," Leo said dryly. "Try me."

"My ex," Fisher said. He set the knife down again and turned, resting his hips against the counter. "Peyton."

"Such a bro name," Leo said, biting into another carrot.

Fisher ignored that. "You know most of it. He didn't want to acknowledge me because he wasn't out. Plus he never had time for me, was always working out or going to games. All he could talk about was hockey. *Everything* was hockey. He was obsessed with it. The only way to shut him up was to —well."

Leo snickered. "Time-honored method."

"I just… I wanted to be that important to him. I wanted to be his focus. I resented hockey because it took him away from me. And when I broke up with him, I told him that. I didn't *quite* stoop to making him choose between us, but I made it pretty clear why it wasn't going to work."

"And he chose hockey."

Fisher lifted a shoulder. "He said he was sorry I couldn't support his dream, and he wished me well, and that was it. He didn't try at *all* to keep me." He shrugged away the old remembered sting. "I swore I'd never be with someone who didn't put *us* first. Didn't matter what he did, he had to be committed to our relationship first and foremost."

"And you think Felix wouldn't be."

"He's a *professional* hockey player," Fisher spat. "It is quite literally his *life*. You think anything could compete with that?"

"You do realize that there are a lot of married hockey players? Happily married ones? Some of them even have children."

"What works for them won't work for me," Fisher snapped.

"Oh, you're special, is that it?"

Fisher glared at him.

"What makes you different?" Leo asked. "And don't say it's because you have a penis."

"It's *not*," Fisher said. "It's just… I don't fit the mold, okay? I'm not what any hockey player is looking for. And that's fine with me."

Leo sighed. "You're just not even gonna try. That's what's so fucked up about this."

"There's nothing to try *for*!" Fisher shot back. "He didn't fight for me, he didn't ask me to forgive him or to try again. He just let me yell at him and then he left. He *walked away*."

"And there it is."

"There *what* is?"

"He didn't make enough of an effort for you." Leo kicked his heels and popped another baby carrot in his mouth.

That silenced Fisher momentarily. "That's… ridiculous," he finally managed.

"Is it?" Leo began ticking off points. "He didn't want a relationship to begin with, even as you guys spent more and more time together, until basically any time you were both free, he was over here. You took him to the farmer's market, Fish. *More than once*, which for you is tantamount to a proposal. You fell in love with him, and I'm pretty sure he was falling in love with you right back, but when the shit hit the fan, when everything went to hell, you got scared and you told him to leave and he *did*. Just like Peyton."

Fisher opened and closed his mouth. He felt like he'd been punched in the gut.

Leo hopped off the counter. "What's for dinner?"

It took Fisher another few minutes to find his voice. "Fuck if I know."

Leo sighed and pulled out his phone. "Fine, I'm ordering a pizza but you owe me."

Later that night, once Leo had gone home with a kiss to Fisher's cheek, Fisher sat down and turned on his computer. He stared at the search engine for a minute before squaring his shoulders and typing *Felix Papillon* in.

Page after page of results popped up. Felix staring at the camera, wearing the teal and white Seabirds jersey. In the middle of a game, his helmet perched precariously on the back of his head—*how did it stay like that*, Fisher wondered—smiling brilliantly at someone just offscreen. Another picture of him, this time on a plane next to Saint, their heads together in discussion.

The next picture was of Felix in a suit, arm around a handsome man with blond hair and perfect skin. The caption read, *Felix Papillon and partner, aspiring actor Paul Brandon, at the Seabirds 2019 annual charity gala.*

Fisher was startled by the stab of jealousy that knifed through him. Felix looked so *happy*, his smile wide and pride in his bearing. Fisher took a breath, willing himself to calm, and looked closer. He didn't think much of Paul, he decided. His smile didn't reach his eyes, and while he was admittedly handsome, there was a sameness to his features that left Fisher unmoved.

He went back to the search engine and typed *Felix Papillon Paul Brandon* in. More pictures and articles came up, fluff pieces about their life together, interviews with them sitting side by side on a loveseat, their thighs brushing. Henry was draped across Felix in one of the photographs, eyes closed as Felix smiled down at him.

Was this who had hurt Felix so badly? Maybe Fisher was reading too much into things, but he thought there was a difference to the way Felix held himself in the pictures. The Felix he knew was coiled tight, tense and wary, always guarded as if against a blow. This Felix was… joyous, leaning against Paul with his head thrown back in a laugh as Paul grinned down at him.

It made Fisher's chest ache. He searched for *Felix Papillon Paul Brandon breakup*, but the only things he found were a few throwaway mentions of an amicable separation, of Paul moving to Los Angeles to pursue his craft, how they were still close. Then *how* had Felix been hurt?

Wren had mentioned his personal details had been leaked online. Fisher went back to the search engine again. *Felix Papillon doxxed* brought up a dozen articles, and he clicked on the first one without looking too hard.

Felix Papillon, starting goalie for Portland's own Seabirds, released a series of three posts across several forms of social media this morning, inviting fans to follow the clues hidden within the pictures. The winner will receive an exclusive one-on-one training session with the 2017 All Star Games attendee, a signed, game-used stick, and box seats to the Seabirds' next home game.

"Jesus Christ," Fisher breathed.

Followers were skeptical at first, the article continued, *believing his account to have been hacked. But they were soon convinced by the cross-posts on Twitter, Instagram, and Facebook. Who will be the first to reach the end of the treasure hunt? Stay tuned to find out.*

Fisher clicked on the next article. *FELIX PAPILLON VICTIM OF VICIOUS PRANK,* the title read. Under a picture of Felix glaring at the camera in full hockey gear, sweaty and furious about something, the article laid it all out.

This morning, Felix Papillon's Twitter and Instagram accounts were hacked. Sensitive information and pictures of him were released without his knowledge or consent, including his home address, financial details, and his phone number. The 'treasure hunt' was actually an elaborate hoax designed for maximum harm.

"What the *fuck?*"

Papillon is as notoriously private as he is charming, able to deflect invasive questions with a wry joke in his soft French accent or a quick jab at a teammate that leaves everyone laughing. A call to his agent yielded the following statement: "The attack on Felix this morning was dangerously personal, revealing information he's guarded closely his entire professional life and causing him great emotional and financial damage. Make no mistake, this was malicious in intent, and we ask that Felix's privacy be respected in the aftermath."

Felix had been forced to fill out restraining orders against three people and lost several hundred thousands of dollars before he was able to plug the leak and change all his information, Fisher read on, horrified to his core. The mere *thought* of his life being laid bare like that, of the vultures picking through it all, made him nauseated. No wonder Felix had been so devastated, so wary of showing any vulnerability after that.

Fisher put his head in his hands. After all that, Felix had allowed Fisher to know the location of his house, an act that had clearly taken every ounce of courage he possessed. *Has he already moved again?* Fisher wondered. Surely that would have been his first act once Fisher had rejected him so forcefully. Guilt gnawed at his stomach.

So *who* had done it? Fisher dug deeper, reading article after article, but no one seemed to have any answers. A few enterprising internet detectives noticed that Paul Brandon and Felix had quietly separated several days before, and there were plenty of rumors that it had been Brandon behind the attack, but Felix had only released a single statement through his agent on the subject.

Paul and I parted ways with nothing but affection for each other, it read. *He chose to move to California to further his career, and I wish him all the best. I have no doubt we'll be seeing him in leading roles very soon, just as I have no doubt he could never do anything so vicious and wantonly dangerous to anyone, let alone someone he once cared deeply for.*

"Oh Felix," Fisher whispered. He sat back against the cushions, staring into space. A lot more made sense now, the way Felix had been so skittish, terrified of revealing any part of himself. Fisher was honestly surprised Felix had been willing to even give him his phone number, let alone allow him in as much as he had.

He clicked through a few more articles, scanning for Felix's name. There was no shortage of discussions about him, mostly speculation and gossip running wild, none of it substantial. Finally, he closed the computer. His little house felt empty in a way that it never had before Felix had burst into his life, cold and lifeless. Fisher hated it.

"I have to think," he said aloud. Maya pricked her ears questioningly. "Let's go for a run," Fisher told her, and she bounced to her feet immediately, tail sweeping in wide circles.

IT WAS LATE FOR A RUN, the sun inching toward the horizon and the air cold enough to sting. Fisher ran until his muscles were warm and loose, Maya keeping pace easily beside him, until they came out on a hill that overlooked the city. There was no one else around, so Fisher unclipped Maya's leash and let her explore the interesting smells while he stretched. Portland was spread out before him, lights coming on all over the city as the sun slipped down.

If he squinted, he could just barely see the dome of the arena where the Seabirds played their games. Unbidden, his mind went to Felix, just like it always did. What was he doing right now? Had he already moved on? Forgotten about Fisher and found another fuckbuddy to scratch the itch? Was he out looking for someone else, or was there a game that night?

Fisher whistled for Maya, who loped over, tail going. "Time to go home," he told her.

IN BED THAT NIGHT, he stared at the ceiling. Sleep stubbornly refused to visit. Finally, he picked up his phone and did a search for Paul Brandon.

He was in Hollywood, Fisher read, currently starring in a tv show airing on HBO. Fisher had never heard of it, but Paul certainly looked the part of a prosperous actor, hair perfectly tousled and teeth gleaming white as he smiled at the cameras on the red carpet.

There were plenty of articles about him, lauding his acting ability, his charm and charisma. A few of them mentioned Felix in passing, but none went in depth.

Fisher gritted his teeth. He needed to *know*, to understand what had happened between Paul and Felix. An idea took hold and he sat up in bed, staring at nothing as he thought it through, working out the logistics. It could work. He could *make* it work.

He called Leo.

"We're going to LA," he said with no preamble. "Pack a bag."

28

———

"Okay, run it by me again," Leo said, tugging on his seatbelt. A flight attendant was making her way down the aisle and she paused to check their belts, giving them both a smile before moving on. "I was half-asleep last time."

"We're gonna go find Paul Brandon, and I'm going to talk to him."

"And I'm here because…."

"Because you know people."

"I know people in *Portland*," Leo protested. "Not Hollywood!"

"Really? So no one you know has ever moved to LA and hit the bigtime?"

"Not like… the A-list," Leo said, but he was frowning, the little furrow between his eyes that appeared when he was working through a problem. "Wait, there's—no, they quit acting altogether. Oh, how about—" He pulled out his phone and began scrolling through his contacts. Fisher watched as Leo's fingers flew over the keys, sending texts.

The captain's voice came over the intercom, asking them to put their phones away, and Leo scowled but obeyed.

"I'll have an answer by the time we land." He sounded confident.

Fisher patted his knee but didn't answer.

LOS ANGELES WAS BUSTLING, loud, and crowded. Fisher hated it immediately. He tugged his ballcap low on his head and hailed a taxi. Leo had his phone out before the car arrived, scrolling through messages. Fisher opened the car door and bundled him inside. He was sliding in the other side when Leo crowed triumphantly.

"I *knew* she'd come through!" he said, brandishing the phone. "That's my girl!"

"Who?"

"Eliza," Leo said, already back to texting. "She doesn't have Paul's address, or a phone number, but she knows his favorite bar and he's there almost every night."

"Paul maybe has a drinking problem?" Fisher muttered, drumming his fingers against his knee.

"That or he's networking." Leo shrugged. "You have to know everyone in this business, and the who's who list is constantly changing."

"Sounds exhausting." Fisher stared out the window, barely seeing the buildings.

"How's the job hunt going?" Leo asked.

Fisher made a noncommittal noise that could have meant anything. Truth be told, he hadn't even really started looking, short of pulling up a few websites and putting in his information, but he hadn't followed up and submitted applications anywhere.

"You *are* hunting, right?"

"I will," Fisher said, glancing at him. Leo looked disapproving. "I have some savings, Leo. Don't fuss so much, you'll get wrinkles."

Leo glared at him. "I will fuss if I want to. Your savings won't last forever, and it's not like I can support us both on a minimum wage income."

"I love you for even considering it as an option," Fisher said, looping an arm around Leo's neck and ruffling his hair. "But I'll start seriously looking soon, I promise. I need to do this first, that's all."

Leo freed himself and smoothed his hair back, muttering under his breath. "So what are we doing, just lurking at this bar all day hoping Paul shows up? It's not even two yet."

"I thought we'd see the sights first," Fisher said. "When are we gonna get another chance to see Los Angeles, huh?"

Leo perked up. "Can we go to the Black Cat Tavern?"

"It's already on my list," Fisher told him.

Leo wriggled with joy. "This is gonna be great."

THAT NIGHT, exhausted and sunburned, they collapsed at a table in the bar Eliza had told Leo about. Fisher had stretched his aching feet out and was making short work of a cranberry juice when Leo elbowed himsharply. "Is that him?"

Fisher looked up to see a blond man making his

way through the tables, smiling at the diners as he passed them.

"He's shorter than I thought," Fisher mumbled.

Leo snickered. "I love it when you're catty. Makes me feel better about myself."

Fisher poked him in the side and Leo yelped. Paul was heading for the bar at the back of the restaurant. He settled on a stool and Fisher downed the rest of his cranberry juice.

"I'm going in."

Paul had both elbows braced on the bar, staring at his whisky when Fisher slid onto the stool next to him and caught the bartender's attention.

"Tequila, keep 'em coming."

Paul glanced at him but Fisher didn't look, watching the bartender pull a bottle off the shelf and pouring the first shot. When it was set in front of him, Fisher nodded.

"Leave the bottle." He picked up the shot glass and held it out to Paul. "To shitty exes." Paul's eyebrows went up but he touched the glass with his own.

Fisher knocked the shot back and took a deep breath as the alcohol slid down his throat, spreading fiery tendrils through his chest.

Paul still hadn't spoken, but he'd swiveled on his stool to watch Fisher, curiosity on his face.

Fisher poured another shot. "To self-centered exes who refuse to compromise to be in a relationship."

"Been there," Paul said, meeting his glass. His voice was deep and smooth, a wry smile tucked into the corner of his full mouth. He topped up his drink. "How's this one—to exes who always put their job first."

Fisher didn't have to fake the bitter laugh. "Perfect." He knocked his glass against Paul's and downed the shot. "God, men are trash. Did you feel like you were the afterthought the whole time? Like you were only kept around because their job didn't have a dick to keep them satisfied?"

"I sure fucking did." Paul's mouth twisted. "'Hey, let's do something tonight, just the two of us.'" He pitched his voice higher. "'Oh, I have to work tonight, I thought you knew that.'" He snorted. "He said he had to go out of town when I had surgery. Can you believe that?"

"Asshole," Fisher said, pouring another shot. "What kind of surgery?"

Paul looked suddenly shifty. "Don't tell my fans, but it was a nose job."

"Fans? Are you famous?"

"What, you don't recognize me?" Paul grinned, leaning toward him, and Fisher pretended to study his face.

"Are you an actor? I don't watch a lot of tv but I'd remember seeing you—you're way too handsome to forget."

Paul laughed, tossing his head back to expose his throat, and Fisher forced himself to laugh along.

"Yeah, I do a bit of acting," Paul said when he'd sobered. "Not enough, though, if you don't know who I am."

Fisher propped his chin on one fist and looked closer at him. "What have you been in? I'll make an exception for you."

Paul's smile widened. "Couple of rom-coms, an

action comedy, and right now I'm starring in a tv thriller on HBO."

"Wait, seriously?" Fisher widened his eyes, swaying toward him. "Shit, what's your name? I'm gonna google you."

"Where's the fun in that?" Paul countered. "My first name's Paul but I'm not giving you my last name yet. You'll have to earn it." His tongue darted out to touch his lower lip, and Fisher swallowed the knee-jerk desire to punch him.

"What do I have to do?" he asked instead.

Paul looked him up and down and bit his lip. "I have a few ideas. What's *your* name?"

"Stephen," Fisher said. "With a PhD."

Paul burst out laughing again and Fisher laughed with him this time, scooting his stool a little closer.

"That's cute," Paul said. "Almost as cute as you. What's your PhD in?"

Fisher made a disparaging noise. "Doctor of Musical Arts. Very boring."

"I refuse to believe anything about you is boring," Paul said, touching Fisher's forearm. "So you're a musician?"

"I've written a few songs about my sordid love life," Fisher said, leaning into his touch. His skin crawled but he was committed. "Maybe if you're lucky, I'll give you a private showing of them."

Paul licked his lips again. "That sounds... nice." His pupils were blown.

Fisher sat back. "So tell me about this ex, the one who didn't appreciate you. How'd you meet?"

It took Paul a minute to gather his wits. "Well... not naming names, but he plays hockey."

"I do love a good hockey ass," Fisher mused.

"I was a fan for a while," Paul continued. "Went to all his games. He was *hot*, right? And I knew he wasn't straight, so I managed to find out he was gonna be at the local hospital for a charity thing, and I engineered a meeting. By which I mean I had my arms full of stuffed animals and I 'accidentally' ran into him." His eyes invited Fisher to laugh with him. "He fell for it, of course."

"Of course," Fisher said, pouring another shot to stifle the urge to punch him.

"God, he was needy though," Paul sighed. He tilted his glass, examining the amber liquid. "Always wanting to be with me when he wasn't working. At first it was sweet, but it got to be a drag. Asking me where I was, who I was with."

"Stifling," Fisher offered. He wrapped his hands around his glass to hide how they were trembling.

"Exactly! See, you get it." Paul drained his glass in two quick swallows and signaled the bartender for another one. "And the sex wasn't that great. God, and his asshole cat. I hated that fucker. He *bit* me when I tried to pet him once, can you believe it? And F—my ex refused to get rid of him even though he was *clearly* dangerous."

Fisher made a sympathetic noise.

"But the worst part by far was the hockey. He lived, breathed, and shat hockey. That was all he could talk about. His team's playoff chances, his *precious* best friend who is, apparently, God's gift to hockey in general, whatever problems they were dealing with. It was so *boring*. And then *he* acted all hurt when I tried to tell him that—tactfully, of course!"

"Of course," Fisher agreed.

"All I said was maybe he should pick up a hobby. Something that had nothing to do with hockey. God, you'd have thought I asked him to change his entire personality!"

Because you basically did, Fisher thought, gritting his teeth. Aloud, he said, "Is that why you broke up?"

"No," Paul said. He had moved closer somehow and was looking up at Fisher through his lashes. "He needed a push. Something to break him out of his rut, make him realize there's more to life than hockey. His fans, the press, all of it—it was so invasive and we never had a moment of privacy. Everyone all up in his business all the time. I knew he'd be grateful once he was away from it, you know? So I told him he needed to choose. Me or hockey."

Fisher didn't have to feign the shock. "You gave him an ultimatum?"

"For his own good!" Paul said. He put a hand on Fisher's thigh, thumb rubbing against the inseam.

Fisher somehow managed not to jerk away. "So what happened?"

"Well, considering I'm coming onto you pretty hard right now, it's pretty easy to guess, don't you think?"

Fisher huffed a laugh. "Hey, I don't know, maybe you were recruiting me to go home with you where he was waiting so we could have a threesome."

Paul's pupils dilated and he licked his lips. "That sounds… very appealing. But not with him. He was a real stick, didn't even want the lights on during sex. Adding a third would have probably broken his brain."

Fisher managed to hide the laugh and leaned into him, letting his eyelids droop. "Sounds like you're better off. So what'd you do when he said no? Did you fight it, try to make him see it was for his own good?"

"Nah. I just walked away." A thin smile flickered across Paul's mouth. "But I did leave him a parting gift. Something to show him those 'fans' of his never really cared about him."

Fisher couldn't take it anymore. He nearly fell off the stool in his haste to pull away, leaving Paul blinking up at him in surprise.

"Something wrong?"

"You have no idea," Fisher said tightly. He was shaking with rage, with the need to hurt Paul the way he'd hurt Felix, and he knew he couldn't let the leash slip or he'd never stop. He took a step away. "Change of plans. I'm gonna walk away right now and you're gonna let me go, or I'm going to break your nose."

Paul shot to his feet. "I'm sorry, *what*? Who the fuck are you?"

"No one you know," Fisher spat. "Let's keep it that way." He turned, then spun back. "And just for the record, Felix was the best thing to *ever* happen to me, in every possible way, and that *includes* his hockey."

Paul's eyes went huge with shock, but Fisher was already walking away, jerking his head sharply at Leo, who scrambled to join him.

Fisher was so furious he couldn't talk. He blew through the restaurant doors and picked a direction at random. Behind him, Leo was already out of breath trying to keep up, but Fisher didn't slow. He wanted to scream, to punch something, to *punish* Paul for what he'd done, and the fact that he couldn't just made him angrier.

He lost track of how long he walked before the worst of the rage subsided and he was able to take a deep breath and slow down. Leo was nowhere to be seen. *Shit.* Fisher sent him a quick text.

Where are you?

Waiting for you, Leo responded. *Gave up a couple miles ago.*

Sorry, Fisher sent, and hailed a passing taxi.

They stopped to pick up Leo, who'd found a convenient brick wall to sit on, and Fisher asked the driver to take them to the airport.

"Ready to talk about it?" Leo asked.

Fisher rubbed his face. "He's definitely responsible for doxxing Felix."

Leo swore under his breath.

"Doesn't regret it, either. In his mind, it's Felix's fault for not giving him what he wanted. The doxxing was his way of showing Felix that his fame is a lie, that he can't trust his fans. Something like that, anyway. The details are fuzzy because I was trying to keep from murdering him."

"I applaud your self-restraint but also regret it," Leo said. "I think he'd definitely look better with a bloody nose at the very least."

Fisher slumped against the seat with a noisy sigh. "God, poor Felix. It's blindingly obvious Paul gaslit the fuck out of him. No wonder he didn't trust me." He rolled his head on the seatrest to look at Leo, who was watching him with amusement and sympathy in his green eyes. "Do you want to go to a hockey game with me?" Fisher asked abruptly.

Leo's mouth fell open. "You mean…."

"No." Fisher shook his head. "Too… much. Too soon. But there's an AHL league nearby, isn't there? We could go to one of their games."

"Okay," Leo said carefully. "But can I just ask… why?"

"Because," Fisher said, "I'm in love with a professional hockey player and if I want to have even the slightest chance of getting him back, I need to do some homework."

Leo flung his arms around Fisher's neck with a delighted squeal, and Fisher laughed, blinking hard and hugging him back.

"I *knew* you'd get your head out of your ass eventually!" Leo said, planting a smacking kiss on Fisher's cheek before sitting back and beaming at him. "We need to bring Wren with us. She can actually teach you about this shit."

"I'll call her as soon as we're home," Fisher said.

Leo took his hand. "I'm so proud of you," he said softly.

Fisher lifted a shoulder but didn't pull away. "I have no fucking idea what I'm doing," he admitted, voice low. "What if he doesn't—what if I drove him away for good and he wants nothing to do with me?"

"Absolutely no fucking way that's even possible," Leo said. "He loves you too, Fish, I *know* he does. And we're gonna help you get him back."

Fisher blew out a breath. "Okay. Okay. We're doing this."

29

———

"I NEED TO TALK TO YOU." Saint looked upset, and Felix shoved his helmet to the back of his head and reached for his water bottle.

"What happened? Is it Caz?"

Saint shook his head. "After practice. Don't go home until we've had a chance to talk."

"Okay, cherry." Felix watched him skate away, faintly puzzled. It had been a month since his life had blown up in his face, but he liked to think he was slowly putting the pieces back together. There were days when all he could do was hold his phone, staring at the black screen and aching to write down everything he was feeling so Fisher would *know*, but he never did it. He always put the phone away and went to pester Saint or Kasha or Vanya, anyone who could help distract him.

They had a homestand over the next four days, and Felix was looking forward to a little time off. Their bye week was coming up, and Carmine had been voted into the All Star Game, something he complained about but was clearly delighted by.

As if summoned, Carmine appeared, puck on his stick and a determined light in his eyes.

Felix dropped his helmet into place with a jerk of his head, and crouched, all other thoughts driven from his mind.

SAINT FOUND him after practice as Felix was coming out of the shower, toweling his hair dry. His jaw was set in the expression Felix had come to recognize as his 'giving bad news' face.

"You're starting to worry me, cherry," Felix said as he got dressed.

"Have you heard from Fisher?"

Felix froze. "Is he hurt? What happened?" He turned, fumbling for his shoes and nearly dropping them in his haste. He had to go, he had to—

"He's not hurt!" Saint said, grabbing his arm. "Fee, *stop*. Sit and listen to me for a minute."

Felix sank unwillingly onto his locker as Saint sat beside him.

"Don't be mad at me but I checked up on him," he said after a minute. "I wanted to make sure he was okay. He didn't come back after you two… talked, and I just—well. I'm nosy."

"No, you care," Felix said.

"He lost his job," Saint blurted.

Fuck.

"Because of me," Felix whispered. His lips were numb.

Saint shook his head. "No. *No*, Fee, it wasn't because of you."

"How do you know?"

"I talked to his assistant. Wren?"

"How did you get her number?"

Saint almost smiled. "Kasha. I asked him to give her my number and for her to contact me. She did, and we've been talking. Apparently there was a parent at the school who was harassing Fisher, trying to force him into something?"

Felix nodded. "I know. Fisher hadn't decided what to do about him, last we spoke."

"Wren said he showed up right after you left and Fisher snapped. Yelled at him, told him exactly what he thought of him. This dirtbag went straight to the dean and accused Fisher of sexually assaulting *him*. The dean gave him a choice of quitting and getting a good reference, or getting fired and fighting it."

"He chose to quit." Felix folded forward, elbows on his knees. *Fuck, Fisher.*

"How do you know that?" Saint asked, genuine curiosity in his voice. "Why don't you assume he'd try to fight it? He has a chance at a good case, with a decent lawyer."

Felix lifted his head. "Because it's *him*," he said, and sighed. "He won't want this dragged out in the open. The thought would horrify him. He'd rather quit and keep his dignity."

"You really do love him," Saint said quietly.

"I told you, not everyone is as lucky as you and Caz," Felix said, bumping shoulders with him gently. "I'm better for the time I spent with him, no matter how it ended. I just wish—"

"That you could fix it."
Felix nodded.
"I have an idea."

30

———

Fisher was jerked from sleep by his phone ringing. He pried one eye open to see the time—close to eight a.m. Being jobless was wreaking havoc with his schedule.

He fumbled for the phone, nearly dropping it, and got it to his ear. "Hello?"

"Am I speaking to Fisher Montgomery?" a brisk voice asked.

"Yes," Fisher said. "Who is this?"

"My name is Harper Curtis, and I am the dean of Primrose House. Have you heard of us, by any chance?"

Fisher rolled upright fast. "I—yes, of course I've heard of you. Everyone knows about Primrose House. What—how can I help you, ma'am?"

"We recently had an opening for one of our kindergarten classes, and I understand you parted ways with your previous employer not too long ago. I would like for you to apply."

Fisher opened and closed his mouth.

"Is that something you're interested in?" Harper asked.

"*Yes* ma'am," Fisher managed. "Yes, of course. I'm—thank you so much for thinking of me. If I may ask, how did you find me?"

Harper made an amused noise. "That's not something I'm able to divulge. I also want to caution you that I'm not offering you the job—merely the opportunity to apply for it. If you get the position, it will be because you're the best candidate for it and for no other reason. When can you come in for the initial interview?"

Fisher's head was spinning. What was even happening? How did the dean of *Primrose House* know who he was, let alone that he was currently looking for a new job?

He dragged his brain into gear. "Any day from Wednesday on is fine," he said.

"Excellent. Let's have you come in Thursday morning at eight. I'll send you an email with directions and instructions. I'm looking forward to meeting you, Fisher." With that, she disconnected, leaving Fisher gaping at nothing.

After a minute, he called Leo.

"How the fuck would I know how to contact the principal or headmaster or whoever of Pygmalion House?" Leo demanded.

"*Primrose*," Fisher said, a bubble of laughter swelling in his throat.

"My point stands. It wasn't me, Fish."

"Maybe it was Wren," Fisher mused. "Gotta go."

Wren answered on the second ring. "Hey Fisher!"

"Did you give my name to the dean of Primrose House?" Fisher asked.

"Did I *what*?"

Fisher slumped at the honest bafflement in her voice. "Well, if you didn't, then I would *dearly* love to know who did."

"Maybe—" Wren hesitated as if not wanting to say his name.

"It wasn't Felix," Fisher said immediately. "He doesn't have kids, he doesn't *want* kids, he has no reason to know Primrose House even exists."

"Are we still on for tomorrow?" Wren asked.

"Yeah, of course. The Embers are about to clinch a spot and I'm not about to miss it."

Wren giggled. "If Peyton could see you now, huh?"

"Shut it," Fisher said without heat. "Speaking of hockey, how's your boyfriend?"

"*Not* my boyfriend," Wren said immediately. "But he's good." Her voice softened on the words and Fisher swallowed his laugh.

"You haven't told him anything, right?"

"We don't talk about you, Fisher. Kasha's a sweetheart, but his first loyalty is to Saint. Anything I said would go to him, which means it would go to —" She hesitated. "So no. I haven't told him anything."

"How are the kids?" Fisher asked.

"They miss you," Wren said. "Trying to explain you're not coming back isn't going well. I wish—"

"I know. Me too. Have you seen anything of Calum?"

"Ugh. No, the nanny drops Max off now."

"Well, at least you don't have to deal with him

too. Tell the kids I said hi, and I'll see you tomorrow."

Who else could it have been? He didn't have time to ponder it. He needed to get his suit dry-cleaned, book a haircut, and run some errands he'd been putting off so he'd be ready for Thursday.

"So HAVE you figured out yet how you're going to do it?" Wren asked.

Fisher shook his head, mouth full of hotdog. The warmup music was so loud he had to lean in and shout once he'd swallowed. "It's not like I can manufacture a reason to run into him somewhere, especially after what Paul did. And it's not exactly the kind of conversation you have over text, you know?"

Leo leaned over Wren's other side. "Text him, ask him to meet," he suggested.

"So he can leave me on read?" Fisher snorted. "No thanks. There has to be a middle-ground between text and ambushing him. I just have to figure out what it is. *And* what to say that he'll actually believe."

"Tell him you've been learning about hockey," Wren said. "What's a hat trick?"

"Three goals in a game." Fisher rolled his eyes.

"Fine, what's a natural hat trick?"

"Three goals in a row," Fisher said promptly. "Saint got a natural hat trick his second year."

"And a Gordie Howe hat trick?"

"A fight, goal, and assist in the same game. Carmine got one of those this year."

Wren kept going, quizzing him on various terms

and positions. When Fisher didn't know the answer, he searched it up and then wrote it down, committing it to memory. He looked up after the third time to Wren watching him.

"What?"

"Nothing," Wren said. She looked suddenly guilty. "It's just—you're so serious about it. Like this is a test you don't want to fail."

"In a way it is," Fisher said. "I need Felix to know I'm committed."

"You know he wouldn't care if you never learned the first thing about hockey, as long as you supported *him*?" Leo asked.

"I know." Fisher squirmed in the too-small seat. His knees were almost up against the glass, but at least they could see everything. "But it's like—my way of apologizing, I guess."

"It's supposed to be *fun*," Wren said. "Not… penance, or whatever you're doing."

"It's not penance!" Fisher protested. "I'm taking it seriously because I take everything seriously. Ask Leo."

"Before he adopted Maya, he took an actual *course* on how to care for a dog," Leo said. "Like paid *money* for it. This is what he does."

Wren studied Fisher. "So you don't hate it?"

The players took the ice to a scattered chorus of cheers from the crowd that had gathered to watch the warmups, and the conversation stopped briefly so they could watch. Black, silver, and teal jerseys swirled on their end of the ice, the players lining up to take shots on the goalie, in his crease and ready.

Fisher watched everyone, cataloging what he saw, making mental notes of questions to ask Wren later or look up on his own. When they finally left the ice, he turned back to Wren.

"I don't hate it," he said. "I really don't. I expected to, not gonna lie. I thought it was all senseless violence. Bloody knuckles and missing teeth, you know? But you were right. It's so much more than that. It's… beautiful, in a weird, physical way. And I *get* it. The more I watch the goalies, the more I see why Felix loves it, why he won't give it up. Only a monster would ask him to walk away from this."

Wren smiled up at him. "I think you're ready."

"You're definitely ready," Leo added.

"Great," Fisher said, slumping in his seat. "Now I just have to figure out how to make him believe me. And also apologize for being such an asshole."

Wren patted his arm. "Something tells me you're not gonna have to try very hard."

"I've got it!" Leo said. "We go to a Birds game, right? And we get there for warmups, and you, Fisher, you bring a sign for Felix. Something that says 'PLEASE TAKE ME BACK' or something suitably romantic and sappy. Put it up against the glass and wait for him to see it. It's foolproof!"

"That's ridiculous and we're not doing that," Fisher said flatly.

"It's perfect and we *are*," Leo argued.

The lights were dimming and the smoke machine was ramping up, so Fisher just gave him a glare before he settled in to watch the game and did his best to put the dilemma away at least temporarily.

31

———

One week later

"Tell me again what you're gonna say," Leo ordered.

Fisher gripped the wheel. Traffic was heavy but at least it was moving. A flashy sports car swerved in front of them and Fisher stomped on the brakes, swearing.

"*Assholes.*"

"Fish," Leo prompted.

"Right. So I'm gonna start with apologizing, obviously."

"Obviously." Leo propped his feet on the dashboard. "Go on."

"Put your feet down," Fisher said. "Do you *know* what would happen if we were in a wreck and your legs were like that?"

Leo rolled his eyes but obeyed. "So, apology. What exactly are you gonna say?"

"Not a hundred percent sure," Fisher admitted,

changing lanes as the cars in front of him slowed to a crawl. "Figured I'd let the moment guide me."

"Boring, but you do you, I guess."

"Can you not critique my groveling technique?" Fisher snapped. He braked hard again as a truck roared by on the shoulder, music blaring. "Mother*fucking* idiots, where's a cop when you need one? I'm just going to tell him this whole thing is my fault, and ask him to forgive me. Is that good enough for you or would like to write me a script?"

"Would you use it?" Leo shot back.

"Nope," Fisher said, slanting a grin at him. "Fuck this, I'm taking 213. Maybe it'll be at least a little more bearable."

"Traffic lights," Leo observed.

"Can't be worse than this," Fisher snapped. He took the exit for the highway that connected with 82nd Ave, watching in his mirror to make sure his lane was clear.

"*Fisher*!" Leo's voice was high with terror, and Fisher looked up just in time to see the massive semi barreling straight for them. The collision was screaming metal and shattering glass, crushing force hurling them both hard into the unforgiving embrace of their seatbelts, and then Fisher's temple connected with the window and the world went black.

32

———

FELIX HADN'T HIT a hot streak like this in a long time. It was like he knew, deep in his core, what the opposing team was going to do, three moves before they did it. Every shot they made, he was there to block, snatching the puck out of the air or blockering it away, scrambling back to get set up again as everyone went after it.

He wouldn't even let himself *think* the word, but he knew it was coming. He could feel it. Nothing was going to stop him. He left the ice after the second period, fierce delight fizzing in his blood, and made his way to the locker room with the team. No one spoke to him. They knew his routine by now. But there were taps against his pads, the occasional fist held out for a bump as the players listened to Flanahan talking strategy.

Felix listened with half an ear, drinking water and running his own plays in his head. A phone rang somewhere and he blinked, looking up. The other players seemed equally baffled.

"Whose is that?" Flanahan snapped.

Saint cleared his throat. "I think it's Felix's."

The phone stopped ringing and then started again.

"Why would it be mine?" Felix asked. "I'm not expecting a call. Unless—*Maman*—" He shot to his feet and scrabbled in his coat pocket, hanging from a hook in his locker. It wasn't his mother, he realized, but the rush of relief was mingled with a spike of adrenaline when he saw Fisher's name flashing on the screen. "What—"

"*Answer* it," Saint said.

Still Felix hesitated, frozen in place, staring at the screen. This wasn't happening. *Couldn't* be happening. He'd made his peace with never seeing Fisher again, he couldn't handle—whatever this was.

Saint made an annoyed noise and snatched the phone out of his hand. "Hello?"

Felix watched him, unable to look away. The rest of the team seemed equally spellbound, waiting breathlessly.

"*What?*" Saint said, and Felix jerked, fear running down his spine in an icy rivulet. "How bad?" *Oh god.* "Text him the address," Saint snapped, and hung up.

"What is it?" Felix demanded. "Saint—"

"Fisher's been in an accident." The words hung in the air, hard and uncompromising, and dread turned Felix's bones to dust. "That was Leo. He said —it's... not good."

"I have to go," Felix said, and suddenly he could move again. He dragged his jersey off, dropping it to yank at the buckles of his chest protector. He couldn't seem to make his fingers work right, and he swore, filthy and vicious as he fought the clasps.

Then Saint was there, unbuckling the straps, helping Felix peel it off and drop it to the side. Felix was frantic, breath coming in sharp, short pants, as Saint dropped to his knees to start working on his leg pads.

"Coach," Felix said, looking up suddenly. "I have to—"

"Of course you do," Flanahan said. He didn't look happy, but he didn't seem angry, either. "Vanya, start warming up. You're in."

Between them, Saint and Felix had him out of his gear in record time. Felix grabbed a pair of sweats and dragged them on over his UnderArmour, hands shaking with his haste, and shoved his feet into shoes. Saint held out his phone.

"Leo texted you the address," he said. "Go."

Felix just nodded, grabbed the phone, and ran for the door. In his car, he put the address in the text into the navigator and peeled out, tires making an ungodly screech as he roared from the parking garage.

Please let him be okay, he thought as he wove between cars, heedless of traffic laws. *Please, Fisher, don't you dare—* He couldn't even finish the thought, gripping the wheel until his hands ached.

Somehow he made it without being pulled over. The flashing red and blue lights told him he was there before he rounded the corner and hit the brakes so hard he left a trail of rubber on the asphalt.

Fisher's beaten up SUV was on its side, the hood crumpled in a ragged semicircle like something massive had tried to take a bite out of it. Nausea rose in Felix's throat and he scrambled out of his car, running for the wreckage.

A fireman caught him before he got there. "Sir, *sir*, you can't go over there!" The hands were rough, the voice uncompromising, and Felix twisted in his grasp.

"Please, I have to—*Fisher!*" His legs threatened to give out. Was Fisher still in the car? Was that blood on the pavement? His heart was hammering so hard he couldn't breathe. "I'm his—please, I need to know he's okay. *Please—*"

The fireman's grip loosened but he didn't let go. "Are you family?"

"I'm—" Felix swallowed tears, clutching the man's reflective vest. "I'm not—is he alive?"

"*Felix?*" Fisher sounded shocked, worried, but *alive alive alive* and Felix's knees nearly buckled.

He tore away from the fireman and bolted for Fisher, coming from the direction of the ambulance. There was blood and soot on his face, streaking his beard, and Felix swallowed a sob, pulling up short.

"You're hurt," he said, hands out, terrified to touch.

Fisher felt at his head, wincing. "I'm fine. Cuts and bruises. Felix, why are you here?"

Felix took a step forward, hands still out. One more step, Fisher looking startled but holding his ground, and Felix was able to press his fingertips to the dark cotton shirt Fisher was wearing, over his heart.

"You're alive," he whispered, and blinked hard. "Okay. That's good. That's so good." Fisher was distorted in his vision when he looked up, blurry through the tears, and Felix came back to himself with a jolt. "I'm sorry," he said, stepping back. His voice sounded oddly formal to his own ears. "I should not have—I just needed to know—"

Fisher caught his wrist and Felix went very still. Fisher's fingers were warm and strong, thumb sweeping soft over Felix's jackrabbiting pulse point.

"I'm fine," Fisher said, voice low. "Did you think I wasn't?"

Felix swallowed hard. "I—Leo called. Said you were in an accident." He looked up suddenly. "Is *he* okay?"

"He's fine." Fisher's eyes were so intense, Felix thought he might be drowning in them. "Felix—"

"I'm so sorry I didn't tell you," Felix blurted, and Fisher's face went slack with shock. Felix forged on. "I lied to you and it was wrong, I'm sorry Fisher, I'm so sorry, I know you can't forgive me but I was just so afraid of losing you—"

Fisher took one quick step forward and cupped Felix's face in both hands. "I love you," he said, eyes so dark Felix was drowning in them. "I love you and I never should have reacted like that. *I'm* sorry, Felix. You did *nothing* wrong, do you hear me?"

Felix swallowed a sob and reached for him but Fisher was already there, closing the distance so their mouths could meet. Fisher tasted like blood, bitter copper in Felix's mouth, but his breath was warm and his lips were soft, and Felix closed his eyes and held on tight, standing in the bitterly cold night and feeling nothing but Fisher around him.

It was several minutes before they broke for air, and even then they clung to each other, unwilling to move even a few inches apart.

"*Je t'aime, mon pécheur,*" Felix whispered, and Fisher's smile spread wide and sweet over his face.

"You'll have to translate that," he said, but his twitching lips gave his words the lie.

"Or you'll have to learn French," Felix countered, and pulled him in for another kiss.

33

───────

It took a while to sort everything out. Fisher and Leo had been on their way out for the evening when a semi had lost control and barreled into them, crumpling Fisher's SUV like it was tinfoil. But the restraint system had saved their lives and they'd been able to climb out the shattered window, shaken up and with cuts and bruises, but nothing worse.

"You told him I was *dying*?" Fisher demanded of Leo, who had a scrape on his forehead and his arm in a sling for a wrenched elbow.

"In my defense, I wasn't exactly at my most logical," Leo said. He pushed his lower lip out, scowling. "I'm injured, don't yell at me."

"Christ, Leo, you scared the *shit* out of him," Fisher said. He turned to Felix, who was shivering in his thin undershirt, and seemed to realize what he was wearing for the first time. "What—Felix, where were you when Leo called?" He took his jacket off and wrapped it around Felix's shoulders.

Felix tugged it closer, taking a deep breath of Fisher's warm cologne. "It's not important."

Fisher narrowed his eyes. "Felix."

"At a game," Felix said reluctantly.

Fisher's mouth fell open. "You left a *game*? A game I assume you were *playing* in? Because you were worried about me?"

"Of course," Felix said.

"But we weren't—aren't—I *yelled* at you the last time we spoke, and you still left in the middle of a game to make sure I was okay?"

"Yes...," Felix said slowly. He couldn't decipher Fisher's expression. "Are you... angry? I know you told me to never come near you again, I'm sorry, I was just so worried—"

"*Felix*—" Fisher cut himself off and reached for him, hauling him into a crushing hug. He buried his face in the crook of Felix's neck, his breath ragged, and Felix held him, giving Leo a questioning look over Fisher's shoulder.

Leo shrugged. "Can we go home, maybe? I can't afford a hospital."

"I can," Felix said, still holding Fisher. "Do you need one?"

"Nope." Leo smiled at him. "But I do want to get out of the cold."

Fisher raised his head and wiped his face.

"Are you crying?" Felix demanded, suddenly alarmed.

Fisher hiccupped a wet laugh. "Felix, this whole time I've been afraid we wouldn't work because you're too dedicated to your job to care about me. And you—" He shook his head, words failing him.

A paramedic approached, holding a clipboard.

"If you're refusing transport, I need you to sign this," she said. "The tow will be here soon to get your vehicle. Do you have a ride home?"

"Yes," Felix said instantly.

"One of the officers will wait for the tow truck," the paramedic said when Fisher handed the forms back. "You're free to go."

Felix bundled them into his Porsche immediately, Leo making awed noises over the leather seats.

"Don't get blood on 'em," Fisher said to him.

"I don't care if you do," Felix responded, turning the car on. "Back to your place? Leo, where do you live?"

Leo made a face as Felix glanced in the mirror. "I'd rather not deal with my stupid roommates. Fish, can I crash—poor choice of words, sorry—at your place tonight?"

"Of course," Fisher said. He reached across the console and put a hand on Felix's thigh. There were dark circles under his eyes, but his smile was genuine when Felix laced their fingers together and looked at him. "Hey," he said softly. "I really missed you."

Felix squeezed his hand, watching the road. "I missed you too, *pêcheur*."

They didn't speak for the rest of the drive, Felix too relieved and wrung out to think of anything to say, and neither Leo nor Fisher seemed inclined to break the silence either.

When he parked at the curb, Leo was the first out of the car, saying something over his shoulder about the bathroom before slamming the door.

Fisher sat with Felix a minute, watching him in the amber glow of the streetlight.

"I've been trying to think of how to apologize to you for a month now," he said.

Felix blinked. "You—but it wasn't your fault."

"Don't even start," Fisher said. He stroked Felix's knuckles. "We both know it was my pigheadedness that got us into this."

"No," Felix protested. "I *said* I didn't want a relationship, I let it go on too long without talking to you even when I realized I wanted more. I was afraid to admit it to you. It was stupid."

Fisher smiled at him, sweet and a little sad. "You were only afraid to say anything because I had such a stupid fucking hangup about hockey. And then I got mad when I found out, like it was your fault somehow?" He shook his head. "I've been a complete idiot. It doesn't *matter* what you do, baby. And I've been trying to figure out how to tell you that for a while now."

"You're—okay with the hockey?" Felix whispered, a lump in his throat.

"It's part of you, and I'm all in," Fisher said. "I'm done being an idiot." He paused. "Well, about this, anyway." His teeth flashed with his grin, but then he sobered. "I've watched all your games."

It was not unlike being hit in the head by a two by four.

"You what?"

"Well, all I could find," Fisher amended. "I wasn't ready to pay for tickets until I'd apologized to you properly, but I've watched all your interviews and games, the specials—did Saint really wear a giant teddy bear costume?"

Felix couldn't stop his snort of laughter. "He did.

We chirped him for *months* on that. *All* my interviews? There are… a lot."

"Well, I didn't have the real thing, I had to make do somehow." Fisher sobered. "Will you—come inside with me? Just for a little bit? Or do you have to go back? It's okay if you do, I should have asked—"

"I don't," Felix said. "But I have a better idea. Come home with me."

Fisher's eyes went wide. "Really?"

"Is Leo safe to be left on his own?"

That made Fisher laugh. "He's not a toddler."

"No," Felix protested, laughing with him. "I mean with his injuries!"

Inexplicably, this made Fisher's eyes soften. "You know that was one of the first things that drew me to you?"

"What?"

"How *kind* you are." Fisher brought Felix's hand to his mouth and kissed along his knuckles, lips slow and lingering. "That first night—remember it?"

Felix coughed a laugh. "Difficult to forget."

"You put a pillow under Leo's head after—when we were done."

"I did?"

Fisher's mouth curved against Felix's skin. "And you asked how he was the next day. You thought to ask about him tonight even though you were clearly out of your head with worry about me. You're so kind, love."

The word made Felix shiver. It still didn't feel quite *real.*

"But back to your question, I'm sure he'll be fine. In fact, he can walk Maya for me. I'll just go get a change of clothes. As long as I can use your shower?"

Felix laughed at him, twisting his wrist to reach up and flick the tip of Fisher's nose. "Of course. You go in, I'll tell Saint everything's okay."

Once Fisher was out of the car, Felix pulled out his phone. He hadn't bothered calling before, because Saint and the rest of the team had still had a hockey game to play and media obligations after, win or lose. He was probably still talking to the press, but at least Felix could leave him a message.

Saint answered on the first ring. "Fee?"

"How are you already free?" Felix asked.

"Caz took the interviews, I was able to duck out early. Are you okay? Where are you? Which hospital? How's Fisher?"

"Fisher's fine. No hospital. Bumps and scrapes, that's all."

"But Leo—"

Felix leaned his head against the seatrest and closed his eyes. "I don't know if he deliberately overexaggerated the severity of his injuries or if he was truly so shaken up that he thought it was that bad. But they're both fine. Just sore."

"Thank God," Saint said. "And you?"

"I—Saint, he loves me still." Tears inexplicably stung Felix's eyes and he took a shaky breath.

"Of course he does," Saint said instantly. "Does that mean—"

"*Oui*," Felix husked. "He—I told him. A-apologized. He said… it was not my fault, that he never should have reacted as he did."

"Goddamn *right*," Saint said. "Sorry, Fee, I didn't say it before because it wasn't what you needed to hear, but he acted like a fucking *idiot* and I wanted to kick his ass."

Felix's laugh was waterlogged. "No need. Not anymore. He's—I'm taking him to my place tonight."

Saint caught his breath. "Are you—no. Okay, Fee. I'll see you… tomorrow? Will you be at practice?"

"Yes," Felix said. Fisher was coming out of the house, Leo backlit in the doorway as Fisher made his way down the steps, a backpack over one shoulder. "I have to go—wait. Did we win?"

"Vanya got you your shutout," Saint said, laughing quietly.

"Good for him. Okay, I'll see you tomorrow."

"*Je t'aime*," Saint said.

"*Je t'aime aussi*," Felix said, and hung up as Fisher opened the car door, giving him a quizzical smile.

"Is he sufficiently reassured? How badly does he want to kick my ass?"

Felix started the car and Fisher slid inside, tossing the backpack on the seat behind him before leaning over to kiss Felix's cheek.

"How did you know he wanted to do that?" Felix asked.

Fisher snorted a laugh. "Pretty obvious, really. And well-deserved."

"No." Felix took his hand as he pulled away from the curb. "You had your reasons."

"My reasons were stupid, let's talk about something else. How have you been? The team's close to clinching, isn't it?"

Felix shot him a startled look. "How did you know that?"

"I'm all in," Fisher repeated. "I haven't gone to your games yet but I told you I've watched them all. You're incredible, by the way. You're so *fast*, I don't know how you do it. And the flexibility makes a lot more sense now."

Overwhelmed, Felix pulled to the side of the road and stopped.

"Felix? What's wrong?"

"I just—" Felix managed, and reached for him.

Fisher met him halfway and Felix hiccuped against his mouth, fighting the tears.

"Don't cry, baby," Fisher whispered, kissing along his jaw. "It's okay now. Will you take me home? I need to hold you properly."

THE DRIVE DIDN'T SEEM to take long at all, Felix sneaking looks at Fisher every few minutes to reassure himself he was really there and finding Fisher looking back at him every time.

He led the way to his front door, Fisher close on his heels.

"This is nice," Fisher said as Felix turned on the lights. "It's… cozy."

Felix rubbed his arm, suddenly diffident. "My first house was too much. In every way. When I ended up having to move, I looked for something that fit me better. It means I can't host the holiday dinner, but otherwise it's perfect."

"We need to talk," Fisher said.

A jolt of fear rooted Felix's feet to the floor. "Already?" he said, trying for a joking tone, and

Fisher's eyebrows went up. He took two quick steps and kissed him, hard and deep.

"Not like that," he said when he lifted his head. "But I think we need to… clear the air."

"Ah. Yes. I suppose you're right. Do you think it can wait until we've showered? I came from the game, and you're covered in blood. I would like to be clean for this talk."

"Lead the way," Fisher said, stepping back.

He whistled approval at the bathroom with its gleaming marble floor and huge glassed-in shower as Felix pulled towels from the cupboard and set them on the counter. He looked up to see Fisher looking at him in the mirror, and turned.

"You first," he said.

"Not together?"

Felix almost laughed. "I think if we both get in there, we won't talk. And as much as I want to—you know—"

Fisher's eyes crinkled with his smile.

"I think you're right, we do need to talk first."

"Being all responsible and mature," Fisher grumbled, but his eyes were soft, and he kissed him, quick and gentle. Then he pulled his shirt off over his head and Felix's mouth went dry. It had been too long since he'd seen Fisher naked, and judging from the smile playing on Fisher's face as he stepped out of his pants, muscles bunching and sliding under smooth skin, he knew exactly the effect he was having.

"I'll, uh—go get a change of clothes," Felix said, and escaped.

Henry was asleep on Felix's bed, and he rolled over and stretched with a rusty meow when Felix stepped inside.

"'Allo, *bâtard*," Felix said. "You'll be nice to Fisher, yes? No biting this one."

Henry yawned and blinked sleepy crystal blue eyes. Felix bent and dropped a kiss on his head and went to find clothes.

When he got back to the bathroom, the door was open and Fisher was already tugging soft pants up over his hips, his chest still bare and hair curling damp against the base of his skull.

"How are you feeling?" Felix asked.

"Sore," Fisher admitted. He raised an arm and twisted to inspect his ribcage in the mirror, grimacing at the bruise blooming under his skin. "Seatbelt did a number on me."

"It means you're alive," Felix said. "I'll take it." He hesitated but Fisher didn't seem to be going anywhere, pulling a shirt over his head and then leaning against the sink. "You can wait in the living room," Felix suggested. "You'd be more comfortable."

Fisher's lips twitched. "I'm comfortable right here."

Felix sighed and skinned out of his shirt before pushing the sweats down and off. When he straightened, Fisher was watching him, arms crossed over his chest and eyes hot. Felix swallowed hard and turned to flip the shower on.

Definitely the fastest shower he'd ever taken, he decided when he was done rinsing his hair and shut the water off.

Fisher hadn't moved when Felix stepped out, and he said nothing as Felix got dressed. Only then did he reach out one long arm to catch Felix's wrist, gently hauling him in.

"Hey," he said as Felix stepped close. "How are you doing, sweetheart?"

"Better," Felix said. He couldn't help pressing his face to Fisher's throat, taking a deep breath of his warm skin before raising his head. "Do you want something to drink? I should have offered, before—"

"No," Fisher said immediately. "Let's talk."

Felix took him through into the living room and they settled on the couch, Felix cross-legged on the cushions so he could see Fisher's face.

He found himself at a loss once they were situated, though. Where to even begin?

"Tell me about Paul," Fisher said, and Felix stiffened. Of course he wanted to know about—him.

"You figured it out, I guess," he said, drawing his knees to his chest, and Fisher put a hand on his calf, solid and comforting.

"That he was the one who doxxed you?" Fisher's mouth twisted. "Yeah. But I have a feeling he did a lot more than that."

"It took me a long time to… see it," Felix whispered. "He was so charming. When he was with me, it was like no one else existed. It was a heady thing, yes? I was drunk on it, it was all I could think about. He was funny, he was smart, he was—he seemed kind. He knew how to make me want him. He gave me attention, got me wanting more, and then he'd back away. Hot and cold. I wanted him to want *me* as much as I wanted him. I—" He swallowed. "I despaired, thought he didn't love me, that I wasn't good enough, or smart enough, or educated—I didn't go to college. He'd tease me about that, how I didn't have an education, hold it over me—but subtly. He never said it outright, so if I got offended, well… I was the one overreacting, being unreasonable."

Fisher's mouth was pinched in a flat line, eyes hard and cold.

"I should have seen it sooner," Felix said, looking away.

"No." Fisher sounded angry, but not at him. "No, none of this is your fault. You were too deep in it to realize. You loved him, didn't you?"

Felix put his head on his knee and nodded silently. He held out a hand without looking, and Fisher took it, squeezing.

"He wanted me to quit hockey," Felix continued after a minute, eyes closed. "I loved him, I wanted him to be happy. I… thought about it. I am ashamed of that, now."

"You shouldn't be."

Felix lifted a shoulder. "But I told him no. That I loved the game too much to quit, that I have several good years left, the fans counted on me, my team needed me. I couldn't just walk away, even if I hadn't signed a contract."

Fisher squeezed his hand again. "Good for you."

"He was angry," Felix said, looking up. "So angry. He said I was being stupid, that the fans didn't truly love me. That they'd drop me when I hit a slump, demand I be traded, turn on me and tear me to shreds when I couldn't perform well enough. I told him it didn't matter, that it was part of the price, and one I was willing to pay." He stopped, remembering Paul's handsome face twisted in fury, how his stomach had been so tied in knots from the confrontation that he'd vomited after Paul had stormed out.

"So he was trying to teach you a lesson?" Fisher asked softly.

"I suppose." Felix sighed. "He wanted to hurt me as much as possible. It worked."

"But you never told anyone it was him?"

"What good would it have done?" Felix countered. "He knew my passwords, he used my own phone while I was asleep. There was no proof of anyone 'hacking' me. It was my word against his, and I saw no point in accusing him. I just wanted it all to go away. And eventually, he did."

"I met him," Fisher said abruptly, and Felix reared backward in shock.

"You *what?*"

Fisher met his eyes, but guilt lurked in them. "I wanted—I'd read about what happened. All the speculation and rumor that it was Paul, but you refused to confirm it. You said *good* things about him. It didn't make sense to me. I understand if you're angry, if I crossed a line. I probably did. But I needed to know if it was him, and if it was, how he could do such a horrible thing to you."

Felix wrapped both arms around his knees, a shiver wracking him. "I'm not angry," he managed after a minute. "What—what did you say?"

"Well, I didn't give him my name," Fisher said. He didn't try to touch him, tracing the embroidery on the cushion in his lap with one long finger. "I—" He grimaced. "I had to flirt with him. Made me feel filthy."

"Bet he liked you," Felix murmured. "Tall, dark and handsome? You're just his type. He always said I was too thin, that he liked more muscle."

"God, I *really* should have punched him," Fisher

said. He rubbed his face and blew out a breath. "There's no point in going into specifics, in any case. But he all but admitted to having done it, doxxing you."

Felix nodded, unsurprised. "He'd told me, the night before. That I would regret my decision, that he would show me how wrong I was. I didn't know what he meant, not then."

"I'm so sorry," Fisher said. He held out a hand, his eyes unsure, and Felix took it immediately. "The more I learn, the more obvious it is to me just how much he fucked with your head. And then I went and yelled at you, drove you away. Had the fucking nerve—or stupidity, whichever you prefer—to blame you for not telling me, as if I'd ever done anything to earn your trust that way."

Felix squeezed his hand. "Tell me about *your* ex."

Fisher huffed an almost-laugh and rubbed his face with his free hand. "You sure you want to hear about that?"

"I want to know what made you *you*," Felix said steadily. "Will you tell me?"

"It doesn't look good for me," Fisher replied, dropping his hand.

"Was there cheating?" Fisher asked. "Abuse? Did you hit him or manipulate him?"

"No!" Fisher looked genuinely horrified, and Felix's chest eased. "No, nothing like that. He didn't do that to me either. We just...." He sighed. "Weren't good for each other."

"How?"

Fisher's lips twitched. "You're really gonna just drag the whole story out of me, huh?"

"What's good for the goose, as my *maman* would

say," Felix said, smiling back at him. "I want to know… what made you the way you are."

"He wanted to go pro." Fisher's eyes went distant as he remembered. "It was all he thought about. Everything he did was geared to that. Diet, working out, practices. He loved the sport like no one I'd ever met. And at first, I thought that was sexy. He looked *good* dripping with sweat, in just his pads and shorts. He was hot and he knew it, and for a long time it was just a part of who made him who he was."

"What changed?"

Fisher sighed. "There wasn't a single defining moment. Just a few things that built to a lot of things until I resented his game as much as I loved *him*."

"Things like what?"

"Like a math tournament that was important to me, but he had practice. Not a game, I wouldn't have asked him to skip a game, but I thought— surely he'd be willing to skip one practice to support me. But he wasn't. It was stuff like that, things he did that showed me that there was hockey, and there was me. But I would never matter as much to him as hockey." He hesitated. "This is the part that looks— not good." He glanced at Felix, who raised an eyebrow, waiting, and Fisher sighed as if giving into the inevitable. "I broke up with him. But the way I did it—I made it obvious it was because of hockey. That if he… backed off it, maybe, then we could stay together. I didn't *quite* give him an ultimatum, but I'm still not proud of how I did it."

"You wanted to matter as much," Felix said, and Fisher's head snapped up.

"Yes, exactly! I just wanted to know he cared

about *me* as much as he cared about the game, and he didn't. So I blamed hockey. If it didn't exist, I'd have had Peyton. I told myself that until I believed it, but I know now that if it hadn't been hockey, it would have been something else. Football or soccer. Doesn't matter. I was never going to be able to compete."

"I see why you hated it," Felix whispered. "Do you—" The question stuck in his throat. "Do you still?"

"*No*," Fisher said, cupping Felix's face briefly. "No, I don't. And yeah, at first I was only learning about it because I wanted to support you, but the more I watched, the more interesting it got. The interpersonal dynamics, the speed of it, how everyone knows where they need to be—and the *goalies*." He shook his head, awe clear in his eyes, and Felix couldn't help the smile.

"You like the goalies, then?"

"One in particular," Fisher teased, and took a quick kiss from him. "But yes, goalies in general are definitely my favorite."

"Aren't you worried, though?" Felix said, unable to help himself. "It's my *job*. I have a duty to perform, to play as well as I can. Why would you not assume I'm just like your ex?"

"You left a game for me," Fisher said simply. "Peyton would never have done that. It never would have *occurred* to him. And even before you did that, I just—" He lifted a shoulder. "I knew. Once I had time to think about it, once I got over myself. Of course you weren't like that. You *care*. You've cared from the beginning, haven't you?"

"Just about," Felix admitted. "But I travel so much. I'm so busy. You're okay with… that?"

"I knew you traveled before," Fisher pointed out. "You've always made time for me. I think you still will, won't you?"

Felix nodded, swallowing around the lump in his throat. "Always, *mon pêcheur.*"

"Can I take you to bed now?" Fisher asked.

Felix tilted his head, smiling at him. "I would like that very much."

"Oh thank God," Fisher said, and lunged.

He bowled a laughing Felix over, bearing him to the cushions in a flurry of arms and legs. Felix let him, wriggling beneath him until he could open his thighs and wrap his legs around Fisher's hips to pull him closer.

Fisher bent his head to kiss him, making a soft noise as their lips met. "Missed you so much," he murmured, kissing his way along Felix's jaw. "God, do you even know what you do to me?"

Felix shivered. Fisher's mouth felt like reverence pressed into his skin, worship and prayer as he nipped at Felix's earlobe and then set his mouth on his throat just below his ear and sucked hard. Felix twisted, hands coming up to grip Fisher's shoulders. He could feel his pulse hammering under Fisher's lips, heartbeat thundering in his ears as adrenaline careened through him.

"Bed," he managed to gasp, but Fisher didn't move, still pinning him to the couch and apparently doing his best to suck a permanent mark into Felix's throat.

Felix got a hand up and into Fisher's hair, the strands silky soft and curling around his fingers.

When he pulled, Fisher moaned but didn't lift his head.

"My love," Felix managed, and Fisher jerked like he'd been hit. He lifted his head, pupils blown.

"Say that again."

Felix twined his arms around Fisher's neck and tugged him down until he could brush their noses together. "You already know I love you," he said.

"Yeah, but hearing it—" Fisher dropped a kiss on the tip of his nose. "Please?"

"My love," Felix said, giving in. "I love you like air, like water. Like the things I don't notice but that I need to survive. I *need* you, with your Halloween and Christmas decorations and the glitter in your hair and the way you love *me*, so fierce and strong and steady. I love the way you touch me like a prayer you never thought would be answered, the way you tease me, how you make me laugh. You *see* me, you know me. The real me." He'd slipped into French somewhere in there, but Fisher was just staring at him, wonder in his eyes.

Felix cleared his throat, suddenly self-conscious. "Sorry. I got carried away."

"I'm in love with a poet," Fisher said, and kissed him again. Then he rolled off the couch, pulling Felix with him. "We need a real bed, because I'm going to make love to you until you forget all those pretty words of yours."

"All of them?" Felix teased, pointing in the direction of the bedroom and letting Fisher tow him that way. "I know a lot of words, *amor*, in several languages. You think you're up to it?"

Fisher got him through the door, pulling on Felix's shirt until he lifted his arms and let him drag it up and over his head. "How many languages do you speak?" he asked, almost absent as he spanned Felix's ribcage with his huge hands.

Felix tried to remember how to talk. It wouldn't do to let Fisher win *just* yet. "French, English. Some Russian, enough to get by. A little German, but only a very little. *Ich bin der Torwart der Seabirds*. And a few words in Swedish, I guess."

"Got my work cut out for me," Fisher mused, and pushed him toward the bed. He stopped abruptly when he caught sight of Henry, who still hadn't even bothered moving.

"Fisher, this is Henry," Felix said, leaning back into his frame. "I can't promise he won't bite you. He's a little bit of a bastard."

Fisher held out a hand for Henry to inspect. Henry sniffed him, yawned, then rubbed a cheek against Fisher's fingers.

"Oh," Felix breathed.

"Is that good?" Fisher asked, voice rumbling in his chest. "I don't really know cats."

"That's good," Felix said. He scooped Henry off the bed in a swift motion and dumped him outside the bedroom, shutting the door before turning back to grin at Fisher. "I don't think he needs to see this."

Fisher skinned out of his shirt and Felix went to him, catching his wrist before Fisher could take his pants off.

"Let me?"

Fisher swallowed and dropped his hands. Felix took a minute to appreciate the sight, the soft curling hair on his chest that thickened on his abdomen to disappear below the waistband of the pants. Fisher twitched but managed to hold still as

Felix hooked his thumbs in the elastic and tugged the pants down and off.

"Beautiful as ever," he murmured.

Fisher's cock was thickening, liquid pearling at the tip, and Felix couldn't resist wrapping a hand around him and stroking.

"Fu-*uck*," Fisher managed, hips jolting.

Felix hummed and let go, smiling as Fisher protested wordlessly. He stepped back and pushed his own pants down, and Fisher's forehead creased.

"What?"

"Have you lost weight?" Fisher asked. He traced a path along Felix's abs, frowning.

"A few pounds," Felix said, shivering. "That time of the year."

"It's January," Fisher said. "What do you mean?"

"Pushing for playoffs," Felix explained, and comprehension dawned in Fisher's eyes. "It'll get worse if we *do* make the playoffs, which I think we will. The trainers have a hard time keeping weight on me."

"Jesus, baby," Fisher murmured, and pushed him onto the bed, crawling on after him to settle between his thighs. "Guess I'll just have to up my cooking game, huh? Make sure you're getting enough calories." He ground down and Felix arched against him with a gasp. The sudden pressure was overwhelming, sparks skittering along his nerves as his body woke up to the memory of Fisher's touch.

"Lube," he managed, flopping a hand in the direction of his bedside table.

Fisher laughed as he leaned across him to rummage in the table, coming up with the lube and

—Felix could *feel* the fiery blush as Fisher held up his dildo, eyebrows arching.

"That—um. Forgot about that."

Fisher's lips twitched. "Replaced me already, huh?"

"Don't flatter yourself," Felix retorted, snatching the dildo away. "You *wish* you could make me come like this can."

"That sounds like another challenge," Fisher said. Mischief danced in his dark eyes. "Maybe I should make you come *with* that."

The mental image made Felix's mouth go dry. On his knees, Fisher behind him, working the rubber dildo inside him slowly, Felix helpless to do anything but take it.

"Oh, you like that idea," Fisher said. "I think we're going to have to do that at some point. Right now, though, I really want to get my dick inside you."

Felix choked on his laugh. "They say romance is dead," he teased, and Fisher grinned at him, settling on his knees between Felix's thighs.

He stroked a hand over the muscle, squeezing and kneading, and Felix spread his legs more, a wordless invitation.

"Condoms," Fisher said suddenly. "*Fuck*, I don't —do you have any?"

Felix shook his head. "There's been no one but you since we met," he said, suddenly shy with the confession, but Fisher's eyes softened.

"Me too, you know that, right?"

"I… hoped," Felix admitted. "But I didn't know how to ask."

"It's easy," Fisher said, that teasing light back in

his eyes. "You just say, 'Fisher, I'm in love with you and I want to be monogamous.' See? Easy."

Felix thumped his shoulder, making Fisher laugh. "Easy when you know the answer, maybe," he retorted. "Not so much when it could have driven you away permanently."

Fisher's smile slid off his face. "I'm sorry. I've been so stupid. If we'd just *talked*—"

"Enough," Felix ordered. "No more blame. Make love to me, Fisher."

"I can do that," Fisher said. He nudged Felix's thighs apart a little more, settling between them with his thick brows drawn together. Studying the situation. Love swelled in Felix's chest, making it hard to breathe, and he tilted his hips in a wordless invitation.

Fisher's lips quirked absently and he uncapped the bottle of lube, spilling a generous amount into his palm. His finger was wet and cold when it touched Felix's skin but it warmed quickly as Fisher traced small circles around his hole.

Felix squirmed, planting his heels on the bed and trying to push into the contact, but Fisher would not be rushed. He put his dry hand on Felix's knee, steadying him maybe, grounding them both, and stroked the sensitive skin behind Felix's balls with his finger, pressing and retreating until Felix was breathless and desperate.

Finally, Fisher seemed to relent, adding more lube before sliding a finger knuckle-deep inside. The noise Felix made was definitely not dignified, and Fisher's lips twitched again, eyes still intent on his work as he slid deeper, bit by bit until his knuckles were pressed against Fisher's ass.

"You feel so good," he whispered. "You're so hot, so tight." He pumped his finger in and out a few times and Felix groaned, reaching for himself. Fisher slapped his hand away. "Not yet. Not until I'm inside you."

"You're—ah—inside me now," Felix panted. "Please, I need to—"

"You can hold on," Fisher said calmly. "Can't you? For me?"

It took Felix a few minutes controlling his breathing before he was able to swallow and nod. Fisher smiled at him, eyes warm with pride.

"I'll make it worth it," he promised, and added a finger.

Felix's grasp on reality dissolved, awareness narrowing down to Fisher working him open on his fingers, murmuring encouragement and endearments under his breath as if he wasn't even aware of it.

His skin felt tight, too tight for his body, a pressure coiling in his chest tied directly to the ache in his balls. He writhed, fist jammed against his mouth. He thought vaguely Fisher was up to three fingers, but he couldn't be sure. All he could process was the relentless push-pull, splitting him open and filling him up.

"I think you're ready," Fisher said, and Felix whimpered as he pulled his fingers free. Fisher petted his knee, soothing him as he shuffled forward. His eyes were still so intent on his task, slicking his cock and lining up, and Felix reached for him without thinking, desperate suddenly to kiss him.

Fisher leaned back from his grasping hands, lips quirking. "Wait, baby, wait—" He pushed and the head of his cock slipped inside, making them both groan. Fisher tilted forward, sliding deeper and planting his elbows on either side of Felix's head, fully blanketing his body.

"*Now* I can kiss you," he said, and rolled his hips at the same time. His nose brushed Felix's cheek as their mouths met, breath mingling hot and desperate, and Felix made a noise like a sob as Fisher worked somehow, impossibly, deeper. He laid claim to Felix's body, touching it like he owned it, tangling his hands in Felix's hair and *still* kissing him, demanding everything from him. Felix gave it gladly, his own hands roaming over Fisher's biceps, his shoulders, everything he could reach. He exulted in the feel of satin skin under his fingers as Fisher fucked him, slow and deep, the movement of his hips pulling Felix closer to the edge with each thrust.

His orgasm was wound tight, caught in his chest. He was going to come any second now, without even a hand on him, and he wasn't *ready* for it, he didn't want it to be over.

"Stop, *stop*," he gasped, and Fisher went still instantly, lifting his head. There was horror in his eyes.

"Am I hurting you?" He tried to pull away and Felix wrapped his legs around Fisher's hips, yanking him back.

"Don't—just need—" He couldn't find the *words*, and damn him, Fisher saw it, realization dawning on his face mingled with delight.

"I made you forget your pretty words," he said. Crowed, really, and Felix would punch him for it, or kiss the stupid grin off his face, but all he could do was pant for air, Fisher still so hard and thick inside him that he thought he might shake apart right where he was. He fumbled for Fisher's head, pulling him down into a clumsy kiss, trying to pour everything he was feeling into it.

Somehow, Fisher got it. He kissed him back, lips and tongue sweet, cupping Felix's face. When he rolled his hips, Felix gasped. Fisher raised an eyebrow.

"You want me to keep going?"

Felix just nodded, still unable to find words, and Fisher grinned briefly. Then he pulled out and slammed home, and Felix's eyes rolled back in his head. He arched into it, grasping desperately at any part of Fisher he could touch. Heels scrabbled in the sheets. Hands tangled in hair. Fisher grunted with each thrust, eyes gone distant as he chased his pleasure.

Felix had been riding the knife-edge for so long that he couldn't pinpoint the moment he tipped over. It felt like unspooling, thread being pulled from its container, unwinding in his chest as his entire body lit up with it. His toes curled, every muscle locking up as he rode the bliss. Dimly, he heard Fisher swear, thick and choked, and redouble his efforts, fucking him through it until Felix collapsed back against the bed, abruptly boneless.

Fisher slowed and then stopped, buried deep inside him. Felix opened his eyes, blinking until he could focus. There was urgency in Fisher's eyes, but he didn't move.

Felix licked his lips. He felt so *good*, liquid and warm, well and truly fucked out. "Do it," he rasped.

Fisher groaned raggedly and dropped his face into Felix's throat as he began to thrust again. His breath was hot, mingled filth and endearments falling from his mouth. Felix welcomed the overstimulation, shivering as Fisher stiffened and drove deep, freezing.

"Fuck, fuck, *fuck*," he chanted, shuddering all over, and spilled in Felix's core. His arms shook from the effort of holding himself up, body rigid, and Felix pulled on him until Fisher groaned and collapsed on top of him.

It was several minutes before either of them could speak or move. Felix let himself drift, Fisher's body a heavy, welcome blanket.

Finally, though, Fisher stirred, lifting his head. "Fucking *Christ*," he said wonderingly. "I always wondered why people made a big deal about makeup sex. I think I get it now." He nosed along Felix's jaw, and Felix stretched beneath him and turned to capture his mouth.

"Have to shower again," he said after a minute.

Fisher wrinkled his nose. "As long as we can do it together this time."

THEY MADE their way into the bathroom and Felix turned the water on as Fisher rested a broad hand at the base of his spine. When the water was warm, they stepped in and Fisher muscled Felix under the spray.

"Let me," he said. "You've had a long day."

That made Felix laugh, as water cascaded over his shoulders and chest. "I have? You were in an *accident* today."

"So you can take care of me in a minute," Fisher said, already squeezing body wash into his palm.

His hands were warm and gentle as he soaped Felix up, ghosting soft over his cock and pulling him in against him to reach around and clean up the mess he'd left.

Felix wrapped his arms around Fisher's shoulders and held on, still half-drifting from the combination of adrenaline, exhaustion, and endorphins.

He dragged himself back to awareness when Fisher finished rinsing him off, though, and insisted on doing the same to him. Fisher let him, a smile in his dark eyes as Felix cleaned him up, and they kissed under the spray, sleepy and languorous.

When they were dressed, Fisher helped him strip the bed and change the linens before they climbed back in. Felix curled up against Fisher's chest, sleep tugging at him.

Still, there was something else to be said.

"It won't be easy."

"Hmm?" Fisher's nose was in Felix's damp curls and he didn't seem inclined to move.

"This. Us." Felix tucked his fingers in the hem of Fisher's shirt. "The—my fans. They will say... things. Hurtful—they'll judge you, Fisher, say vicious things about you."

Fisher tightened his grip. "I can't control what anyone else says or does," he said, voice a low rumble in Felix's ear. "If they're jealous, that's their problem. I won't read the comments, okay? I promise."

Felix nodded fractionally against his chest. "They don't speak for me."

That startled a laugh from Fisher. "I know *that*, or we wouldn't be here right now."

Felix leaned back enough to see his face. "I heard you lost your job."

"Mm." Fisher traced a line down Felix's backbone. "Did you hear I got another one? A better one? The pay's better, the staff is incredible, and half of them are queer too. Plus Wren left Saint Mary's and got a job at the new place. She's not my assistant, but I still see her every day, eat lunch and talk hockey with her." His eyes were keen. "You wouldn't happen to know anything about why the head of Primrose House called me for an interview, would you?"

Felix ducked his head, burying his face in Fisher's shirt. "Primrose House?" he said, trying for a normal tone. "Is it a good school?"

"It is." Fisher sounded amused. "It's so good, in fact, that Roderick Murphy's children attend it. You might know him? Saint's winger?"

Felix gave up. "I might have asked Roddy to put in a good word for you. Suggest you for consideration. It was actually Saint's idea."

Fisher tipped his face up and kissed him. "Even when we were apart, you were trying to take care of me," he murmured.

"I felt responsible," Felix admitted, and hurried on when Fisher's brows drew down. "If you hadn't been so upset when that asshole showed up, you might have been more… temperate. Been able to turn him down without risking your job."

"No." Fisher shook his head. "I was never going to get out of that situation easily. It's not on you. And anyway, it's behind us. I have a much better job now, one where you can come eat lunch with me sometimes if you want. Although Wren will probably faint dead away when she finally meets you properly."

Felix laughed and tucked his face into Fisher's throat again. "I look forward to it." He closed his eyes, finally able to let himself relax, and fell asleep with a smile on his face.

EPILOGUE

"Fisher, what are we *doing* here?" Wren's voice was about an octave higher than usual. "Why did you tell me to bring my skates? I thought you didn't skate at all!"

"I don't," Fisher said, ushering her through the sliding doors into the foyer of the practice rink. "But some friends of mine do. I thought it might be fun if you skated with them."

Wren's eyes went huge and she stopped dead. "Fisher. You didn't. Tell me you didn't."

Fisher played dumb. "Didn't what?"

"*Fisher.*" Wren sounded nearly hysterical and Fisher took pity.

"It's just a few of them," he said. "And they're all really nice. Plus you already know Kasha, and you've met Saint."

Wren buried her face in her hands. "I can't believe this," she said, muffled through her palms.

"Look, you only have yourself to blame," Fisher said, and Wren snapped her head up to glare at him.

"How do you figure?"

"You shouldn't have told me how much you love playing and how you thought about going pro before you decided to go into teaching instead." Fisher shrugged, shoving his hands in his pockets. "If you think about it, it's pretty obvious this is all your fault."

Wren's mouth worked. "I can't decide whether to hug you or murder you," she finally said.

"Hug," Fisher said instantly, and held his arms out. Wren launched herself into them and Fisher laughed, holding her tight. "I love you," he said against her hair.

Wren sniffled and pulled away, eyes suspiciously bright. "Love you too. Am I really gonna skate with *Saint*?"

"Well, if you actually get geared up, yeah." Fisher gave her a gentle push toward the locker room. "They're already waiting, get going!"

SEVERAL PLAYERS WERE in the middle of the ice and Felix was between the pipes when Fisher got to the rink itself and made his way down to the side nearest him. Felix caught sight of him and his eyes lit behind his mask. He skated over, pushing his helmet to the back of his head, and Fisher leaned over the boards to meet him with a kiss.

"Hi," he said. He was grinning like a fool and he didn't care.

"Hi yourself." Felix's curls were disheveled, peeking out from his helmet, and his eyes were bright with his smile. "Is she here?"

"Getting her skates on. Completely losing her shit, of course, so be nice."

"I'm always nice!" Felix protested. "I can't speak for Caz, though."

"Mean as a snake, that one," Saint agreed as he skated nearer. He smiled at Fisher, who returned it.

"I'm telling your boyfriend," Felix said, and shoved him. They tussled briefly, grabbing at each other's jerseys and skidding back and forth on their skates as Carmine approached and gave Fisher an eye-roll of solidarity.

"It's always like this," he said, sounding longsuffering, and Felix freed himself from Saint's grip and punched him in the shoulder.

Wren came out the side door and made her way toward them, everything in her bearing screaming uncertainty.

"Wren!" Kasha shouted, and bolted for her. He scrambled over the boards and scooped her up in a huge bearhug as she shrieked and clung to his shoulders.

"Don't *drop* me, asshole!"

Kasha set her back on her feet, a huge smile on his face.

"Wow," Felix said. "I don't think he's ever looked at anyone but Saint that dopily before. Saint, you have competition."

Kasha bent to say something in Wren's ear, her hands still on his shoulders, and she laughed, cupping his face and kissing him.

"Oh, well that explains it," Saint said under his breath as Fisher resisted the urge to cheer.

Wren's blush reached the tips of her ears when they turned to the group, but no one teased her for it. Instead Saint opened the door for her to step out on the ice and gestured for everyone to gather around.

"I was thinking we'd do a game of two on two," he said. "Me, Caz, Kasha, and Wren. Felix is goalie for both teams."

"Twice the work," Felix complained.

Saint ignored him. "Wren, who do you want for your partner?"

"Uh." Wren shifted her weight and shot an apologetic look at Kasha. "You, if that's okay?" she said, looking back at Saint. "Sorry, babe," she added to Kasha, who looked baffled.

"Why you're apologize? Saint is best. Is right you play with him."

"So me and Wren, and Caz with Kasha," Saint said. "No-contact, we're not breaking the best thing to ever happen to Kasha today, kids."

Wren shot an agonized look at Fisher, violently scarlet, and Fisher grinned.

Even to Fisher's inexperienced eye, it was obvious the men were slowing down their moves for Wren. But it didn't take long before she was showing off some moves of her own, ducking around Carmine to send the puck to Saint, or feinting Kasha before snatching the puck off his stick. Saint whooped when she pulled that maneuver, and Wren blasted it over Felix's shoulder to hit the back of the net.

Maybe he was moving slower to give her a chance, but when Saint caught her in a celebratory hug, Kasha quickly joining them, the smile on Wren's face was so wide it had to have hurt, and Fisher's eyes stung.

"What is this, the minor leagues?" an unfamiliar voice said. It was drenched with disdain, and Fisher turned to see a tall man with blond curls and icy blue eyes, a bag over his shoulder and lip curled.

"Who's asking?" Fisher said, straightening.

The man gave him a look up and down and clearly dismissed him. "Simon," he said. "I'm here to talk to Saint."

"Well, Saint's a little busy," Fisher said. "But they'll probably be done soon."

Simon blew out an irritated breath. "Fucking figures. Not like anyone around here takes the game seriously anyway."

Fisher narrowed his eyes. Simon wasn't even looking at him, glaring out across the ice at the players, who hadn't noticed his arrival.

"Unbelievable," he muttered. "Can't believe this is my fucking life. Waiting for a spoiled child."

"Are you referring to Saint?" Fisher asked, struggling to keep his temper.

Simon sneered. "Like you haven't seen the fits he throws when things don't go his way. If you haven't, give it five minutes. Guarantee you'll get a tantrum over *something*. And don't get me started on that fucking goalie. His wrist's so limp, I don't know how his blocker stays on."

Fisher saw red and he swung without even thinking about it. His fist connected with Simon's nose with a satisfying *crack* and Simon went over backward, red blooming on his face.

"*Fisher!*" Saint was there, putting himself between them just as Simon scrambled back up and lunged for him, expression contorted with fury.

"You fucking *coward*," Simon spat. Saint hung

onto his arm as Carmine arrived and grabbed him from the other side. "Fucking coldcocking me? Try me on for size when I'm actually ready for it, you piece of shit!"

"Any time!" Fisher shouted, fists still balled with fury.

Felix scrambled over the boards and grabbed Fisher, pushing him back a few steps. "Did he hurt you?" he said urgently.

"What?" Fisher looked at him. "No. No, I'm fine."

"Then why did you punch him?" Saint asked. He let go of Simon's arm, watching him with a wary air until he seemed satisfied Simon wasn't going to try to get to Fisher again.

"He... said some stuff. Who the *fuck* is this guy?"

Saint sighed. "This is Simon Fall, and as of this morning, the newest member of the Seabirds' defensive core."

ACKNOWLEDGMENTS

Once again, my humble village came together in a big way to help me write this book, this time with a few new members. Thank you so much to my betas—Aaliya, Kat, Caitlin, Jodi, and Juliann. Your feedback helped bring Felix and Fisher to vibrant life, and kept me motivated to write more, if only to hear your outraged screams when I brought down the angst hammer. Here's to the next book(s)! Thank you also to the lovely people who helped make sure Felix's French was correct—Gabe, Florence, and the others who chose to remain nameless. Any mistakes are definitely mine alone. Thank you also to Sarah for her incredible cover art, as always, and help with formatting. I can't wait to see what you come up with for the next book!

ABOUT THE AUTHOR

Michaela Grey told stories to put herself to sleep since she was old enough to hold a conversation in her head. When she learned to write, she began putting those stories down on paper. She resides in the Texas Hill Country with her cats, and is perpetually on the hunt for peaceful writing time.

When she's not writing, she's watching hockey or blogging about writing and men on knife shoes chasing a frozen Oreo around the ice while trying to keep her cat off the keyboard.

Tumblr: greymichaela.tumblr.com
Twitter: @GreyMichaela
Facebook: www.facebook.com/GreyMichaela
E-mail: greymichaela@gmail.com

Want to find out when her next book comes out? Sign up for her newsletter here or follow her on Amazon here

Keep reading for a sneak peek at Goalie Tandem!

ALSO BY MICHAELA GREY

Beloved Scars Series
Broken Halo
Broken Rules
Broken Trust
Broken Promises

Hockey Romances
Blindside Hit
Odd-Man Rush
Roughing
Power Play
Double Shifting

Standalones
Copper and Salt

GOALIE TANDEM

The first thing Theo thought when he met Niklas was *holy shit he's tall.*

The second thing he thought was *so this is who's taking my job.* He'd opened the door to find his agent, Hannah, on the other side, with Niklas shifting his weight beside her, clearly brimming with nervous energy. He towered easily eight inches above Theo, lanky where Theo was compact, all elbows and knees like a gangly colt not quite sure what to do with himself.

Hannah smiled at Theo. "Theo Wallin, meet Niklas Stromberg, your new backup. Niklas just landed, so he's pretty jetlagged, but he wanted to meet you before I took him to the hotel."

Niklas beamed at him, brown hair flopping into bright blue eyes, and thrust one huge hand out. Theo accepted it.

"It's such an honor," Niklas blurted. His eyes were huge and earnest. "I became a goalie because of you. I—"

Hannah cleared her throat. "English," she said gently, and Niklas's face fell.

"Sorry," he said in heavily accented English. "Ah… nice to meet?"

Theo hid the smile. "It's nice to meet you too. Will you come in?" He stepped aside and Niklas ducked his head and sidled past, followed by Hannah. Theo led them into his kitchen and Niklas turned in a circle, eyes wide at the vaulted ceiling, the gleaming utensils on the magnetized racks above the counters, and the spotless marble counters. "Are you thirsty?" Theo asked.

Niklas shot a glance at Hannah, who was tapping something on her phone. Theo could sympathize—Hannah was intimidating even to people who knew her. Niklas chewed his lip, darting a look at Theo and shifting his weight.

"Water is okay?" he finally said.

"Sure," Theo said. He filled two glasses and put them on the counter as Hannah scowled at her phone and then swore.

"Theo, I'm so sorry, I've got a fire to put out right now. Can you take Niklas to his hotel and get him settled in?"

Theo swallowed the sigh and nodded. He followed her out the door to get Niklas's gear and she was peeling out of his driveway before he had the strap over his shoulder. Niklas, right behind him, grabbed the bag, babbling apologies.

"You not—is okay, I'm get—"

"She's gone, you can speak Swedish," Theo said, and Niklas heaved a huge sigh of exaggerated relief.

"I *do* know English," he said, looking embarrassed. "But… she scares me, and it just… *poof*, you know?"

Theo gestured for Niklas to follow him back inside. "She scares everyone. It's why she's so good at her job. Are you hungry?"

"*Yes*," Niklas said fervently, right on his heels.

Theo showed him where to put his bag in the front hall and then offered him a stool at the kitchen counter. Niklas hooked his feet around the rungs and watched as Theo pulled a lasagna from the refrigerator.

"It's a little early for dinner, but something tells me you need the calories," he said.

Niklas made a small affirming noise and Theo glanced up. Niklas immediately looked away, his cheeks going pink.

Amused, Theo went back to cutting a slab of lasagna and putting it on a plate. "How was your flight?" he asked as he put it in the microwave. When he looked up, Niklas jerked his eyes away again, cheeks turning even pinker.

"It, uh, was fine," he told the ceiling.

Theo snorted and grabbed two beers from the refrigerator. He popped his and drained half the can without stopping for air. When he put it down, Niklas was staring at him again, his eyes huge.

"Get it over with," Theo told him. "You'll feel better once it's out."

"You're the reason I'm here," Niklas said immediately, clutching the edge of the counter. "I saw you play in the Olympics when I was eight—" Theo managed to hide the wince, but just barely. "—And ever since then I just *knew*. I knew I was going to be a goalie. I knew I was going to play in the NHL. Play with *you*."

"Technically, you can't play *with* me, not if we're both the same position," Theo pointed out dryly, but Niklas didn't seem to register the sarcasm.

"I have posters of you on my walls," he said, eyes earnest. "I've watched every single one of your games. At least all the ones I could find, and most of them more than once. You're my favorite player in the whole world."

They stared at each other for a minute. Niklas didn't seem inclined to say anything else, and Theo didn't know *what* to say. The ding of the microwave startled them both, and Theo coughed as he turned to retrieve the food.

Putting the plate in front of Niklas, he handed him a fork and then leaned back against the counter, arms folded.

If you think I'm so great, why are you here to take my job? He didn't say it, kept the words locked behind his teeth with an almighty effort. It wasn't the fault of the young man currently digging into his pasta like he hadn't eaten in a week. But Theo couldn't help the jolt of resentment in his chest, like the kick of a mule when he looked at Niklas's big hand folded carefully around the fork that looked so small in his grip.

The team needed to get bigger. Faster. Stronger. They needed a brick wall in net to make up for their inconsistent defense, and that brick wall was eating Theo's food, utterly oblivious to the conflict in Theo's head.

"You're not eating?" he asked, looking up.

Theo shook his head. "I'm not a growing boy."

Niklas visibly bristled. "I'm nearly twenty-three."

"And I'm thirty-four," Theo said, hiding his smile. "You're fully grown, sure, but you're also still filling out. At least I *hope* you're fully grown, how tall are you, anyway?"

Niklas ducked his head, looking abashed. "Six five," he mumbled. "Sorry."

"For what, being tall?"

Niklas glanced up. His blue eyes were unhappy. "You're not."

Theo flinched. "Thank you?"

"Sorry," Niklas blurted. "Sorry, I didn't mean it that—" He shoved a hand through his hair. "I wanted… to be like you. And I'm…." He gestured vaguely at himself.

The light dawned. "You can't help your height," Theo said gently. "And your height helps *you*. It means you can make the big saves with less effort, cover the net more efficiently. I have to work twice as hard to cover as much ground."

"You make it look easy," Niklas said, glancing up again.

"Well, I've been doing it for awhile. Besides, you can't play like me. You have to play like you."

Niklas sighed and nodded.

"So tell me about yourself," Theo said.

Niklas's eyes went wide. "Oh," he managed, "I'm not interesting."

Theo raised a brow. "Really? What do you like to do in your off-time? Surely you've got some hobbies?"

"Not much," he mumbled. "I play Call of Duty some, I guess."

"Anything else?"

Niklas ducked his head, a blush dusting his cheekbones. "No," he told the counter.

Theo watched him narrowly for a minute. Whatever Niklas wasn't telling him, it wasn't his business.

"As long as it's not illegal, I don't really give a shit," Theo said, glancing at the clock above the stove. "We should probably get you to your hotel, you must be exhausted."

"I'm okay," Niklas insisted, then immediately yawned.

Theo laughed. "Okay, whatever you say."

Niklas slid off the stool and took his dishes to the sink, where he proceeded to wash them over Theo's protests.

"A good guest cleans up after himself," he said, chin jutting out as he scrubbed, and Theo gave up, reluctantly charmed.

He watched him for a minute as Niklas frowned at the dish in his hand. He didn't *want* to like this young man, his replacement and physical reminder that Theo was getting closer to retirement every day, but he couldn't really help it. Niklas was so earnest, so sincere, and it didn't hurt that he was easy on the eyes.

Soft brown hair fell over his forehead, silky straight and cornsilk fine. His bright blue eyes were narrowed in concentration, tongue peeking from his mouth, and Theo had seen dimples when he smiled.

Theo wondered idly about his sexuality. Did he like men or women? Both? Niklas didn't read as gay, but he played hockey. He'd have learned to conceal it from an early age, act like the others, even flirt with women to keep his secret.

Or maybe that was just Theo. Niklas had

finished the dishes and was drying his hands, looking up at him expectantly.

"Do you have a place to live yet?" Theo asked.

Niklas shook his head. "Hannah said she would show me some places. Maybe tomorrow. I don't want to buy anything yet, I'll probably be sent down soon, you know? And what if I don't fit? If I get traded, I don't want to go through all that."

Theo regarded him. "You've got a good head on your shoulders."

Niklas blushed. "My mama taught me a lot."

"Not your father?"

"Eh, he's okay," Niklas said dismissively. "Not really involved, you know? He was always busy with work."

"Do you want to stay here?" Theo asked, and then snapped his mouth shut, horrified with himself.

Niklas's eyes went huge. "You—really? Do you mean it? *Really?*"

What was he going to say? *Haha just kidding, let's get you to the hotel?* Theo was an introvert, not a monster.

"Of course I mean it," he said out loud, and the smile that spread over Niklas's face was almost worth the regret in his gut. "Just for a while, yeah? Until you find a place of your own."

Niklas nodded fervently. "I'll be so quiet," he promised. "I'll clean—every day. And do laundry. Dishes. Whatever you want."

"You're a guest, not my maid," Theo said, startled. "I mean it, don't you dare try to clean my house because you feel grateful or something."

"I won't," Niklas said. "But if I see something that needs cleaning?"

"Then I guess you can clean it," Theo said, amused in spite of himself. "Come on, you can pick a room."

Sign up for Michaela's newsletter here to find out when Goalie Tandem is available!

www.ingramcontent.com/pod-product-compliance
Lightning Source LLC
Chambersburg PA
CBHW071234190726
48292CB00007B/2274